Advice on wo  **e happily marr**

Peter Holiday: "There's no cure for love."

Michael Holiday: "Women are...unique. If a woman is worth fighting for, then fight for all you're worth. If it's love, it'll work out in the end. Just hang in there for the duration."

Jared Holiday: "Either you are in love or you aren't. Just don't fight it."

Raymond Holiday: "Accept it. It'll save you a lot of aggravation."

Criticism from the last single
Holiday man...

Richard Holiday: "Thanks for nothing, guys!"

Doorstep Daddy

LINDA CAJIO

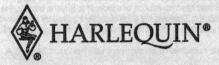

HARLEQUIN®

TORONTO • NEW YORK • LONDON
AMSTERDAM • PARIS • SYDNEY • HAMBURG
STOCKHOLM • ATHENS • TOKYO • MILAN • MADRID
PRAGUE • WARSAW • BUDAPEST • AUCKLAND

Doorstep Daddy

LINDA CAJIO

ISBN 0-373-16752-0

DOORSTEP DADDY

Copyright © 1998 by Linda Cajio.

Prologue

Dear Richard:

All four of those cousins of ours finally got married, and all in the same year. Amazing! Ran into
a mutual acquaintance here in Barbados who told
me the news. Ought to keep up with the other Holidays more. Family is not your thing, I know. The
weather's terrific and the beaches pure white. Eat
your heart out. Celeste and the kids love it. See
you when you get home and we get home.

Bob

Richard Holiday chuckled and slipped the postcard into
his breast pocket. He leaned back in the plane seat and
closed his eyes. So the other side of the family had a
rash of marriages last year. Scary thought. Still, Peter,
Michael, Jared and Raymond Holiday had been bache-
lors for a long time—like he was. He wondered what
had changed his cousins' minds all at once, then decided
better them than him. He just didn't have time for a wife
and kids.

He shivered as if a ghost had just wafted through him.
Must be the air-conditioning, he thought.

He'd rarely seen his second cousins, or maybe it was

third cousins or fourth. Or maybe they were once-removed. He was never sure how relation counting worked. Their grandfather and his grandfather had been half brothers, if he understood the connection right. He hadn't seen the guys in years, even though they all lived in the Philadelphia area. Better to let his older brother, Bob, handle the family thing. Bob was better at it. He had a beautiful wife and three great kids. Richard hadn't seen them in several months, as an extended trip to Singapore, Malaysia and Indonesia had kept him away from home. His import-export business was growing like crazy with the entry of Pacific Rim nations into the world economy.

He grinned, thinking how his gift of an old phone system to the newly elected Fijian government had garnered him the appointment of part-time consul to represent that country, and eventually several more, in Philadelphia. Not bad for a guy who quit college in his sophomore year. It helped that his roommate had been from the islands and had political connections. Bob would howl with laughter when he heard of Richard's latest appointment—especially when he found out the duties mainly consisted of getting fresh fish, flowers and exotic fruits and vegetables out of the airport and through customs for the local restaurants. Once an importer, always an importer, no matter how one gussied it up.

Richard smiled to himself. He was thirty-four years old, had an expensive high-rise apartment in the city, a BMW two-seater convertible, his own business and money in the bank. He came and went as he pleased, with the occasional woman on his arm and in his bed, and he adored his niece and nephews. That was enough for him.

Life was excellent. Unlike his whatever-they-were-in-relation-to-him cousins, he had no desire to change the way he lived. Certainly he was nowhere ready to.

He leaned back in his seat, content.

Chapter One

"Flap your wings, Uncle Richard."

Richard groaned at his nephew's request. "Not again!"

"*Please,*" Jason whined.

"Peas Fap!"

Richard sighed at the baby voice. His nephew, Mark, not quite three, repeated everything he heard. Richard had made the mistake of cursing in front of the little guy after cutting a finger. Mark had happily repeated the swear words. Seven-year-old Jason loved his uncle Richard's Batman costume, unfortunately. The boys' older sister, Amanda, looked at her uncle with a sad gaze. Amanda needed something to cheer her up.

All the kids did. He hadn't been home from his Micronesia trip for two weeks, when his brother, Bob, and his sister-in-law, Celeste, had been killed in a car wreck. Richard was the children's godfather, but he'd never imagined in his worst nightmare that this would happen. Yet it had.

The kids had come to him of course, and his life had completely changed. He tried to fill in the blanks as a parent and make a good life for them, but he was a woeful greenhorn. His mistakes had been endless. He barely knew what little boys were like, and he had no clue what to do with a young female adolescent, let alone help all of them through their loss. Raising them in the city hadn't been working. Neither had trying to run his business from his midtown office. He had finally chucked the hapless baby-sitters, au pairs and day-care centers, bought a home in the outer suburbs and moved his business into his home. That had been two months ago, and things weren't much better, either in his learning curve or in the children's happiness. But he was trying.

Which was why he was trudging along the street in a rented Batman costume on Halloween.

"Should I?" he asked Amanda.

The thirteen-year-old shrugged. "Halloween at home was better than this."

She had joined her brother in his plea to celebrate a traditional Halloween and go neighborhood trick-or-treating. They'd all dressed up—little Mark was Robin, Jason was Hercules and Amanda was a goddess in white and gold. She had been as excited as Jason when they'd left the house. Now she looked embarrassed.

"The streets are a little empty," Richard admitted with a frown as he looked around the small yet exclusive homes in the Green Briar development. They'd been to five houses and so far no one had even answered the door. No other family was out trick-or-treating. He decided they must be a little early. It wasn't even six yet, although it was dark. Probably that was it. "I guess I'd better flap. That ought to wake everyone up. Amanda, you push Mark's stroller while I flap."

"I'll go ring the doorbell!" Jason shouted, and ran off.

"Jason!" Richard yelled, but the boy didn't stop. That

was the problem with Jason. He was uncontrollable at times. "Damn!"

"Damn!" Mark repeated.

"Hel—" Richard swallowed the end of the curse. "No, Mark. Bad word."

"Hell," Mark said, anyway.

"We better hurry up," Amanda said wisely, trotting after Jason and taking Mark out of earshot. She wore a ghost of a smile.

Richard brought up the rear, flapping as he went. The bodysuit, with its washboard torso, chafed and seemed to cut into his circulation. He gripped the winged cape and moved his arms as best he could. He wondered if he looked as idiotic as he felt.

The door opened and Jason shouted at the top of his lungs, "Trick or treat!"

Richard stopped in midflap. The woman on the doorstep blinked at the strange-looking family in front of her. She was tall and slim, her jeans tight-fitting and her Penn State sweatshirt loose, giving her the air of a teenager. Her face was heart-shaped, her features delicate and exotic like a fairy's. Blond hair framed her face in a cloud of curls, the hall light behind her adding the illusion of a halo.

Richard's heart pounded and his blood turned thick in his veins as awareness seeped through his being. A boy, not much older than Amanda, stood next to her, but he barely noticed the kid. His attention was all on the woman.

Her surprised expression vanished, replaced by growing amusement. Richard realized how ridiculous he must look in his costume. Awareness died and humiliation shot to the fore.

"Poopies!" Mark yelled happily, sending the humiliation factor rocketing skyward.

"Oh, God," Amanda muttered, knowing what it meant.

Truer words had never been spoken, Richard thought.

"Is that my trick?" the woman asked Mark, bending down and tweaking Mark's nose. "It works, pal. I surrender."

Richard cleared his throat. "My nephew likes to announce his personal business after he finishes it. I'm not sure why."

The woman grinned. "He's probably pleased with himself. Kids are shameless, aren't they? They look great, too. So do you."

Richard could feel his face heat. He was blushing like a schoolboy. What was this reaction to her? "Thanks."

"Joey, get the Halloween candy," she said to the boy who stared from behind her.

"We don't have any, Aunt Callie," the boy, Joey, replied.

Richard groaned under his breath. They finally got someone at home and there was no candy. What a disaster this Halloween was.

The woman, Callie, turned to the boy. "What do you mean, you have no candy?"

"Nobody does trick-or-treating here," Joey said, shrugging. "The moms have that neighborhood party, instead, for the little kids. Us older kids...well, we go to our friends' or something. But nobody goes around here."

"Ah, that explains it," Richard said, enlightened. His niece gave a little squeak. He wondered why, but was too relieved with the boy's explanation to ask. "I'm glad that's all it is. I thought Halloween had been banned or something. I'm sorry, guys. I didn't know.''

Amanda looked unhappy, which explained the squeak. Jason looked crestfallen.

Richard grimaced. Once more he'd screwed up and the kids had suffered—except Mark who grinned and stuck out his tongue.

"Uncle Richard, let's go," Amanda whispered, her voice quavering.

"We aren't getting anything?" Jason asked, tears in his eyes.

"I have something at home, Jason—"

"Oh, yes, you are, Jason," the woman said. "Joey, get the cookies and those packaged cakes and the big bag of gumdrops."

"But, Aunt Callie—"

"The sooner you get them, the sooner *we* go." Wherever he and his aunt were going motivated the boy, because he raced down the hall to the back of the huge house. She turned to Richard. "The cookies aren't wrapped, but I assure you my sister and her family are perfectly normal and nothing will be wrong with them."

"You don't have to do this…"

"I've got a buff Hercules, a beautiful goddess, a poopie Robin and Batman. Now that's deserving of a treat." She gasped, then laughed. "I didn't mean you were poopie. Sorry."

Amanda giggled. Jason laughed.

To Jason she said, "So which Herc are you? TV or movie?"

"Movie," Jason shouted, happy again.

"I thought so. By the way, I did clean the wax out of my ears today, so I can hear your normal voice really well. But maybe you're saving wax in your ears and you can't hear yourself shouting. If you're planning to make wax candles, now's the time.''

Jason laughed again. ''You're funny.'' He didn't shout this time.

She focused on Amanda. ''You look great. Taking your younger brothers around? I always had to take my little brothers and sisters around, too. I permanently borrowed a candy bar or two from them as payment when they weren't looking. Think about it.''

''Okay,'' Amanda said, smiling in pleasure.

Richard gaped. She had Jason laughing *and* listening, and she had Amanda smiling. *Smiling.* How had she done it? He realized he should introduce himself. And do it quick before she got away.

''I'm Richard Holiday,'' he said, holding out his hand to her. ''And these are my niece and nephews, Amanda, Jason and Mark. We live up the road.''

''Callie Rossovich. This is my sister Gerri's house. The boy's her son, Joey, and she has a daughter, Kristen, who's upstairs dressing.''

She took his hand. As her fingers touched his, Richard felt as if he'd been jolted. Never had a woman's touch affected him in quite this way. She pulled her hand back, as if affected, too. God, he hoped so. He wouldn't like to think he was all alone in this.

''Poopies!'' Mark announced again.

The woman smiled. ''Yes, dear, I know. You said it earlier, and what a good boy you are for telling us again.''

The kids giggled. Richard chuckled, admiring her aplomb with Mark. He'd met her only five minutes ago and he was admiring a heck of a lot about Callie Rossovich.

Joey returned with treats for the kids. A woman resembling Callie came with him. Obviously this was Callie's sister, Gerri. She was more elegantly dressed than Callie, yet she lacked the vivaciousness. Callie's sister stared at him as if he'd grown three heads.

"I can't believe you don't have Halloween candy, Gerri," Callie said to her sister as she doled out the treats.

"Well, nobody comes around," Gerri replied defensively. "And we have that party for all the neighborhood children, so I buy for that."

"Looks like you forgot a few here. Hercules, the goddess, Robin and Batman who live up the street."

"But I wasn't in charge of the invitations!"

Callie sniffed, obviously not accepting that explanation.

"It's okay," Richard said. "I'm Richard Holiday. We moved into the development only a couple of months ago."

"A couple of months!" Callie exclaimed. "Gerri!"

"I didn't know," Gerri said.

"It's okay," Richard began, feeling badly for the woman. He felt worse for his kids. Because he'd been too busy to introduce himself to people here, the children had missed out on a big party. And on Halloween.

"No, it's not okay," Callie said. "I was about to take my niece and nephew out trick-or-treating in the old neighborhood. It's great for kids. Why don't you and your children come with us? I can vouch for every house we go to. Say you'll come."

"I couldn't impose," he said, half wishing he could take her up on her offer. The kids had had little fun lately.

"You're not imposing, so that's settled."

"Yeah!" Jason shouted.

"Joey, go finish getting ready," Callie said to her nephew. "And tell your sister to hurry up. She's got to be witchy enough by now."

"Poopies!" Mark yelped.

"I better go change him," Richard said.

"I'll do it," Amanda offered, turning the stroller around.

Richard gave her the keys to the house. Changing Mark was a chore at best. Amanda never offered before, but he wasn't about to question her. God forbid she should change her mind.

"I'll make sure the children get on the party list," Gerri told him. "We have a Christmas one and a summer pool party. All the families come."

Richard smiled at her. "Thanks."

"Come in," Callie said, opening the door wide. "We've never had Batman in the house before. Call your wife and tell her to come back with the kids."

"I'm not married," Richard said.

"Oh," Callie said. She had a funny look on her face. "Well, come in, anyway."

Jason skipped over the threshold. Richard stepped across it. The house was beautiful, but it felt cold, and not from the brisk autumn air wafting inside. Callie was the only warmth. From her smile and her green eyes, she exuded the emotion. And he responded to it.

He liked that.

CALLIE ROSSOVICH grinned at the wonder on the newcomers' faces. The three-hundred block of Walker Street had been the subject of several news stories over the years for its decorations. All the row houses joined in whatever was the current holiday fun.

This time, orange and black streamers rippled over the

street. Ghoulish lights and swaying Frankenstein mon-
sters highlighted picture windows. On porches and pat-
ios, scarecrows guarded speakers blasting moans of the
undead. But best of all, children of every size and age
paraded back and forth under the watchful eyes of parents. And half the adults were dressed in the spirit of the
evening.

"Wow," Richard said. "I've never seen anything like
this before."

"Oh, there're a few places like it in the city," Callie
said, smiling affectionately at her childhood home. She'd
grown up on this street. "The northeast is pretty close-
knit, and south Philly even more so. But we're the only
block like it in the Roxborough section. Everyone's lived
here forever—"

"Can we go, Aunt Callie?" her niece, Kristen, asked
impatiently.

Kristen and Jason, both the same age, stood together,
treat bags at the ready. They had overcome any shyness
after five seconds in each other's presence.

"What are the rules?" Callie prompted Kristen.

"We stay on this street only, and we play I spy,"
Kristen answered. "Which means I hafta be in sight of
you all the time."

"I spy you and you spy me," Callie said to Richard
by way of explanation.

"And we don't eat *any* candy unless you look at it
first. If we mess up, we hafta walk with you."

Callie grinned at her niece. "The kiss of death. Okay,
you two can go."

"Same rules for you, Jason," Richard called out.

To her nephew she said, "Joey, why don't you take
Amanda around with you? Then she won't be stuck with
the young kids or the old you-know-whats."

Joey glanced at Amanda, who looked as if she wanted the ground to open and swallow her. Callie hadn't missed the touch of lip gloss and enhanced eye shadow the girl had obviously put on while changing her brother.

"Okay," Joey said, without whining. Usually he whined if asked to perform a task he didn't like. Gerri spoiled him, in Callie's opinion. But Gerri had always been the material girl in the family.

The four kids vanished, leaving her with the cutest Robin and the sexiest Batman she'd ever seen. Robin was easy to handle. She just pushed his stroller. Batman was another story.

Tall and blond, Richard Holiday reminded her of Val Kilmer in looks, as well as choice of clothing. His features were clean-cut all-American good-looking male, and he had golden brown eyes. Like a lion's, she thought. The bodysuit made her wonder what he had underneath. His legs and arms in the clinging tights looked muscular. Nothing overly so, but worthy. *Very* worthy. And when he smiled…he lit her bat light every time.

He'd looked so helpless when she'd answered her sister's door. She'd felt badly that his niece and nephews had missed out on the party. Leave it to the airheads in Gerri's neighborhood to goof up on the invitations, Callie thought. She wondered what he thought of her invitation. No doubt he felt he was slumming. She hoped so; she needed something to smother her attraction to him, and snobbery would help.

What had she been thinking, so impulsively giving a man an invitation? No matter how innocent, she'd been foolish. She was being nurturing again, and she had to stop. Now.

"You sure the kids will be okay?" Richard asked as

they strolled along with Mark's stroller. Richard pushed, yet he hardly looked domestic, despite the Halloween costume. His voice was deep and disturbing, like water over a stone.

"Sure," she said, pointing to both sets of kids. "See? We spy them and they spy us. Of course, we do the majority of the spying, but it works."

He chuckled. "It does so far. I don't exactly know what I'm doing yet, so I get nervous about the kids."

"Hey, nieces and nephews are great," she said. "You take them out occasionally, enjoy them, then send them back to their parents for the tough stuff. I know I do."

"Actually I'm raising them," he replied. "My brother and his wife died in a car wreck and I'm the children's guardian."

"I'm so sorry," she said, laying a hand on his arm as sympathy welled up inside her.

His body, however, was hot and strong, eliciting much more than sympathy for him. A shiver of awareness ran through her veins. The sensation was so strong she awkwardly dropped her hand away.

"Thanks," he said, smiling as if unaffected by her touch. Now there was a downer, Callie thought. He added, "It hasn't been easy for the kids. I'm a lousy substitute parent. We went through a couple of idiot au pairs and a Nurse Ratchet-type nanny or two. My midtown apartment was not the place to raise kids, either. They've been good about it all, but it's not helping matters."

Oh, God, she thought. This man could have her wrapped around his little finger in a heartbeat. Who *couldn't* respond to that story? Not her. Definitely not her.

She cleared her throat of the suspicious lump of emotion that lodged there and got practical. "You'll find your way. Raising kids is more about organization than anything else. I'm the oldest of six, and I had to help out a *lot*."

The truth was, she practically raised her younger siblings. Both her parents worked and worked hard. They'd always been a poor family, and she'd done what she had to do. Now she was free and finally getting on with her life. She intended it to stay that way—provided she stopped responding to a sexy Batman with a heartrending story.

"Help me," she muttered. More loudly she said, "Come on. We'll go to my parents' house first and see if they recognize me."

"But you're not dressed up for Halloween," he said, frowning.

"Don't bet on it."

"I take it you don't live here with your parents," he said as she led him up the steps of a row house.

She laughed. "I've been out for about a year, ever since my younger brother graduated from high school. I have an apartment in Jersey. Not far from you and Gerri, actually."

That proximity sounded more promising than a casual throwaway. She pushed the disturbing thought aside.

Her parents' house looked no different from the others on the block. But she knew every brick, every crack of the place. She'd grown up here. Or rather, she'd been a grown-up here when she should have been a kid. She'd spent many a Halloween giving out candy or taking her younger siblings around, instead of dressing up and going with her own friends.

Grinning away the twinge of resentment, she knocked. When the door opened, she said, "Trick or treat!"

Her father, rail thin as always, laughed at her. "And what are you supposed to be, kid?"

"A lady nearing thirty with a couple of friends in tow," she replied, opening the door wider to reach into the candy bowl. "This is Richard Holiday and his nephew, Mark. Richard, this is my father, Ellis Rossovich."

"Friends, eh?" Her dad peered around her. "Hell, I thought you were Batman and Robin. You Callie's new boyfriend? About time she got one."

"No, he's not my boyfriend, so don't embarrass him with any crazy ideas," Callie said matter-of-factly, knowing that would be her father's conclusion. She dropped some candy into Mark's plastic pumpkin bag, then tweaked his nose, much to the toddler's delight. She added, "Richard is Gerri's new neighbor. He was taking his kids around there, which is useless, so I brought him here with Kristen and Joey."

"Where are my grandbabies?" Ellis asked.

"Taking Richard's niece and nephew around. Don't worry. They'll get here eventually. You know they love to make you guess who they are."

Her father cackled. "I can't tell half the time, either. Give me a hint."

"No way. Put your glasses on for once."

"I hate those things. Well, come in. You're letting in the cold and I ain't no rich man."

The lament never changed, Callie thought in amusement. "Maybe later when the kids are finished, I'll bring them in for cocoa. We've got to take Mark around first. He shouldn't miss all the fun."

Her father turned and called out, "Steph! Callie's here, but she's taking some guy and his kid around the block!"

Callie's face flushed at her father's unintended double entendre and the sound of footsteps beating a quick path to the front door. Richard grinned at her.

Stephanie Rossovich was breathless and flushed. Callie eyed her mother critically. She'd suffered a mild heart attack last year. The drawn exhausted look her mother had carried for many years had lessened with the long recovery period and her mother's return to light duty at work. Still, Callie could never remember her mother not looking worn-out. Even with Callie doing the cooking, washing, ironing and baby-sitting, her mother had been the one to bear six babies in ten years. She had also worked full-time at night in a lamp factory. Her mother had aged before she should have.

Callie wasn't falling into the same trap. She would get her college diploma—it would take her eight years to do it because she had to go to evening classes—but she would get her degree, and then she'd consider marriage and children. Now was her time to catch up on all the things she'd missed.

"Callie!" Her mother came outside and kissed her on the cheek. Rasputin, the mangy old Persian cat, came with her.

"You need a coat, Mom," Callie said, frowning at her mother's thin sweater.

"I'll get it in a minute. Who's this?"

Callie made the introductions, emphasizing Richard's being Gerri's neighbor. Rasputin stretched up on arthritic legs to sniff Mark. Mark sniffed back, nose to nose with the feline.

"Kit-kat," he announced, before whacking the cat on the top of the head in a toddler's version of petting.

Rasputin, a veteran of little kids, scooted back out of the way.

"Mark!" Richard admonished. "Be nice."

"Here." Callie scooped up Rasputin and gave him a soothing pat on the head to ease any bruised feelings. She knelt in front of the stroller, took Mark's hand and gently stroked it over Rasputin's shoulder. "Nice boy. Nice kitty, Mark."

Mark grinned and stroked the cat on his own when Callie let go of his hand. Rasputin began to purr.

"Not bad, huh?" she said to the toddler.

"Nice kit-kat," Mark said.

Smiling, she looked up at Richard. His gaze, lambent as it focused on her, held her captive. She felt as if she were looking into her own soul. And his. He smiled lazily, sending her blood flowing thickly through her veins.

"Not bad at all," he replied.

Chapter Two

"She was real nice."

Richard glanced up from his cereal, Jason's comment to Amanda penetrating his normal morning fog. The fog had gotten worse since he'd been staying up half the night to run his business. He lived on about five hours sleep a night, tops.

"Yeah," Amanda said. "I thought Halloween would be dumb, but it was really good after we went with her."

Yeah, Richard thought, not at all insulted by his niece's comment. Halloween had been great—after they met up with Callie Rossovich. Not only did she look like an angel, she acted like one. They were all still talking about it days later. If he hadn't had the kids to cope with, he would have thanked Callie in a unique manner.

"Toes! Toes! Toes!" Mark suddenly demanded at the top of his lungs.

Beeps erupted, adding to the din.

"What the hell!" Richard snapped, his heart thudding in the aftermath. Talk about a wake-up call.

"What the hell!" Mark shouted, throwing his milk cup across the room.

The beeps started again.

"It's my chickies and dinosaurs," Amanda said, pressing buttons on three different electronic virtual-pet games. Richard had bought them over the weekend for her, and she had hung them on a key chain in a never-ending portable-complaint session. All they did was beep for attention. "They're just waking up. Omigod! The bus'll be here any minute and I haven't even done my hair yet!"

His niece burst into tears, great sobs racking her shoulders. Mark screamed for "Toes" while Jason shoveled in the last of his cereal and waved goodbye, then shot out the door before Richard could stop him. Oh, well, he thought. One kid was together enough to get out the door on time. Why prolong the agony?

"Finish getting ready," he told Amanda, "and I'll drive you." He glanced at Mark. "As soon as he has some toast."

Richard handed a piece to the child. Mark stopped screaming and slammed the toast down on his high-chair tray several times.

"That's right," Richard muttered. "Beat it to death before you eat it."

Mark grinned, then shouted for milk—after announcing a bodily function. Richard shuddered. He wondered how he would get any work done today with Mark in his present mood. When nap time came, Richard bet he'd be joining the kid. If he could *get* Mark to nap.

He noticed Amanda still busily pressing buttons.

"Hey! You've got school eventually. Better get moving now."

"But I have to feed them. And play with them. If I don't, they'll die." More tears watered in her eyes.

Richard groaned. He wished he'd never bought the stupid things. "Forget them. Just get ready for school."

"You don't understand!" Amanda shrieked, and ran from the room.

Richard slumped in his chair. He ran a hand down his face, pulling the skin in frustration, while wondering if he should just go hang himself from the rafters. The day had barely started, yet it couldn't get worse. He looked at Mark, who grinned through a mass of toasted bread-crumbs. "I'll never get it right, will I?"

Mark threw the toast at him. "Uncle Richard silly guy."

Richard picked it off his lap. "I always liked confirmation."

Amanda eventually came back downstairs, looking subdued and ready for school. Richard glanced wistfully at the table full of dirty dishes and hoped they would magically clean themselves while he was gone. He and Mark got Amanda to school with no mishaps, although Richard had to sign her in since she was late. He tried to talk to her, but she was too sullen, walking dejectedly out of the school's main office. He didn't have a clue what to do to make her happy. Or any of the kids.

On the way home he thought about Jason's comment at breakfast. Besides being beautiful, Callie had a way with children. She certainly understood what made them happy. One look at his three lambs and she knew they needed the best trick-or-treat place in the Delaware Valley.

He noticed Callie's sister, Gerri, coming outside when he turned onto his street. He stopped and rolled down the window.

"Hi," he called out. "Remember me? I'm the local Batman."

"Of course." Gerri's smile didn't begin to match Callie's for warmth. "I was going to call you to apologize again and invite you as guest of honor for a housewarming."

"Oh." The housewarming took him by surprise. He didn't know what to say. Thank-you seemed best, so that's what he said.

"We'll have it next Friday at my house."

Mark kicked his legs restlessly in his car seat. Richard knew he had less than a minute before the toddler volcano blew again. "I'm sure I'm free. I hate to impose, but would it be possible to call your sister? I'd like to thank her again for taking the Halloween dummy, namely me, under her wing."

Gerri's eyebrows came together in a frown, but she rummaged in her bag before removing a pocket computer. She pressed buttons, rather like Amanda. The notion of adult virtual pets came to mind. Richard shuddered yet again.

"Here it is," Gerri said. "Got a pen?"

Richard felt in his pocket and came up with a half-broken pencil he'd found in the foyer as he was leaving to take Amanda to school. He had no paper, then glanced at Mark's car seat and decided to improvise. "Go ahead."

She gave him Callie's home and work numbers. Richard vowed to have nicer thoughts about Gerri from now on as he wrote the numbers on the plastic side of the seat. Mark watched him, fascinated with the moving pencil.

"Thanks," Richard said, moving the pencil out of Mark's reaching fingers.

"Oh, you're welcome." Gerri snapped her minicomputer shut.

Richard waved goodbye before she could talk more.

Back in his own house, he settled Mark with some toys and a Barney tape, then dialed Callie's work number.

"County Office on Aging."

Richard gave a start; Callie's place of work was completely unexpected. Not that he knew what he'd expected, but this wasn't it. He asked for Callie and was patched through.

"Hi, it's Richard Holiday, the Batman man," he said when she came on the line. "Your sister gave me the number here, so I hope it's okay to call."

"Richard," she said in such a way that he was unsure whether she sounded delightfully surprised or dismayingly surprised. She continued, "How's that cute little Robin? Still giving you his special brand of crime fighting?"

Delightfully surprised, Richard decided. He laughed, feeling as if the morning was truly starting now. "The child lives for it. I wanted to thank you again for helping us the other night with Halloween. The kids had a great time. So did I."

"No problem. You all looked like such poor lost souls how could I resist?"

"We're lost all right," Richard admitted ruefully while Mark chattered to his television friend. "You were a miracle worker. I'd like to take you out for dinner some night. When are you free?"

"I don't..." She paused. Richard held his breath until she added, "I have classes three nights a week, but I could do it Friday. Is that all right?"

"It's perfect," he said, and meant it. A strange kind of excitement rose inside him. Sexual, but more than that. He couldn't explain it.

"I'll see you Friday, then," she said.

"Wait, wait. Don't hang up. I don't know where you live."

She laughed. She had the most delicious laugh. "Peach Tree Apartments. Three-A. It's off Connors Road."

"I know it. Can I ask you something?"

"Sure."

"Do you understand thirteen-year-old girls?"

She laughed uproariously. "Oh, God, yes. I was one once. Having trouble with yours?"

"I'm glad you were one. You can explain them to me on Friday. I have a list."

"Okay. But basically just duck and run for the next few years when you see them coming. That's the only way to survive."

"Great," he muttered.

He hung up the phone a few minutes later, feeling pleased. He had a date.

"Want joos!" Mark yelled.

"No problem." Richard held out his hand. "Barney's over, so let's go get juice, clean up the breakfast dishes, and then it'll probably be time for lunch. We can clean that up and make dinner."

Mark happily took his hand.

Oh, brother, he thought. When was he supposed to work?

He'd have to ask Callie.

CALLIE CAREFULLY TOUCHED the mascara to her right lower lashes—just as the doorbell rang.

Her hand jerked at the sudden noise.

"Dammit!" She stared at the dark tracks coursing across her upper eyelid to her temple. She'd had just this last bit to do and she would have been perfect. Now Richard was here and she was a mess.

Why was she going on this date? Okay, so she was a sucker for a pretty face, and he had one. And she hadn't been out in a long long time with a man. Even if she wasn't in the market for a relationship, surely she could go on a date. One date. She only wanted to look good for it, after all.

"I'm coming!" she called out, while running a washcloth under hot water to begin repairs to her face.

The doorbell rang again...and again.

"Sheesh!" Callie grimaced at the impatience of the man. Her blood pressure shot up as the bell rang several more times. Why was he ringing so much? He couldn't be that restless. Even a guy fresh out of prison would let a few moments go by before ringing the bell again, she thought. So why was Richard going nuts with the bell?

Callie realized there could be a problem. Mrs. Fogelman, the widow across the hall, was on the frail side since her latest surgery. Maybe she was hurt or something.

The doorbell rang for the fortieth time.

Callie strode out of the apartment bathroom to the front door. She opened it—and died a thousand deaths.

"...told you not to ring it again!" Richard was saying to Jason. Mark was in his stroller, next to his uncle, who straightened. "Hi, I'm—"

He stopped, his jaw hanging open as he stared at her face.

"What's that?" Jason asked, pointing to her forehead.

Callie put her hand over her mascara mess. "I was trying to paint my forehead and I missed. Come in."

She desperately wanted to ask what the boys were

doing with Richard as he pushed the stroller across the threshold, and she hoped his answer would be that they were dropping them off at a baby-sitter's. But she couldn't ask; that would be impolite. Jason raced in behind his uncle.

Callie caught the boy. "Slow down, kid. I've got a speed limit in my living room and you're over it. Here." She walked him to the television and turned it on, then set up a video game, her secret passion. "Take that energy out on Go-Go Karts."

"Wow." Jason concentrated on the screen, his fingers pressing control buttons.

Callie turned away deliberately from Richard, so he couldn't see her face. "I'll just be a few minutes."

She escaped to the bathroom.

When she looked in the mirror, she groaned. "Oh, God. *The Rocky Horror Picture Show.*"

She emerged from the bathroom.

"Poopies!" Mark yelled.

"Thank you, Mark," Callie replied gravely. "I always did hate a child's honesty."

Richard grinned at her. "You look beautiful."

Callie smiled at the compliment. "My war paint's all in place at least. What more could a guy ask?"

"Nothing," he assured her. "I'm sorry I have to bring the boys with us. I don't know anyone who could baby-sit, and I think Amanda's too young. I also think she's too young to be home alone, but I lost that argument."

Callie's heart sank at the idea of a group date. In her moments of weakness, she'd envisioned an intimate dinner for two in a dark corner of a fine restaurant. Maybe a club afterward for some slow dancing. Maybe a goodnight kiss that left her breathless and dreamy-eyed. Maybe a little more than a kiss. And definitely a phone call the next day, asking to do it all over gain. She would have said no, but she wanted the good part first before not wanting a second date.

"I hope you don't mind," he said belatedly, as if he'd just realized he'd made a mistake.

"Oh, no, I don't mind," she replied. What else could she say? *Hey, buddy, if you're looking for sex, don't bring the kids?* She wasn't looking for sex, but it had been more than a year since her last date, and it would be nice if a man was looking for *anything* personal from her. Her feminine self-esteem needed a wallop. With a forced smile, she added, "Kids are fun."

"Good." He looked relieved. Callie decided that wasn't a bad thing between a man and a woman on a first date. "I've made a reservation at the White Dog Café in the city."

Callie had been to the upscale bistro, hardly a place for kids. Disaster would be a mild word for their date if the date weren't headed away from the pass right now. "The White Dog's a great place, but I think Jason and Mark would be bored there. How about a Chuck E Cheese, instead?"

"Oh." Richard blinked as if the lightbulb of a great realization had just come on. "You don't mind?"

"No. We'll save the White Dog for another time." If they had another time, she thought. And they'd do it without the kids.

Richard took out a cell phone and called to cancel the reservation. He also called home and talked to Amanda.

"I won!" Jason shouted.

"Hurray!" Callie said. "And besides your trophy, you'll get a free dinner at Chuck E Cheese. Right now."

"Oh, boy!" Jason beamed. "Can I have pizza and a hot dog?"

"Sure. I think I'll have that, too." When in Rome.

"We better change Mark first," Richard said as the youngest Holiday made his familiar announcement once again.

Callie sighed. What a date.

CHUCK E CHEESE was mobbed, three raucous birthday parties not helping matters.

"I think I should have called in a reservation here," Richard said ruefully.

"Don't worry," Callie told him while snagging Jason before he could run off and explore. "It clears out fast. My sister Helena brings her kids here all the time. She's got three boys and is more down-to-earth than Gerri." She chuckled. "That's not saying much, but Helena's on the mark about kiddie restaurants."

"Shall we find a table, then?" he suggested with Cary Grant aplomb.

He could have been Cary Grant, Callie decided when they reached the after-dinner soda stage. Or Tom Hanks, only cuter. Richard had that same ability those two men had to calmly accept the unexpected. Unfortunately he did call Amanda every few minutes, just to check on her. The poor girl must be ready to strangle him, Callie thought in amusement.

They kept an eye on Mark and Jason, who were with other children in the restaurant's play area nearby. The noise level was horrendous, but Callie pushed it to the background as best she could.

"I killed her babies," Richard said. "I think she hates me."

Callie gasped. "I beg your pardon?"

"Those virtual-baby-pet things," he explained. "Amanda got in trouble for taking them to school, so she handed them over to me and I…I forgot to feed them when they beeped."

"Oh, Lordy," Callie said in sympathy for the drubbing he no doubt got.

"She screamed at me and burst into tears," Richard added. "I don't know why she always does these histrionics. It's just a game."

"Maybe her reaction has to do with losing her parents," Callie told him. "Maybe the game symbolizes her ability to keep her parents from dying. Maybe she doesn't want anything else to die."

His beleaguered expression cleared. "I never thought of that. I bet you're right. What a doofus I am."

Callie giggled. "I haven't heard that word in ages."

"What else describes an old idiot?" He shook his head. "I'll talk to her tomorrow, although I have no clue how I'll keep up with her virtual pets and Mark, too." He ran a hand through his hair. It fell back into perfect place. "I'm so behind with my own stuff now."

"Have you considered day care?" she suggested wryly. "A couple of hours a day might help you."

"We had problems with that before," he replied dubiously. "I gave up on it, along with au pairs and housekeepers."

Callie shrugged. "You'll work it out."

"I hope. Amanda's so moody all the time. She cries about everything."

"Women," Callie murmured dryly.

He chuckled. "Okay, so I'm a crumb in the women's pages."

"Amanda probably thinks so." Callie wondered if the girl's weepiness had a simple physical cause. She decided to be blunt; the man needed help, after all. Tons of it. "Has she gotten her period yet?"

Richard's jaw dropped in clear astonishment. "Oh, God. I don't know."

"'Atta guy," Callie said, shaking her head, mildly exasperated with men's ability to stick their heads in the sand. "I'm sure you would know. After all, somebody's got to buy things at the store for her needs. But a girl's hormones go nuts in the months before her period starts, and sometimes they get very weepy about everything. She probably can't figure out what's wrong with her, either."

Richard rubbed his forehead. If he felt as over-whelmed as he looked, he was in deep trouble. "This is women's territory."

"Oh, no. You don't get off the hook with that, buddy. This is *parents'* territory," Callie countered, looking him straight in the eye. Kids screamed and raced all around them. She ignored the chaos. "Talk to her about this, too. Tomorrow, Richard. She's probably scared to death something will happen and she has to cope alone. I'd apologize profusely for the virtual pets, while I was at it. A little humbling goes a long way."

He reached across the littered table and took her hand. His was warm and strong as it closed around her fingers, sending bursts of heat along her veins.

"I will. Thanks for listening, Callie. I don't know what the hell I'm doing raising kids—but they've got no one else."

Callie swallowed around a suspicious lump of sympathy. This man was helpless, hopeless and sexy. She could be a goner if she allowed herself. "You'll be fine."

"Not without your help. You're a great date."

A scream of pain erupted from behind them.

Callie wryly noted how Richard dropped her hand like

a hot potato even as they both rushed to soothe Mark, who was crying. Richard picked up the toddler and awkwardly patted him on the back. Callie pressed her hand over Richard's and rubbed Mark's back with him. Mark quieted.

"I didn't do it," Jason said.

Callie focused on him. "That's an interesting thing to say."

Jason looked shamefaced. "Maybe I pushed him, but I didn't mean to."

Richard said in a stern tone, "You have got to be more careful. He's just a baby."

"But I didn't mean to!" Jason wailed, beginning to cry.

Callie sighed. Dumb male strikes again. She rubbed Jason's back, just as she'd helped Richard do to Mark's, a pure calm comfort gesture. "Hey, it was an accident. Everyone has them, Jay, and Mark's not broken. But when big guys like you are playing around the rug rats, you've got to be a little less like speed demons, okay?"

Jason nodded, sniffing back his tears. When he regained his eight-year-old macho male dignity, Callie patted him one last time. She'd done this sort of thing so many times with her brother and sisters, soothing kids and making them happy, she could do it in her sleep.

"Go hug your brother and tell him you're sorry," she said. "When we make mistakes, we have to make up for them, too."

Jason went to Mark. Richard squatted down while holding Mark, and Jason made a nice apology to his little brother. Mark reached out and hugged Jason. The adults sighed at the sweetness of it.

"Well-done, Jay," Callie said. "You're a good kid."

Jason grinned. "Can I play skee-ball now?"

"Sure. I'll spot you a dollar for games and bet you fifty cents that I win."

Jason laughed and took her hand, dragging her to the skee-ball machines.

"I'm going on a hot date with your nephew, just so you know where he is," she said over her shoulder to Richard.

He grinned. "Don't corrupt him too much."

"Pooh! You're no fun."

As she skillfully managed to lose three games, she chatted with Jason about school, which he liked and hated, the latest toys, which he wanted, and video games, which she wanted. She was aware of Richard watching her. It felt good to have a man's gaze on her body. A sudden wave of heat washed over her that ignited her long-dormant senses. She hadn't realized how much she needed to feel like a woman. Richard gave her that feeling with a glance. This might not be the date she wished for, but she'd found a deep satisfaction from it. Unexpected, she admitted wryly. Maybe she had a little Cary Grant in her, too.

Yet she wanted a monastic life—temporarily maybe, but remaining uninvolved was a necessity for her right now. She'd been responsible for so many for so long, and she'd finally achieved freedom to do what she needed for herself. It wasn't selfish; it was survival. Her dream of college would wither if she got involved with someone, let alone someone with kids. Others would have demands on her time again, and she would sacrifice herself once more. She had to be strong for herself for a while. That was all. Maybe this group date was the best kind of date, light and casual and, above all, friendly. No future implied.

Mark was practically asleep in Richard's arms after

skee-ball. Callie had paid her losses to that slick shooter, Jason. Jason looked happy—and nearly out of gas.

"Time to go," she said.

"I got the message," Richard said, nodding at the dozing toddler he held.

"I won, Uncle Richard." Jason held out his take, a dollar and a half.

"Wow. Dinner's on you. Just kidding. Congratulations, although I ought to yell at Callie for teaching you how to gamble."

Jason grinned at his uncle, clearly forgiving him for his earlier reprimand.

As they walked out, Richard said, "You're a sensational date."

Callie grinned, very pleased he thought so. "Thank you."

"And you're a good friend."

Her pleasure faded as a strong, more tender emotion surfaced. Be careful, she told herself. "I'm happy to help."

"I think you're my guardian angel. You've saved me tonight from a lot of future torture. I hope."

He repeated the "guardian angel" sentiment at her apartment when he dropped her off. It pleased her until she realized he wasn't walking her inside for a goodnight kiss. Logic told her he couldn't leave two young children alone in a car, even for a few minutes.

He did cover her hand with his. "I'll call you."

She smiled. "Good night, Richard."

His fingers squeezed hers, as if sending her that kiss he couldn't physically give. "Good night."

In her bed later Callie found herself as dreamy-eyed as if he had kissed her senseless. Get a grip, girl, she thought, shaking off the gooey feeling. The guy brought kids on a first date, a nightmare signal in any self-respecting woman's book of prospective mates. And any self-respecting woman would have run for the hills.

She *was* running. Now if only she hadn't had such a good time beforehand.

"THAT'S ALL OF IT."

Richard stood in the huge hangar-warehouse as trucks waited to pick up fruit from Malaysia. USDA inspectors swarmed over the boxes before finally releasing the shipment. In his capacity as Malaysia's local representative, Richard signed off on the paperwork while ignoring Mark's grunts to get the stroller moving. He had no other choice but to bring the boy with him as he got the Southeast Asian country's merchandise pushed as quickly as possible through the system.

"Okay, kid, we're off," he told Mark, turning the stroller toward the entrance. He waved his hand, motioning the trucks to move in.

Mark screamed happily at the vehicles, calling them by name. Only he didn't quite get the word right.

"*Trucks*, Mark, with a *T*," Richard corrected firmly as the warehousemen nearest them roared with laugher. "*Trucks.*"

"Tucks!" Mark shouted.

"Close enough, my friend." Richard decided he had handled that Callie's way—with humor, not outrage or admonishment for perfection. He could live with "Tucks." Boy, could he live with it.

He'd had that talk with Amanda about the virtual pets and about her life changes. She'd blushed furiously, and he'd been embarrassed, too, but he'd also tried to be as easy and matter-of-fact as he could. He didn't think he'd made too much of a mess. Amanda had seemed better since, controlling her outbursts…well, toning them down a bit. And maybe that was because she now had some insight into the cause of her behavior. All thanks to Callie.

He wanted to see Callie again to talk about *her* this time. She had mentioned night classes, but they'd never got around to talking of them on their date. They'd never got around to a lot of things. He intended to make up for that.

He would call her for another date as soon as he got home. And he would see her at the housewarming her sister was giving him. That would be great.

Chapter Three

"We're so honored to have a diplomat among us."

Richard couldn't understand his neighbor's excitement about his title. If they'd been at the warehouse with him and Mark, they wouldn't have been nearly so impressed. He'd been dressed in jeans and a ratty University of Pennsylvania T-shirt. About the closest he came to class or elegance had been his five-year-old loafers. The air he breathed had hardly been rarefied. "Sucking diesel" was the slang expression for inhaling truck exhaust. All in all, his diplomatic post meant he was no more than an exotic paper-pusher.

Richard smiled at the speaker, a woman from around the corner whose husband ran a Fortune 1000 company. "It sounds niftier than it is," he said, "believe me."

"Oh, I doubt that." The woman was so positive, Richard didn't have the heart to disabuse her of her notion.

As she talked with him, Richard had to admit that Gerri's housewarming was niftier than *he* had thought it would be. The place was packed, which was gratifying. Most of the guests talked in bunches, clearly old neighbors and friends, but they welcomed him graciously, and he couldn't complain.

For once he was without kids, too.

Since Gerri's house was on the same street, he'd left Amanda in charge of the boys. She was only a few minutes away, he would only be a few hours, and Mark had had his bath and been stuffed into his pajamas before he'd left. He felt at a loss as to what to talk about with these people, his world lately revolving almost exclusively around children, but his neighbors were quite skilled in the art of conversation. He was getting back into adult-conversation shape. Only one thing was missing. Callie.

When Gerri crossed his path in her hostess duties, he stopped her. "Is Callie coming?"

"No," Gerri said, looking surprised. "Why would she?"

Richard realized he might have made a faux pas. "I mentioned I expected to see her here when I talked to her the other day. I didn't think…I mean, she is your sister, and I assumed she'd be invited."

"Oh, dear." Gerri's face mirrored distress. "I don't invite family to neighbor things. I didn't even think about it. I'm sorry."

"I'm sorry, too," Richard said. It occurred to him that Gerri knew perfectly well he was more acquainted with Callie than with ninety-five percent of the people in the room. To leave Callie off the list because she didn't mix family and neighbors was incredibly rude to the guest of honor, who ought to have one familiar face in the crowd.

"I can call her now if you like," Gerri said, gesturing toward the kitchen where there no doubt was a phone.

"No, that's okay. She's probably busy."

Gerri brightened considerably. "Oh, yes. She must be. She's quite the free bird now."

Richard's housewarming mood deflated after that. People were welcoming still, but they seemed to have no true depth of character. He didn't feel much better when Callie's nephew, Joey, came downstairs and greeted him.

"Hi, Mr. Holiday," the boy began innocently enough.

"Hi, Joey." Richard smiled at him. He looked a little like Callie with his blond hair and fair complexion.

"Is…is Amanda allowed to go to soccer matches after school?" he asked, blushing bright red. Richard sensed girl interest, and he wasn't sure he liked it directed at his sweet, innocent, if occasionally hurricanelike niece. In fact, he was sure he didn't.

"Well, yes, I suppose," he said dubiously, having a feeling Amanda would kill him if he said anything else. "I'd like to see her support her school's events."

"Oh. I don't go to her school," Joey said. "I go to a private one. All the kids around here do."

Richard stared at him. He'd had no clue she was on the wrong side of the school tracks, too. Before they moved, he had thoroughly researched the schools, and they were excellent, in the top ten percent of the country. Why would all these people send their kids to private school when the local one had a great reputation? Unless they were total status-symbol seekers—or knew something he didn't. He would have to ask Callie. In the meantime he said, "I'm sure Amanda can go to your school's soccer match if she wants to."

The boy smiled. "Great. Thanks."

Joey practically skipped into the kitchen. Richard frowned after him. Nice boy, he thought. Polite. And he had better be as sweet and innocent as Amanda while he was with her. Unfortunately Richard had once been an adolescent. Masses of uncontrollable hormones weren't the exclusive property of young females. While girls got moody and weepy, boys got horny—and eventually desperate for an outlet. Richard glared at the swinging single door.

Worried about his niece, he managed to get away from the housewarming the moment it was acceptable to do so. He used the excuse of an early-morning appointment. People assumed it was some diplomatic thing, all hush-hush. He let them.

"Everything okay here?" he asked Amanda when he came through the door.

She nodded while staring at the den's television set. "I thought you'd be late."

"I was concerned about you, how you were doing. Mark went to bed okay?" he asked. "And Jason?"

"Yes," she snapped, glaring at him.

"I'm just asking," he replied, a little tired of the sulkiness. He wished he knew what to do with her. When her parents first died, she'd been clingy, something he understood perfectly. Now, however, she was distant, belligerent even. He wondered if she should see a grief counselor. He sat down opposite Amanda in the other wing chair. "Everyone was nice and very glad we've moved in. They gave us lots of things we can't use."

She wasn't amused. "That figures."

"I was joking." He paused, then decided he should play his ace. That was bound to make her happier with him. "Joey's bringing the gifts over in the morning."

She glanced at him again, although in a barely interested manner. "He is?"

Richard nodded. "He talked to me about asking you to a soccer game at his school."

She bolted upright. "What! You didn't say anything stupid, did you, Uncle Richard?"

Richard straightened happily, knowing he was on solid ground. "No, I didn't. I'm not that dumb. You'll be happy to know I told him it would be okay with me if he asked you to go."

"Uncle Richard!" she wailed, horror in her voice. "You *didn't*."

Richard gaped at her in bewilderment. "What's wrong with that?"

"He didn't ask me and now he won't!" She leaped from the chair and ran out of the room.

Richard slumped. "When will I learn to keep my mouth shut?" he muttered. "Especially when I didn't know I opened it?"

A few moments later he got up. He'd wronged Amanda—somehow—justified or not. He needed to tell her he was sorry. He'd also wronged Callie over the invitation. Well, no, he hadn't; her sister had. Still, he owed Callie an apology, too.

He dialed her number. When she answered, he said, "Hi, it's Richard. I hope I'm not disturbing you."

"No." She said nothing else. He wished he knew if she was in her nightgown, ready for bed. Did she wear a gown or pajamas? Baby dolls. She had to be the baby-doll type.

He got hold of his wandering libido. "I wish I'd had control over the housewarming guest invitations because I would have done more than assumed someone I actually liked would be invited. In fact, you would have been first on the list."

She chuckled. "Was it that bad?"

"I could have used an interpreter for all those square jaws." He sighed. "I thought you would be there, and I am not happy you weren't."

"Don't worry about it." Her voice sounded warmer.

"I knew you were naive and probably not on the same wavelength, although you were sweet about it. My sister's a nice woman, but she doesn't think sometimes. I love her, anyway."

"But I invited you. You should have come."

"Well…I thought it might be better not to after I talked with Gerri earlier in the day and she didn't say anything about the party."

"It's my fault," he said, thinking he should have yelled like a drill sergeant at Gerri. That might have gotten the message across to the woman.

"It's not your fault, idiot, although you might not be so generous when I tell you I got you two totally useless horse-head bookends that glow in the dark."

"I'll cherish them forever." He meant it, too. "Will you come over for dinner tomorrow?"

"Um…" She hesitated.

"Please. I'd like a friend. I need one. You can protect me from Amanda."

"Oh, Lord. What did you do now?"

"Nothing. I think. And everything, so I'm told," he said, and filled her in. "So when Joey asked me, I said it was okay by me if Amanda wanted to go. You'd have thought I was the chief torturer at the Inquisition when I told her. What did I do wrong?"

Callie chuckled. "Teenagers hate even the idea that they're under any kind of parental control, let alone to have it acknowledged to their peers. Especially to peers they're attracted to."

"Don't say that part."

Callie laughed this time. "Richard, that's what it's all about when you're that age. Amanda is a teenager, plain and simple."

"I think those are the most frightening words after

'nuclear explosion,'" he said. "Although, I thought it was really polite of Joey to ask me first."

"He's a good kid, despite some of Gerri's nonsense. Matter of fact, you should tell Amanda that."

"I will." He thought of his conversation with Joey. "Hey, is there something wrong with the public school here? I researched the school systems thoroughly before I moved here, but Joey tells me none of the other kids in the development go to the local school."

"I've heard nothing and, believe me, I would have. My sister sends her kids to private school because it's trendy, not for any other reason. Like the material girl she is. Gerri needs to have a show of wealth all the time to prove she's not poor anymore. Everyone has a quirky holdover from their childhood. But as far as the school goes, don't worry about it."

"I don't want to move Amanda or Jason. They've seemed to settle in okay. Since the school system's excellent, I truly don't see the point. But I don't want them to be outcasts, either."

"You're a good uncle."

Her words meant more than anything he'd heard in a long long time. "Thanks. I only wish Amanda thought so. I can't seem to do anything right."

"She's thirteen. No parent can."

"Can I do anything right with you?" he asked softly.

"Oh..." Her voice faltered as if he'd set off an unexpected spark. He hoped so. Talking to her about child-raising held an unexpected intimacy for him. Finally she said, "You do okay."

"I'll do much better," he promised.

"And, Richard...I'll see you tomorrow."

When he hung up the phone, he admitted he liked

keeping her off balance.

He planned to keep her even more so.

"I SHOULDN'T BE doing this," Callie muttered, pulling into Richard's driveway the next evening.

She stopped in front of the house itself, halfway around the horseshoe drive. The house's elegant, French-château facade was miles above her boxlike apartment complex. She bet the inside was to die for. Yet the formality was an odd place for a guy to bring three kids to live. She would have thought someplace less structured and formal-looking would have been more suitable.

Her nephew, Joey, came around the side of the house with Amanda. The pair weren't talking, but walking side by side with just enough distance between them to indicate interest and insecurity.

Callie smiled as she got out of the car. Oh, most definitely a mutual crush, she thought. "Hi, guys. How's it going?"

"Hi, Aunt Callie," Joey said, looking surprised. "Oh, yeah. You're having dinner here, too."

Amanda blushed furiously. "I asked him."

Callie grinned at her. "Great. He's very cute, isn't he?"

"Aunt Callie!" Now Joey blushed furiously.

"Well, you are. And if you're lucky, then Amanda thinks so, too. What's on the dinner menu? Anybody know yet? Do we have to make a great escape for pizza?"

"Japanese," Amanda replied, her blush lessening. "If my uncle doesn't mess up."

"I'll make sure he doesn't." Callie wondered what kind of cook he was. Probably hopeless, helpless and sexy there, too.

As the two teens led her into the house, she knew she

probably shouldn't have come to dinner. Her sister's lack of follow-up invitation had hurt, and Richard's apology had soothed her. Accepting his dinner invitation was partly from vulnerability and partly from the desire to flaunt him under her sister's nose. That Joey was eating here, too, would only rub Gerri's social climbing the wrong way. Her son and her sister, but *not* her. Maybe it would wake Gerri up enough to show some true manners from now on. Maybe.

The quick look at the downstairs rooms they passed reassured her. The house was big, and the furnishings sparse. Toys and papers were scattered everywhere, giving the place the lived-in look of any normal child-harassed household. Not perfection, not even close. She needed to see that, she thought. Or maybe not.

Richard stood among the steaming pots, expertly flipping strips of meat with tongs. He grinned at her and wiped his brow. "Hi."

"Hi yourself." She held up a couple of perfectly nice horse-head bookends. "Here's your housewarming gift. The batteries died so they don't glow in the dark anymore."

"I'm disappointed." He chuckled. "Hey, they *are* nice. Thank you."

"You're welcome." She'd been pleased to find something male and dignified.

A loud banging exploded from behind the cooking island.

"That's just Mark, the Emeril Lagassi of the toddler world," he shouted above the din. "Kid's been back here for an hour having a ball."

"That's all that counts," Callie said, laughing wryly. Richard wasn't hopeless and helpless in the kitchen. At least he was still sexy. He had the best of the three going for him. "Need some help?"

"No, no. Yes. I won't lie. Could you watch the soba noodles while I do the vegetables? Both need major attention, more than a convict on parole."

"Sure."

Callie came around the island. Mark sat on the floor surrounded by every pot and pan Richard wasn't using. The child stacked and restacked a set of plastic bowls, then banged a pan on the floor several times as a reward for his good work.

"Foo! Foo! Foo!" he shouted happily.

"Give him a set of bars and a tin cup to run back and forth across them, and you'd have the next Jimmy Cagney," Callie commented.

"He thinks he's cooking." Richard hollered, "Amanda! Go find Jason and tell him it's dinner in five minutes. By the time you find him, it will be."

Amanda looked murderous. She probably didn't want Joey to know she had to look after her brother, Callie thought, remembering the time a boy she'd liked had been scared off by her responsibilities. They just weren't cool.

"Joey, make yourself useful and go with her," Callie said to the boy.

"Sure, Aunt Callie." The boy looked happy to help. Young love did that.

After the pair left, Richard cleared his throat loudly. "Joey's a nice boy."

"Yes, he is." Callie didn't look up from the soba pot.

"Do you think she's too young to...to be around a boy like that?" he asked.

Callie shrugged. "Hard to say."

"Okay." Richard looked bewildered.

Callie shook her head. "Look, they're both pretty young, so I'd be surprised if it went beyond holding hands and an occasional peck on the lips."

"I don't even want *that*," he exclaimed.

Callie laughed. "Richard, you're sure to make it worse if you don't relax. She has a crush, her first probably, on a boy who's got his first crush, too."

"Okay." He shook himself. "I'm relaxed."

"Yeah, like a wolverine's relaxed. You need to talk to Amanda about sex."

"Oh, God! Can't I have one normal conversation with the kid?"

"Nah. She's a teenager. Look, you want her to respect her body, right?"

"Lord, yes."

Mark banged pots.

"And you want her to know what to do if a boy ever pressures her in the future."

"Is there no end to this?"

"Foo! Foo! Foo!" the next Jimmy Cagney shouted.

"You want her to know these things ahead of time, *before* her first real date."

Richard paused. "That makes sense."

"Of course it does. Better to do it before she's doing more than walking around the house with a boy. Talk to her about the emotional side of sex, not so much the mechanics. She probably knows that part. Heck, Jason probably knows that, too."

"Great. Another one in the wings."

"Actually I thought Joey and Amanda looked sweet together," Callie said, pulling out a soba noodle with a fork to test for doneness. It needed more time.

"You did?"

"Mmm-hmm. You know, this is fraught with danger

for my nephew. A boy's first crush can devastate him if it goes badly.''

"That's true. Mine dumped me for a kid on the basketball team. It took me six months to get over it.''

"She was a fool,'' Callie said.

He turned her toward him. "I'm glad you think so. But I like my latest crush much much better.''

Callie looked into his gorgeous brown eyes. She couldn't *not* look. His lambent gaze fascinated her. His lips closed the distance in the most innocent and yet exotic of kisses. His mouth plied hers, seeking a mutual response. She could taste his scent, imprinting its uniqueness on her brain. She could feel his breath hot on her cheek. She could hear his search for air to fill his lungs. She could smell the burning of his passion....

It reminded her of bad broccoli.

They broke apart just as the pan of vegetables turned black. Richard yanked the pan from the stovetop, rescuing it before a fire actually started. But nothing edible could be salvaged.

"Damn!'' he cursed, looking disgusted.

"Oh, no,'' Callie murmured, realizing the boiling soba noodles had turned to a lump of glue.

She and Richard looked at each other. "Pizza.''

Richard kissed her again, this time hard and fierce, his tongue swirling with hers in the sudden heat that gripped them both.

When he finally eased his mouth away, he said, "Might as well be in for a lion as for a lamb.''

Callie panted for breath, her head dizzy. He would be in for something if she didn't watch herself. Boy, did she have to watch herself.

Callie called in the pizza order while Richard cleaned

up the Japanese-dinner mess. The kids, no surprise, were delighted with the change.

"Don't tell Mom," Joey said to Callie. "She thinks pizzeria pizza is too oily and has lots of fat."

"No sweat," Callie replied. She winked at Joey.

Joey grinned.

Anything to take her mind off Richard's disturbing kiss, she admitted. Both disturbing kisses. They had shaken her to her toes, each in its own way. She tried to keep her emotions in balance, but like Amanda, she was all too aware of the male and all too gooey-eyed in his presence.

She did bounce back to earth a bit when Richard discovered he didn't have enough cash in the house to cover the bill. The delivery person wouldn't take a credit or debit card.

Callie sighed and got the cash from her purse. "You really know how to treat a girl right, my friend."

He looked humiliated. "I'm sorry. I haven't had a chance to go to the bank lately."

"I'm teasing you," she said, giggling. "But you are one heck of an interesting date."

He laughed wryly, finally seeing the humor in the situation. "Boy, I am a hot date, all right. A hot potato you ought to drop."

"I'll hang in there—until I get my money back." She saw his face. "I'm teasing, I'm teasing. You don't have to repay me."

"That wasn't the part that worried me."

Callie regained her equilibrium during dinner. The kids were great, just themselves, and that made the meal easier. She liked the simple fare, the uncluttered attitude and the general company. The meal Richard had originally planned, while more elegant, wouldn't have been as much fun. Right now she could have been back home in the small row house with her brothers and sisters. She liked the feeling, even though she didn't want to.

When the kids split for other venues, she and Richard lingered over after-dinner sodas yet again. Her lot on dates with him, she thought in amusement. But her curiosity about him got her.

"Tell me what a diplomat does," she said.

"Mostly I go out to the airport and make sure the entry paperwork for a shipment isn't screwed up," he replied. "I also pay bills here in Philadelphia as necessary for the country I represent. I help any businesspeople traveling through the region. Once I had to straighten out hotel reservations when a troupe of Balinese dancers appeared at the Spectrum."

"Is Indonesia your country?" she asked. She wasn't sure whether she was awed by the exotic idea of his being a diplomat or deflated by its reality.

"Only one of them. I actually represent most of the Micronesian states now." He chuckled. "I import from them, and after I gave an old office telephone system to Fiji, they asked me to be the local consul for them. Many countries tap someone they know in a city to be consul, usually someone who does business with them or has family connections in the old country. After Fiji, more and more Pacific Rim countries came to me. They made a kind of business conglomerate of the post after that. I pretty much cover them all."

"Wow. Do you go over there often?"

"A couple times a year for my own business, but sometimes for diplomatic reasons. I import and export goods, mostly clothes and furnishings. And chili mix. People in Sumatra are big on Southwest chili. Don't ask me why."

She sighed with envy. "You've been around the world, and I haven't been farther than Disney World."

"That's like being on another planet," Richard said, laughing.

"True."

"What do you do at the County Office on Aging?" he asked. "I was surprised by that. I would have thought you'd be a teacher or a child-care worker. You're really good with kids."

Callie waved a hand in dismissal. "I love kids, but I've also had enough of them, believe me. Since I was the oldest of six, I had to raise my brothers and sisters. My parents aren't rich—you saw that. I told you about Gerri's quirk. Mine is working with older folks. They're on the opposite end of the caregiving, which is refreshing."

"What do you do there?"

She liked that he was curious about her, too. It felt nice to have a man interested in her. "Lots of paperwork mostly. I help people find housing and nursing care or point them to other resources they need. I track statistics, local and federal, make reports, write grants and get federal funding however I can. It's a glorified secretarial position."

"I bet it's never dull."

Callie chuckled. "Most people think it is. And sometimes it truly is, but not often. Usually I'm run off my feet."

"You have classes, too, at night. You mentioned them. Are they related to the job?"

He had a wonderful habit of focusing in on her face, as if anything she did or said was of immense importance to him. What a gem, she thought. A gem with exactly the kind of baggage she didn't need. "I'm also finally going to college. At night. It'll take me about eight years to get my degree in liberal arts, but I'm getting it."

He grinned. "Wow. So you didn't go right after high school?"

"I couldn't." She shrugged. "I had a scholarship to Temple, but I had to help my family, so I couldn't go then."

"That's obscene!" Richard exclaimed, outraged. "Why couldn't the next oldest take over or something?"

"There was more to it than that," she said. "It was just a tuition scholarship, so it only covered half the cost. We didn't know other tricks to make college more affordable. Lots of things that I eventually learned for my brothers and sisters I didn't know for me at the time." She shrugged again, then smiled. "College won't be handed to me, Richard, and so it'll be all the sweeter when I graduate."

"You amaze me." His tone was gentle.

Callie felt a change in attitude from him. A softer Richard would be hard to resist. He *was* hard to resist. "I'm a normal person."

"Hardly. You sacrificed yourself for your family, a rarity these days."

"Lots of people do it. You're sacrificing yourself for others right now."

"I'm an adult—that's different. Lots of people don't help like you have. Especially not at your age. You're still helping people in your job—"

"It's a normal job."

"Not the way you go about it, I'll bet. And you help idiots like me—"

"Anyone would."

"No one has until you."

"Maybe you just needed to ask."

"I didn't ask you, Callie. You just bullied your way in, for which I'll be eternally grateful."

Amid the half-empty soda glasses and leftover pizza slices, he took her hand. "I think you really are my guardian angel."

Chapter Four

Callie's flesh tingled and she was far too aware of him as a man to be any kind of angel to him. He provoked the most temptingly sensuous thoughts and feelings in her.

"I didn't do anything, Richard. Don't make it out to be more than it is, okay?"

Her voice sounded too reedy to be firm. In fact, she sounded very wishy-washy to her own ears. He had to hear it, too.

"You should take more credit, Callie, for being a beautiful person, inside and out."

"I'm neither."

Why couldn't she pull her hand away? Why was she mesmerized like a rabbit in front of a hungry lynx?

"You're both."

He leaned forward and kissed her again. She responded instantly, just as she had before in the kitchen. This kiss was even more glorious somehow, for she had already tasted its like once and anticipated its effect again. Richard didn't disappoint her. Her body shivered with delicious pulses as his tongue mated with hers.

"Uncle Richard!"

They broke apart in a flash of panic. Callie glanced

to the doorway, expecting to have been caught—certainly Amanda's indignant tone indicated that—but no one stood on the threshold.

Amanda appeared an instant later, and Callie realized the girl had called out, giving an innocent warning of her approach. Good thing she had, Callie admitted, seeing Joey trailing behind the girl. Callie needed a diversion, and Amanda had enough to cope with, let alone catching her guardian kissing the socks off her prospective first boyfriend's aunt.

"Jason won't give over the TV," the girl said angrily. "We wanted to watch something, but he's playing video games."

Richard groaned. "The daily argument. Amanda, you know the game's hooked up to that television. He can't just move to another one."

"Well, I can't take Joey to my room to watch mine," she very sensibly pointed out, her cheeks carrying a tinge of pink.

"How about we hook the game system to your television tonight?" Callie suggested, grateful to have Richard focused on something besides herself.

"I don't want my brother in my room," Amanda announced.

"Oops. I forgot. Little brothers and big sisters' bedrooms do not mix," Callie said. "My brother Steve was the snoop police in my room if he got the chance."

Joey grinned at the mention of his uncle. Steve was almost hyper, extremely enthusiastic about everything.

"We'll put the video game on my television in my room," Richard said, getting up. "But this *one* time, okay?"

Amanda beamed at him. "Okay."

Callie hid a grin, proud of Richard. He was sympathetic and yet set boundaries for the future. He might have hope, after all.

"No! No! No!" Jason shouted when told of the change. He danced around evasively while holding tightly on to the joystick as he still played his game. "If I stop now, I'll get killed!"

"Uncle Richard!" Amanda exclaimed in protest.

"Poopies!" Mark shouted, running around the den in further chaos.

"Boy, somebody's gonna hate me." Richard said.

"Jason's not far from the end of this section he's in," Callie said, recognizing the game the boy played. "When he gets there, he can save and he won't die. Then you can move the system to your television. I'll change Mark. Joey, maybe you'd like to take Amanda for a short walk outside in the meantime. It's not too cold out, and there's supposed to be a full moon. It'll be nice for a walk."

"Sure, Aunt Callie. I'd like that," Joey said with a happy grin. Clearly, walking a girl under a harvest moon appealed to him. He turned to Amanda. "Would you like to go?"

"Sure," Amanda said, looking at him with adoring eyes, television and everything else forgotten.

It pays to have an in with one of the crush twins, Callie acknowledged.

"What am I supposed to do in the meantime?" Richard asked.

"Stand there and look pretty until Jason's done."

"I can do that."

Everyone giggled.

"All righty then." Callie picked up Mark. "Let's go, kid. I bet you're going to be president when you grow up, since you have to announce everything you do. Either that, or you'll be a game-show host.''

"Poopies!" Mark shouted again.

"I rest my case."

Later, when she and Richard cleared the table and loaded the dishwasher, Richard said, "You're becoming a very important person in my life—"

Callie sat a glass down with a dull thud.

"—and in an incredibly short time."

She turned to him. "Richard, I can't be any more than a friend to you."

He paused. "What?"

"I can't be any more than a friend to you," she repeated, knowing she couldn't let things go on as they had. "I've got my life in order finally. I'm going in the direction I've needed to go in for a long long time. You're looking for more than I can give right now. I think you should know that."

There, she thought. She had said what needed to be said, and now he knew things would never work between them. So why did it hurt the way it did?

"What are you talking about?"

Richard knew his demand sounded harsh. Suddenly he felt harsh. He felt sucker-punched, too.

Callie's blue eyes grew wide. "I...maybe I'm confused."

"I hope so." Richard felt confused, damn confused. He'd been having a great evening, making a lot of progress with her, despite the kids' interruptions. She had kissed like the sultry angel she was. Her kisses had promised even more. He was no fool.

"I'm sorry. You...you kissed me earlier and then started talking about how important I am to you. I thought you were talking about us being like, well,

Amanda and Joey. Emotionally and physically interested in each other.''

"I was." He hated the comparison to the kids—he still had trouble thinking of Amanda in terms of being physically attracted to anyone—but he let it slide. The more important thing was Callie's reaction. It wasn't what he thought it should be.

"I can't, Richard."

"You sure *seemed* interested. I don't understand," he confessed in frustration. "You kissed me like you were *very* interested. Why not just say you faked it to be polite and I don't turn your key?"

"Jeez!" Callie grimaced.

"I'm a big guy. I can take it. But I'll tell you that if you say it, then you are the greatest actress since Garbo. And about as flaky."

"It isn't that." She looked away. "The opposite is the problem. I'm attracted."

Richard frowned. "I'm attracted and you're attracted. What am I missing here?"

"I'm just getting my life together. For me." She paused. "I'm not explaining it well. I've given over my life for family ever since I can remember. It was expected of me. It was necessary. I understood all that. But my hopes and dreams had to wait. Now I'm going back to school. I'll have the career I want. But if I get involved with you...well, who knows where it might lead. I can't take the chance that I'll have to sacrifice again for family. It's selfish. I know it is. I hear it, and I'm ashamed. But I can only be your friend."

Richard stared at her. He'd expected to hear all kinds of nonsense about a relationship. This, however, wasn't nonsense. His own experience with his niece and nephews gave him a small glimpse into the all-consuming

demands of child care. She had done it for five brothers
and sisters all *her* childhood, when she should have been
dreaming of college—and boys. She must have only had
her dreams in snatches at best. Now she was on the verge
of her own fulfillment and here comes a guy, with kids,
who wants her, maybe to drag her back into that again.
He couldn't fault her in the least and said so.

"Callie, you are the least selfish person I've ever
met," he told her. "You deserve to not be fettered to
something that will hold you back again. I can't say a
relationship with me will be light. That's not what I want
anymore."

She swallowed visibly. "Maybe it's why you're attracted to me, Richard. But it's not really me. It's just
your need to settle down. I'm the first available woman
to come your way after you've decided that."

"Now you're going to tick me off again," he complained. "I didn't pick on the first available woman, believe me."

"Maybe you won't admit it, but most likely you did."
She grinned wryly. "I've got a psych class this semester.
It's amazing what people unconsciously do when moti-
vated."

"I'm quite conscious of why I feel like I do about
you, believe me."

"Okay."

She agreed too quickly, obviously not agreeing at all.
That really ticked him off. He leaned across the dishwasher's open door and kissed her before she could stop
him. He made sure it was a blistering kiss, tongue thrusting and demanding until she responded enthusiastically.
She moaned in clear pleasure, and he knew he could
give no better message that he was the most *un*confused

man on the planet. He based his interest on more than her being a convenient female.

"Oh!"

Richard let go of Callie at the stunned voice behind them. Amanda and Joey stood in the kitchen doorway. Their faces held shock and their mouths formed perfect circles of astonishment. He cursed himself for not having heard their approach. Both kids' cheeks flamed red at the same time.

"Callie and I were having a discussion," he said finally. He resisted the urge to be flip and say, *I was examining her tonsils with my tongue and can pronounce them healthy.* Now was not the time. "Actually I was kissing Callie because I like her a lot. For herself. She doesn't believe me."

"And it's time for me to go," Callie said, stepping away from him and the dishwasher. "Come on, Joey. I'll drive you up the street. I need to see your mother, anyway."

"But I thought I was staying…" Joey began, glancing at Amanda.

"Not now," Callie answered. "Always retire from the field when you're ahead. You're ahead." Callie took her nephew by the shoulders and turned him toward the hall and the front door. "Thanks for dinner, Richard and Amanda."

"Thanks," Joey said helplessly.

Richard wanted to ask what she meant by her comment about retiring while you're ahead, but Callie was gone and he had to deal with Amanda, who gazed at him as if he'd grown another head.

"That was *disgusting,*" Amanda said after the outside door opened and closed. "How could you do that with Joey's aunt and embarrass me like that!"

She ran from the room. Richard ran after her, catching her as she started up the stairs.

"That's enough, young lady," he said, holding her arm. "I'm your uncle, but I'm also a man. A single man. Callie is a very attractive woman and I like her a lot. I will express that on occasion if she allows me. And you will never say a word again about it. Do you understand?" He didn't wait for an answer. "I will be discreet, because I remember how embarrassed I felt when I was your age and adults kissed in front of me. But when two people care about each other, they express that. So you will respect that and make no comment during or after."

"Can I go?" she asked sullenly.

Richard wanted to shake her, but knew he would never raise a hand to the child. "When you start acting more mature than Mark. Right now you're not, and everyone knows it."

She rounded on him. "What?"

"I'm sure Joey's not treating his aunt Callie like a pariah because she kissed me. Amanda, it's not the end of the world because you saw me kissing Callie."

Tears filled Amanda's eyes. "I... I..."

Richard put his arm around her shoulders and hugged her. "I know. Hey, it was a shock to see your old fogy uncle like that."

She wrapped her thin arms around his waist and cried into his shoulder. "I'm sorry, I'm sorry!"

"It's okay." She was standing on the step, which made her nearly even with him in height. The lack of difference gave the teenager a womanly aura—a frightening thought. But she was just a kid, and she needed love and caring from a parental figure. That was him. He regretted being so woefully below standards.

A movement at the top of the stairs caught his eye. Jason stood there, his gaze round with anxiety.

"How'd the game go, Jay?" Richard asked calmly over Amanda's hiccuping tears.

"I won."

"Good."

"What's wrong with my sister?"

Richard smothered a smile at Jason's tone, all masculine and protective of the female member of the family. "Amanda just needed a cry, that's all."

Amanda sniffled, raised her head and wiped at her wet cheeks. "I'm okay now."

Richard patted her on the back one more time. "Good. I'm glad. Jason, it's time for bed."

The boy glanced between them one more time. "Okay."

Wow, Richard thought. With Jason, bedtime was usually a fight. "I'll be up in a minute to say good-night."

After Jason disappeared, he said, "I hope you really are okay with it, Amanda."

"I guess." But she managed a smile that took any sting out of her dubious words.

"It probably doesn't matter, anyway," he admitted. "Callie told me she only wants to be a friend."

"Oh, no!"

Richard had to grin at her sympathy. Kids were all over the place emotionally. Still, he felt he'd reached a new threshold of understanding with Amanda, a much needed one. "We all need a friend like Callie, so I'll live."

"I guess," Amanda agreed, then burst out, "but she's crazy if she doesn't like you!"

A suspicious lump of emotion clogged Richard's throat. It looked like the family protectiveness didn't stop with the males. He kissed his niece on the forehead in thanks.

Amanda giggled, although she looked ready to cry again.

"You've had a big day," he said. "Why don't you go up to bed, too?"

"Okay."

She moved lightly up the stairs. When she was half-way up, he added, "And if you ever kiss Joey or any other boy like I kissed Callie, you'll be grounded for a month."

She whirled around, all sweeping brown hair and colt-ish figure. "Uncle Richard!"

God help him, he thought, thinking she would break hearts without a backward look. He grinned. "Hey, I'm just being a good uncle."

Amanda snorted in disgust, then smiled and went to her room.

He might have told his niece it was a moot point about Callie, but he knew it wasn't from his end. He intended to make sure Callie eventually knew it, too. When she was ready for him.

Friends.

He snorted in as much disgust as Amanda had.

SHE HAD DONE the right thing and nipped the relation-ship with Richard in the proverbial bud.

"Hey, girly. Am I gonna get any service here?"

Callie glanced up from her computer screen. A man, at least eighty and as feisty-looking as he sounded, glared at her.

"I'm sorry," she said sweetly, refusing to be anything else in the face of rudeness. "I didn't realize you were standing there."

He had just walked over to her, and she knew it. So did he.

"'Course you didn't realize it. You got your nose buried in that thing." He sniffed, nodding at the monitor. "Damn things are a menace. Evil to the core. It says I'm dead."

"I beg your pardon?"

"Those things. Ask it. It'll say I'm dead."

"Not mine," Callie said firmly. Boy, was it ever Monday morning!

"You just go look up my name on that inter-ether thing inside it. Lester Jones. It'll say I died. It's cut off my social security and my pension and my bank!" The man's gaze blazed with righteous anger. "I don't mind being dead, girly, but I really would like to *be* dead before I'm declared that way."

No wonder he was so bitter, Callie thought sympathetically. Heck, she wouldn't want to be dead until the real thing, either.

"Here, sit down, Mr. Jones." She motioned to the chair next to her desk. He sat down with a hard thud. She smiled at him. "I'm Callie, Mr. Jones. I can understand your frustration. I'd be frustrated, too, if I were declared dead without the evidence. Unfortunately I'm going to frustrate you more because this office doesn't handle social security, pensions or bank accounts. You need to contact the state—"

"I already did. They say they'll fix it, but they haven't."

"Social Security?"

"You been in that office?" He harrumphed indignantly. "They couldn't find their way off a sliding board. Not surprised they decided I'm dead."

"Oh." She tried again. "Have you gone to your former employer to rectify your pension?"

"Yep. They say I'm too dead to live, girly."

"Callie."

"Girly." He eyed her sourly. "My bank ain't interested in my being alive, either, in case you was about to get to them. I came to you because you helped my neighbor Marsha Towell get her pension back after her company tried to drop her widow's portion. You fix me up and I'll call you Callie. Not before."

Callie smothered a grin. He was a gem. She remembered Mrs. Towell, a sweet little old lady in tears because she'd made no headway with her problem. Callie's heart had gone out to the woman, and she'd gone out of her way to intervene. Old Lester tugged on the heart-strings, too. She wasn't sure how yet, but he did.

"Bureaucracy sucks," she announced. "Okay, Mr. Jones. There are some people at the state and in Social Security who owe me favors. I'll call your employer and your bank, too. I can't wait to have you call me by my first name. You keep calling me girly and I won't speak for my actions."

The old man grinned lopsidedly. "I'll take my chances...girly."

Callie chuckled.

Lester relaxed with a heavy sigh. "Gotta say it's nice someone thinks I'm alive. I was beginning to wonder if I *had* died and gotten trapped in hell."

Callie shuddered at the thought of never-ending offices where one was spun in ever more frustrating circles. "I'll do my best, I promise. Now, I'll need information from you."

As she took it, she knew he'd probably become overwhelmed and bewildered, or had filled out something wrong, which had caused the problem for him. Computers didn't just decide someone was dead. Some human error somewhere had kicked Lester Jones's name out of the system. Even though he should be able to rectify it through normal channels, occasionally that didn't work. It might not be her job, but she stepped in for people from time to time. She just believed people should help others when they could.

She got all the information she needed from Lester, and he left her office almost smiling. Almost. She had a feeling that the other half of his problem was his bristly exterior. People probably refused to budge on his behalf. She intended to ream him out for his rudeness, *after* she helped him.

She made a few phone calls to people who promised to check into the problem and call her right back. With amusement, she flipped her calendar over two days and wrote down Lester Jones's name to remind herself to follow up with her contacts. If they actually called back before then, it would be a miracle. Bureaucracy held no miracles.

When her telephone rang a short time later, she wondered if a miracle *had* occurred.

"Hello?" she said when she picked it up.

"Hi. Am I calling at a bad time?"

Richard. He didn't identify himself, but she knew the voice too well already. It sent a shiver of anticipation along her nerve endings. She could feel again that searing kiss he'd given her. Every kiss he'd given her. They'd been far too few and far too memorable. How could she be just friends with a man who kissed like that? Her body said it would be a lot more than friends if it had the least opportunity—and that scared her.

"Hi," she said, glad her voice sounded fairly normal.

"I'm helping a dead guy come alive again, but no big deal."

"Is his name Lazarus?"

Callie laughed. "By the time I'm done with Lester Jones, it will be. Poor Lester is a victim of human error—and a first-class curmudgeon."

"Why help him, then, if he's so nasty?"

"Because I'm a very nice person. And because *after* I help him, I'll take him to the woodshed. There'll be so much more pleasure in it then."

"Getting thrashed by you would be a pleasure in and of itself."

Callie's face heated. She was glad he couldn't see the blush. "What can I do for you, Richard?"

"Oh, the temptation. I've always had this thing about women's silk panties—"

"I'm sure they look lovely on you," Callie said, having had enough of the nonsense. "Now, could you be serious?"

"Cut a guy's heart out, why don't you."

"One phone call from me, and you'll be as dead as Poor Lester. And I promise I will *not* rescue you."

"I'll be good."

"Good."

She had to admit the sexual innuendo and the bantering appealed to her feminine ego. Hells bells, it *was* nice for a man to view her as a potential bed partner. She would be very tempted if he didn't want and need more from a woman than she could give. Unfortunately, if he didn't, she knew she would want and need more for herself. Why were men such a catch-22, instead of being such a great catch?

"I called to see how you were after the other night. I didn't handle things well, and I apologize for that."

"I'm fine." After a soul-searching Sunday, she acknowledged. "I didn't handle things well myself, Richard, and I apologize for that, too."

"We're getting good at apologies, aren't we?" He chuckled.

Callie smiled. "Too good."

"I thought about what you said, and I want to be a friend to you, too."

"You do?" The notion didn't sit well with her. It felt like…like a rejection.

"I do. Callie, you're a terrific person, and like I told Amanda, we need a friend like you in our lives."

"You talked to Amanda about me?" she asked, shocked. What was this "need a friend like you in our lives" stuff, let alone discussing it with a child?

"Amanda was upset about catching us kissing. Probably she was upset because Joey was with her. By the way, your nephew is practically living over here now."

"Put limits on the visits so the two of them get their homework done," she said automatically, then returned to the subject at hand. "I really wish you hadn't talked to Amanda about us. There is no 'us' for one thing."

"I told her that." He chuckled again, sounding far too amenable to their new status. "She got defensive of me, which was nice."

"What does that mean?" Callie demanded, as bewildered and confused by Richard as Lester Jones had been by the bureaucratic system.

"Nothing. Just that she thought…well, that I was worth more than friendship." His voice faltered. "You know teenagers. First they're embarrassed by something, then they're defending one's honor if they think the family member's been hurt by someone. I thought it was nice of Amanda. I even had a good talk with her about things, the best talk we've had so far.''

Callie realized how petty and perverse she sounded. Why was she so testy over his agreeing with her about their being friends? She wasn't sure whether she was more annoyed about his conversation with Amanda or with Amanda becoming defensive on her uncle's behalf. Why would either bother her? And bother her this much?

''Oh, okay,'' she said lamely, having no clue what else to say. ''Richard, I need to get back to work.''

''Sure. I should be working, too. Would you like to have dinner on Saturday again? As friends of course.''

''Of course,'' she muttered in disgust.

''I'm sorry. What did you say?''

''Nothing.'' She knew what answer she needed to give and did her duty. ''I'm sorry, but I can't.''

''I see.''

He probably did. She could hear the hurt in his voice. Temptation was a brick wall in her path, but she said, ''Richard, I really can't. That's my youngest brother Jamie's birthday. My parents are giving him a party.''

''Oh. How about Sunday?''

She sighed. ''Richard...''

''Just as friends.''

Oh, Lord. She was beginning to hate that word.

''I don't think it's wise.''

''It is, if we're just friends,'' he reminded her.

Yep, she did hate that word.

''Let me think on it,'' she said.

''You do that so nicely.''

''I try.''

After a telling pause he said, ''My turn to be nice. I'll let you go and call you later on.''

She smiled. ''Okay.''

Several hours later was hardly the "later on" she envisioned when she answered her phone and heard Richard's voice.

"Callie? I hate to ask, but I have no one else to turn to."

Something in his tone made her sit up. "What's the problem?"

"The soccer team from Java is in Philly on a U.S. tour. Their right winger was in a car crash. I have to go to the hospital to handle the paperwork and whatever else they need. I can't take Mark and I don't know how long I'll be. Could I presume on our friendship and ask you to watch him until I get back?"

"Sure," Callie said, in total sympathy with his problem. "I'll come over now. It's only a couple more hours until work's over, anyway."

"Great. Thanks." His relief came clearly over the line. "You're the best friend a guy could have."

Callie looked heavenward.

Just the words she wanted to hear.

Chapter Five

It was after midnight before Richard walked in his front door.

He shut it behind him and leaned against it wearily. What a day and night, he thought. Everything passed by him in a blur of waiting rooms, isopropyl-alcohol fumes and bad translations.

"Hi." Callie's slim form was silhouetted in the foyer doorway. "How's the winger?"

"Resting comfortably." He smiled at her and straightened. "It's not anything more serious than a couple of broken ribs and a concussion. The broken leg's a concern because of soccer, but it should heal. They're keeping him overnight. How did it go here?"

Callie grinned. "Good. Mark was fine. Jason argued television over homework. He lost, so I don't think he's happy with me. Amanda was upset at first when she came home to find me, not you, but then she was okay. We all made cookies. Chocolate chip. Want some?"

"I'd kill for some," he said, following her into the kitchen.

He stopped dead. The room was spotless, all the clutter gone and the toys put away.

"Wow," he said in awe, coming fully into the room. "How did you do this?"

"I told them we wouldn't make cookies until they cleaned up." She laughed. "Even Mark put away his Be-Bop. He threw it in the toilet, but that's a minor point."

"It's the hold-out-the-carrot theory, eh? You didn't tell me that one before." He wondered what kind of carrot to hold out to her. Not only for baby-sitting, but for other things, as well. "You are an angel. But I've always known that."

She smiled shyly, for her. "I was happy to do it."

He wanted to kiss her but resisted. She had drawn a line in the sexual sand, and he wasn't sure how to cross it without disastrous results. "I've only known you a few weeks, but I feel like I've known you all my life. I trust you completely."

"Richard, please. It's okay. No big deal."

"It is to me." He paused. "Callie, I have to take this guy back to Java. Probably the day after tomorrow. The coaches have to stay with the team, you see, and he's not able to go by himself. As consul here, I have to escort him home. This is the sort of thing they pay me the big bucks for." He grinned wryly. "It'll take a long weekend at most. I hate to ask. I wish I had someone else to ask, but my mother's in Florida and she's not in the best of health. And frankly, she's not crazy about kids, so it's never been a good situation. That's why I was named guardian of the kids." He remembered her brother's birthday party. "Wait. You can't, anyway. You have your brother's party—"

"Richard, don't worry about that," she interrupted. "I'd do it in a heartbeat, but wouldn't the kids be more comfortable with a family member?"

"No, there really isn't another family member. I have cousins in the area, but I haven't seen them in years, and the kids don't know them at all. But the kids know you, and I know you. We trust you, Callie."

"Oh, God." Callie took a cookie and bit into it.

"I'd take them if I could, but I can't. The trip will be grueling, and I can't care for them and the player, too."

"I know. It just doesn't feel right for me to stay with the kids."

"It feels very right to me." When he'd realized the player couldn't continue the tour and would have to be carted home, he hadn't known what to do with the kids—until he thought of Callie. Never had something seemed so perfect as leaving Amanda and the boys with her. "You care about them, Callie. They know it. So do I."

"Richard." She sighed. "There are so many reasons why you shouldn't and I shouldn't. When do you leave?"

He smiled, recognizing that the nightmare had a bright corner to it. "Not until the end of the week at least. Prang—that's his name—has to wait until the danger from the concussion passes. I'll pay you, Callie, whatever you want."

She glared at him. "Don't ruin the moment with crass materialism. I might take you up on it."

He smiled. "I owe you my life."

"Now you're talking my language." She grinned back, then sobered. "I better go. I do have to work tomorrow, and I'll have a lot to do if I'm going to be out of the office for a couple of days."

"Do you want me to talk to your boss?" he asked.

"No. I can use my laptop to work from here."

Good luck, he thought, knowing that, for him, carving

out work time among the kids was a lesson in frustration. "I'll have the Javanese government give you a humanitarian award."

She laughed. "I'd like that. Hey, I could be the Java Woman."

"I'll see what I can do," he promised.

"Richard, are you sure you want to do this?" she asked.

"Yes. I'm very sure I want the kids with you," he replied, finally taking a cookie. He bit into it. "Hey! This is really good."

"I think that's the one Mark sneezed on."

The cookie piece went dry as dust in his mouth until he saw her mischievous grin. He swallowed and said, "You love teasing me, don't you?"

"Men are such prime candidates for teasing. By the way, do you have a potty chair for Mark?"

Bewildered, he repeated, "A potty chair?"

She looked at him with obvious exasperation. "You know what a potty chair is. Come on, that wonderful device for getting children out of diapers—"

"Oh. Oh!"

"The light has been switched on," Callie said.

"Oh." The final exclamation came out as a groan. "I don't have one. Why?"

"Mark's ready for training, I think."

Training what? Richard wondered, even though he knew. He just wasn't sure he was ready for it even if Mark was.

"I'll get one for you and train him while you're gone."

"My God," he said. "Can you do it in a weekend?"

"If Mark's ready."

"How can you look at him and *know* he's ready?"

"He reminds me of my youngest brother at that stage, and I trained him." She shrugged. "I don't know how to explain it. I noticed today that his diapers were dry for a couple of hours at a time. Well, we'll try and see how he does. If he's not ready, we'll stop. He'll let us know. Boy, will he let us know!"

"Wow." The possibilities were tremendous with Mark no longer in diapers. "If I come home and I don't have to change him, I'll have died and gone to heaven. Do you have *any* clue what that's like?"

"Millions of women and men know, believe me."

"Yeah, but I *don't.*" He picked her up and swung her around. "Callie, if you could do that, then you *are* my guardian angel."

She gave a deep throaty chuckle.

Her body was soft and lithe in his embrace. His senses stirred, sending a rush of heat through his veins. Without thought, he leaned forward and kissed her. Her mouth opened to his. Their tongues mated. He tasted sweetness and chocolate, a rich combination that imprinted on his brain. He'd never be able to eat that kind of cookie again without tasting this moment.

Her breasts pressed against his chest, her nipples hard even through her clothes and his. He wanted her. She had come into his life like a whirlwind at a time when he'd had to set aside adult relationships. Yet she had already made wonderful changes in his everyday life. He needed a much more intimate change between them, one that was forbidden.

Callie pulled away. "Richard, we shouldn't."

He was sick of that notion. Maybe they shouldn't, but he damn well wanted her to know what they might both be giving up.

He kissed her again, tasting her mouth, tasting her

need as she came to him eagerly. Her fingers dug into his shoulders. Her hips pressed against his. Their thighs brushed together. She might not want to be with a man, but she wanted *him.*

When he let her go this time, her eyes fluttered slowly open as if she was still caught in the grip of the kiss. Her lips were swollen from their passion. That pleased him.

"Don't worry," he couldn't resist saying. "It was just between friends."

"Oh." Her eyes narrowed. He had the distinct feeling she didn't like that remark. Which pleased him even more. It was nice to be the elusive one for once.

"I really have to go," she said.

He walked her to the door, deliberately not touching her. He went outside with her to her car, neither of them speaking, yet the awareness between them nearly tangible. The chill air didn't bother him, although she pushed up her coat collar. He opened her car door and said, "Callie, thanks for everything. You are my guardian angel."

"Your *friendly* guardian angel." Her voice sounded sour.

He kissed her cheek in the most platonic of gestures. "Absolutely. I'll call you tomorrow."

She nodded curtly, then left him standing in the driveway as she backed the car out into the street.

Richard watched her pull away around the corner before he went into the house and shut the door. His friendly guardian angel. He wondered how long that would last and hoped not long at all.

He headed for the kitchen and another cookie.

"BUT I DON'T WANT to clean my room!"

Jason stamped his feet and folded his arms across his

chest, his look defiant.

Callie sighed. Just what she needed: Mr. Macho Man. "Okay, my friend. It's your choice, so I guess you won't be playing your video game tonight."

Jason's arms fell to his sides and his jaw dropped open. "What!"

Callie shrugged. "Your room's a disaster and I am certainly not going to clean it."

"But we have a cleaning lady!" Jason wailed.

"That may be, but she won't be able to set foot on a square inch of carpet, let alone vacuum it. You have to clean it up. The last thing I want is to dig up some experiment in there on how many fruit flies can exist off a dirty dish under the bed. Unless it's a science experiment for school, it's just a plain old mess."

"It is an experiment," Jason said quickly.

"Then show me a note from a teacher that it is, and you're in the clear. Just like your room needs to be."

The boy frowned. "Uncle Richard always cleans up my room for me."

Callie turned her head to one side and then the other to display her profile. Aggrieved, she said, "Do I look like Uncle Richard? I'm much shorter and less hairy, thank goodness."

"But it's not fair," Jason whined.

"Life's not fair, so we have to make the best of what we're given. Cleaning a dirty room is a positive thing." She turned him toward the stairs. "Come on, Jay. I'm dying to play Go-Go Karts and I need a second player. Mark's no good. He keeps trying to eat the joystick."

"All right." Jason trudged up the steps, defeated by his desire to beat the heck out of her at the game.

"Carrots," she murmured, going back into the

kitchen. "Who says kids don't want 'em? As long as you use the right kind of carrot, they do."

Richard had left two days ago with the soccer player and was due back late tomorrow. She'd wondered more than once how she'd wound up here, and knew it was her big mouth.

"Poopies!" Mark announced.

"Okay, big guy," she said, scooping him up and rushing him to the potty she'd brought with her.

Mark was duly praised for a good job. The kid was easy, she thought. He announced his intent beforehand, giving her plenty of warning. What more could one ask?

She heard the front door slam and hurried out of the foyer powder room. She whipped open the front door to find Amanda cutting across the huge yard. Callie had been treated to two days of observing the puppy love between Richard's niece and her nephew. It had been painful to watch, because she had a bad case of puppy love herself. If she wasn't careful, her puppy love could turn into a rottweiler that would eat her alive.

"Hey!" she called to Amanda. "Did you forget to tell someone you were going out?"

"I'm going out!" Amanda called over her shoulder, still walking.

"I have a problem," Callie muttered to herself. This was the third time in nearly as many days that Amanda had not so subtly indicated that Callie's presence was unwanted and unappreciated. She shouted after the girl, "Could you come back here a minute?"

"I'm late!"

"Okay." More loudly she shouted, "You left your bras in the laundry room and—"

Amanda yelped in frustration and came running back to Callie. "Shut up!"

"No, I will not shut up if you leave me no choice by continuing to walk away," Callie stated sensibly. "Look, I know you feel you don't need a baby-sitter, but you're not old enough to be left alone, so here I am. Also, your uncle's doing the very best job he can, but he's not your mom and dad and neither am I. Life hasn't been fair to you, but taking it out on me or Richard doesn't help *you.* I think you're mature and bright, certainly mature enough and bright enough to use some common sense. I'm not asking you to help me while your uncle's gone, because you deserve to be a teenager, not a mini-mom like I was." *Like I still am,* she thought. "But I need to know where you are at all times, who you're with, how long you expect to be gone and anywhere else you'll be going while you're out. And I need phone numbers. It's not too much to ask, so it should be a piece of cake to cooperate with me. You get what you want and I get what I need, okay?"

Amanda's expression was sullen, but she hadn't interrupted. "I'll be at Joey's. Do you need the phone number?"

"I don't believe his parents are home." She knew her sister and brother-in-law played golf on Sunday afternoons."

"So?"

"So my nephew is not allowed to have guests over then." Well, he wasn't if she had anything to say about it. This might be puppy love, but sweet innocence could quickly turn to intimate innocence. A little subtle supervision never hurt. "Tell him he's caught and you are both to come here. Now, I have to go back inside before your brothers burn the house down." She softened her voice, "Amanda, honey, I just care about you, okay?"

"Sure." Amanda whirled and headed for Joey's house.

Callie groaned. "Please spare me, Lord, from teenagers and toddlers—and kids in between. That ought to cover it."

Inside, Mark was still in the powder room, splashing water in the bowl. And not the sink. It could be worse, she admitted.

"Water, Callie!" the boy happily shouted.

"You're genius material," Callie said, lifting him away. "You must have a thousand dollars' worth of toys in this house and you're playing with the potty. There's a lesson here, but I don't want to learn it."

By the end of the day, Jason's room passed muster. Mark played with normal toddler toys, and Amanda actually spent the time at her own house with Joey following her about. Callie was exhausted by the time everyone was finally in bed. Her laptop computer called to her, demanding she catch up on the work she'd brought from the office and from school, but she only stared at the flat gray device, unable to do more.

She had forgotten how much mental and physical work children required. Any notion that she could balance all had been killed in the battle to keep up with Richard's three. She couldn't remember whether her brothers and sisters had been as willful as Amanda, as stubborn as Jason or as headstrong as Mark. She knew the kids had suffered a great tragedy, and she'd tried to allow for that. But nothing had changed her feelings on having a family anytime soon. Kids were just too much work. She could not afford to devote herself to such a situation, not for a long time to come.

Richard had called her from Java yesterday to let her know he'd arrived halfway around the world. Amazing, she thought. She'd clung to the sound of his voice. Just the way he said her name sent shivers of delight through her. And the way he kissed… In a few seconds more the other night, he would have been stripping her bare. And she would have loved it.

Yet he came with children. This long weekend served to remind her of her own goals in life. It reminded her where *she* needed to be right now. She wasn't being selfish, just sensible. As she told Amanda, life was unfair. She couldn't allow it to be any more unfair to Richard, to the kids or to her than it already was.

After she'd nursed a glass of wine through the eleven-o'clock news, she finally turned out the kitchen lights and went upstairs, the never opened laptop tucked under her arm.

The house had five bedrooms. She'd used the guest bedroom for two nights, but as she glanced at Richard's closed door, the desire to sleep in his bed just once overwhelmed her. Granted, he owned the guest-room bed, so it was his, too, but the connection wasn't the same. She wanted to sleep where his body slept, where his unique male scent subtly pervaded the sheets. Where his warmth had heated the silk. She knew his bedclothes were silk. She had peeked.

But she couldn't sleep in them.

Why not? Her brain asked the question of its own accord. After all, she could do it with no one knowing. She went to bed after the kids and got up before them. Richard wasn't due back until tomorrow evening. She could wash the sheets and erase all evidence of her presence in his room. She was much more deft than Goldilocks had been with beds. He'd never know.

Best of all, she would have a delicious memory. One she could revisit any time she wanted. She couldn't remember when she had ever taken a memory for herself. Never had she taken one so intimate.

"No," she said firmly, knowing she really couldn't.

She changed into her night wear, an oversize T-shirt emblazoned with a sleeping bear, before going into the large bathroom. When she came out again, her feet wandered over to Richard's bedroom door. She slowly pushed it open. A wedge of light from the hall illuminated the king-size bed. Its dark coverlet was printed with a jungle-pattern of light greens and oranges, a gentle touch with very masculine overtones.

Callie gazed at the empty bed for a long time. She turned out the hall light and went into the room. As if in a dream, she watched herself pull back the coverlet and sheets. The silk was like shimmering liquid against her palm. She slipped into the bed, the mattress accepting her body as a lover might accept a true mate. She pulled the sheet and coverlet up over her shoulders and turned her face into the pillow.

Richard's scent drifted through her senses, elusive, almost nonexistent but with that wonderful sharp twist of cologne just challenging the edges of her mind. They could put her blindfolded in a room with a thousand men and she would be able to pick Richard out. She hoped.

Callie smiled wryly at the thought. Okay, so she was getting way ahead of herself. But a girl could dream.

She did dream. Of Richard.

RICHARD UNLOCKED the front door, walked into the darkened house and hit the button on the keypad that turned off the alarm system.

He dumped his overnight bag next to the foyer table and sighed heavily. Four in the morning was a helluva time to arrive home, but he was damn glad he had. He knew Callie and the kids didn't expect him for another fourteen hours, but he'd gotten lucky and was able to get out of Java earlier than he'd expected after turning Prang over to Javanese authorities. He'd gotten himself bumped up on flights from Sidney and San Francisco, which helped, but his energy was completely wiped out.

His body, as if picking up on the thought, suddenly felt as if it dropped six stories in six milliseconds, and a wave of wooziness overtook him. Jet lag. He'd probably have the condition for the next few days in payment for his quick trip. Maybe he wasn't as lucky as he'd thought.

Smiling, he went into the kitchen to drink some water, knowing he was probably dehydrated, and that added to the jet-lag symptoms. His stomach growled. He was short on food, too. Maybe Callie and the kids had baked cookies again. He was so hungry at this point he'd even eat one Mark really *had* sneezed on. Well, he might.

The kitchen provided cold water from the refrigerator-door fountain, but yielded only store-bought cookies. They weren't as good as the home-baked ones of the other day. It felt like years rather than days since Callie and the kids had baked them.

Callie and the kids.

Richard drew in a deep breath. He loved the notion of Callie in a unit with his niece and nephews. In a unit with him satisfied his soul. He wished he could get used to it—but Callie had dreams and they didn't include him.

He climbed the stairs in the dark. Glancing at the guest-bedroom door, he wanted nothing more than to go in and wake Callie in the most intimate of ways. He wondered if he *should* wake her, just to let her know he was home early. Obviously his coming in hadn't stirred anybody. But he didn't trust himself to be alone with her and a bed.

He opened his bedroom door. The wedge of light from the hall illuminated his bed. A figure lay curled up under the covers. A spill of angel-blond hair spread across the pillow. Richard sucked in his breath. Callie was in his bed.

He felt as if he was watching her and himself in a surreal scene. She stirred and stretched, her slender form outlined under the coverlet. He shut the door and walked toward her, his body under another control.

"Callie," he whispered, knowing he had to be dreaming. Or she was a jet-lag hallucination.

She murmured in her sleep as his hands found her shoulders. She pulled him to her and kissed him, her mouth opening and her tongue mating with his. He *was* dreaming, he thought. She was not vulnerable like this, trusting and wanting and expressing it without hesitation. He kissed her for long moments. Her hands caressed his back, her fingers tugging at his hair as need apparently rose within her. Finally he eased his lips from hers, knowing he should follow reason.

"Callie, wake up," he said in a low voice.

"Mmm. I'm awake." Her voice sounded far too sleepy for that to be true.

He chuckled. "You can't be."

"I am. You can't be here."

"I got home early." His cheek was against hers, and he could feel her smile.

"It doesn't matter. I took your bed. I'm sorry."

"I'm not. Stay here."

She kissed his cheek, his temple, the corner of his mouth, her own unerring in finding the places that sent streams of heat flowing through his body. He wanted her badly, and to have her like this, willing and sensual, was too much for him. He kissed her frantically, trying to convey all the pent-up longing he had for her.

Callie pressed against him, her breasts buried in the wall of his chest. He could feel her nipples already hardened into nubs. They burned his skin. Her flesh was warm and her hair silken. He tangled his fingers in the strands, the tresses wrapping around his palms as if they had a life of their own. This, he thought, was how the Gorgon ensnared men. Not with snakes, but with such wondrous hair that men wanted to spend their whole lives touching it. A thought flitted through his Callie-drugged mind that they should be cautious with the children in the house. But the kids were asleep, and that was all he needed to know.

Not content with her mouth, he kissed her throat, her chest, then pushed the covers down and kissed her breasts through her practical T-shirt. Not the baby dolls of his imaginings, but he didn't care. Only Callie could turn a simple garment into something exquisite. The thin material moved and shifted, giving his lips only glimpses of the satiny skin underneath. Callie's hands urged him on, and he plucked at her nipples, their hardness unhampered by the cotton barrier. She writhed under his ministrations. Richard's mind spun with the heady combination, his jet lag and good sense long forgotten. She offered him this night, and he would be a fool not to take it. Maybe…maybe if she were open to him one time, she would be open in other ways. The risks were worth it.

Her fingers pushed at his shirt buttons, as if she knew his thoughts and agreed. He helped her remove his shirt, then stretched out on the bed as she stroked his naked chest. He shuddered, shivers of delight coursing through his veins at her touch. Her hands were all over him, wanton in searching out points on his body for her caress. Her fingers lingered on his stomach, her nails lightly raking him.

Her T-shirt was on the floor before he realized he had even taken it off her. Her body was cool like marble and yet hot like lava. He wanted nothing more than to lose himself against her, inside her, to find her woman's flesh gloving his own. The rest of his clothes joined hers in a frenzy of hands, their mouths melding together in a wild kiss.

She wrapped one leg around his hip, urging him more intimately to her. Somehow a caution filtered through the sensuous haze. He could not protect Callie from his needs, not when they were the same as hers tonight, but he could protect her from what could threaten to sideline her dreams again. He reached into the nightstand drawer. The rustle of the wrapper brought Callie's head up in awareness of what he was doing.

"Thank you," she whispered.

His breath came out in a rush, and he smiled.

She kissed him tenderly, accepting his caution. He cared for her more than he cared for his own pleasure. Now she would know it. Her woman's flesh was moist and yielding, enclosing him fully in its heat. Richard closed his eyes, wrestling all the urges of satisfaction that his body demanded at once. Callie's other leg slipped under his hip as she lay beside him, pulling him impossibly tighter into her body. Sweat beaded Richard's forehead, and he thought he would shame himself. He held himself still, absorbing the feel of her as one with him. Never had anything meant more than to have Callie so intimately entwined with him. He allowed himself no expectations beyond tonight.

He moved finally, and Callie joined him in the ageless surrender of body, mind and spirit. Their thrusts together were slow, rhythmic, encompassing hearts, as well as flesh. Callie moaned, her kisses frenzied as pleasure released itself throughout her body. It was so strong Richard felt her flesh pulsing with it. He rose above her and thrust, once, twice, hard and fast, until his own pleasure took him crashing over the edge of a velvet darkness that held her and him in its embrace.

Even as it took him, he knew their relationship would never be the same again. He would worry about it tomorrow, which was already today.

Chapter Six

Callie awoke to the light of early morning.

The male form spooned against her back didn't surprise her. She remembered all too well their lovemaking, taking her by surprise and yet so longed for. How could she ever forget being so intimately together with him?

The kids.

Callie tensed, wondering if they'd discovered Richard and her in his bed. Were they awake even? She prayed not. How could she explain if they had come in before now, seen and left? And if they hadn't seen her with Richard, where were they and what were they doing? What a lousy baby-sitter she was.

Guilt washed over her, relieved only slightly when she glanced at the clock and saw it was a little after seven. Yesterday and the day before that the three children hadn't even stirred before eight. Hopefully they had kept to the same schedule.

Callie carefully lifted the male arm from around her waist. She tried not to notice the strong muscles and tanned skin overlaid with a fine layer of hair. She tried not to notice, either, the strong hands that had touched every inch of her in the deepest part of the night.

She moved away from the man she had explored so

thoroughly with lips and tongue and fingers. Her body cried out in protest as she left his warmth, but she forced herself to slip out from the bedclothes. She found her T-shirt on the floor where Richard had tossed it and flung it over her head. Shoving her arms through the sleeves, she tiptoed to the bedroom door.

She couldn't resist peeking at Richard before she left the room.

"Oh, Lordy," she murmured. He looked so damned virile lying there. Like a satisfied panther. She had put him in that condition, and part of her was as pleased as the other part was horrified at what she'd done.

She cracked open the door. Peering out into the hallway, she was relieved that it was clear and blessedly quiet.

She raced across the hall and into the guest bedroom. Once inside, she shut the door against her foolishness. Sitting on the bed, she wondered where her righteous conviction had disappeared. It had vanished faster than Casper the ghost, that was for sure. Mortified, she covered her face with her hands. Leave it to her to follow a lark just once in her life and get burned royally. And had she ever been burned. Deliciously burned.

"Okay, so you made a mistake," she said out loud, lowering her hands. "It isn't the first time, and it probably won't be the last. Get over it." She lifted her head and straightened her shoulders. "Repeat after me. What is the goal? A full college education is the goal. What will *not* get me there? Being mini-mom again." She paused. "*And* men. A man. Richard Holiday. Incredibly sexy, hopelessly honorable Richard Holiday."

Later, she couldn't look herself straight in the eye while she was in the bathroom. It wasn't easy putting on mascara, she admitted, but managed not to get it across her forehead again. After dressing, she stood in the hallway and listened for noise. The kids were still asleep, thank goodness. One disaster averted by sheer luck.

Downstairs, she made coffee. As she sat at the table, not sipping it, she wondered whether she should just leave. Richard was home now, and he would take his job back. But she bet he was exhausted from living on planes for the past few days, not to mention the...other. See? she thought with satisfaction. She hadn't mentioned it. Her conscience wouldn't allow her to just leave, however. Darn it!

"Hi."

Callie glanced up at Amanda's voice. The girl had Mark on her hip. Both were bleary-eyed and a little wild-haired from sleep.

"He was banging on something in his room, so I thought I better bring him down," Amanda said matter-of-factly, while nodding at her little brother.

"Thanks." Callie watched the teenager for any sign that she was aware of what had happened much earlier in the morning between the adults in the house. The girl looked calm, serene almost, a miracle for a teenager. Impossible for a teenager with some personal knowledge about sex between the adults in the house.

"Are there any cocoa crunchies left?" Amanda asked after settling Mark in a chair. "I'm starved."

"I think Jason left a bowlful," Callie said.

"Good, but could you get more today?"

"Sure. Your uncle Richard's home."

Amanda momentarily turned back from her cocoa-crunchies trek. "Really?"

Callie nodded. "He got in during the night. I guess you didn't hear him."

"No. Wow. He's early. Do we have milk?"

"Yes." Mark climbed onto Callie's lap. His thick wad of night diapers buffered his butt. Training was strictly daytime at this point. She was no fool. Well, not about that. "What were you up to in your room, Mister Blister?"

"Bed go boom," Mark said.

"I don't know." Amanda shrugged. "It looked fine to me. He was just banging."

"God knows what he means by 'Bed go boom,' but I'm not sure I want to. Are you doing something with Joey today, honey?"

"No." Amanda grinned. "He's got school, but ours is closed because of the state teachers' convention."

"The joys of a public education," Callie said with a grin. "So what are you doing today without my nephew who's probably jealous as all heck?"

"I'm going to the mall with Heather." Amanda paused. "If that's okay."

The girl sounded uncertain rather than sarcastic. Kids did like limits, whether they realized it or not, Callie acknowledged.

She smiled at Amanda. "Sounds good to me."

Amanda nodded, happy. It seemed something of what Callie had said the other day had gotten through, and a truce had been declared. "Joey wants to play soccer at my school rather than his because our team's better, but—"

"I know." Callie sighed. She could understand her sister's insistence on private school if the local public one wasn't good. But Amanda's school was excellent. Ah, the trials and tribulations that went with kids.

Mark leaned back against her and sucked on his thumb, his small being perfectly content and trusting.

More trials and tribulations of kids, she admitted, stroking his hair. The fine strands felt like silk.

Feet suddenly pounded down the stairs. Jason sped into the kitchen. He spotted the open cocoa-crunchies box on the counter. "Hey! They're mine!"

"No, they're not," Amanda said, taking a huge spoonful of cereal from her bowl and shoving it in her mouth. "Mmm-mmm."

"They're mine!" Jason shouted at the top of his lungs.

"Hey. Hey." Callie got his attention. "The box still has more, Jason. And you don't have to shout, remember?"

"But they're mine!"

"Good morning to you, too. Honey, they're *everyone's.*" Callie fixed him with a stern gaze. "Jay, when you're paying for your cereal with your own money, then it will be yours and you won't have to share with anyone if you don't want to. But if your uncle Richard buys for the household, the cereal is for everyone to eat. That's only fair."

"Life's unfair."

Callie looked at him and burst into laughter at having her own words flung back so aptly. Amanda giggled. Jason finally relaxed and grinned. Mark even smiled around his thumb.

"What's all the noise about?"

Callie glanced up at the deep male voice, although her heart already knew who she would see. Richard stood in the kitchen. He wore a plaid bathrobe and a sleepy expression. His hair stood nearly on end, yet it made him look adorable. Callie glanced away, her blood already heating. *Adorable.* She had it bad.

"Uncle Richard!" Jason ran over and wrapped his arms around Richard's waist, hugging him tightly.

Richard hugged him back. "I missed you guys, so I came home sooner. I even missed your video games."

"Me, too," Jason said, shooting a dark look Callie's way.

Mark scrambled off Callie's lap and went to his uncle. Thumb still in his mouth, the toddler hugged Richard's leg.

Richard lifted Mark up and patted his bottom. Hearing the sound of the plastic night diaper, he said, "Sorry, big guy. Well, we'll try another time."

"He's just daytime trained," Amanda piped up.

Richard frowned. "I think I'll wait on the explanation for that." He went to Amanda, dragging the boys with him, and kissed the top of her head. "Everything go okay, honey?"

The girl nodded, her eyes shining as she looked up at Richard as though he was a god.

Keeping his hand on Amanda's hair, he gazed at Callie for a long telling moment. "Good morning, Callie. You're up early."

Callie stared everywhere but at his face. "Good morning."

She found the situation incredibly awkward and wanted to crawl under the table and die. Yet she wanted to throw herself at him like Jason had—only in a very *un*childlike way.

Richard frowned at her, then picked up the cocoa-crunchies box. He shook it. "Great, there's some left. I claim it. I'm starved."

Jason yelped in protest. Callie and Amanda looked at each other and started laughing. Callie wiped at the tears of amusement leaking from her eyes.

"What did I do?" Richard asked, aggrieved.

"Nothing. You had to be here." Callie chuckled. "All right. I'll make pancakes for everyone."

"Yippee!" Jason yelled.

"But I already ate," Amanda protested.

"Too bad," Jason said.

"Hey, butt-head, I didn't know we would get good stuff. You can have your cruddy cocoa crunchies back."

"Life's unfair," Jason complained.

Amanda snorted, but with amusement, not anger.

"Nailed you, too," Callie said, going to the stove. "Don't worry. I'll make a couple of dollar-size pancakes for you. You won't have to find much room for them."

"Thanks," Amanda said gratefully.

"There's a joke here," Richard said. "Someone can explain it to me later."

Mark removed his thumb from his mouth and shouted, "Potty!"

"I'll take him," Amanda said. "You just cook."

"That's tremendous," Richard remarked when the two vanished on their bathroom mission. "But will they do the trick again?"

Callie shrugged. "They're kids. Be happy for moments like these. Jay, want to mix the batter?"

"Sure."

Jason helped her get the ingredients for the pancakes. Callie was glad to have one buffer against the inevitable discussion. The inevitable *painful* discussion.

"Regrets?" Richard asked into the silence.

Callie's head snapped up. The buffer hadn't lasted ten seconds.

"I don't have any," he added, gazing at her with piercing eyes. Lord knows, she felt skewered by them.

"What's 'regrets'?" Jason asked, stirring the batter dangerously fast with a wooden spoon.

"It's when you do something you enjoy but feel bad about afterward," Richard replied. "Even if you don't need to."

"That's dumb."

"Out of the mouths of babes," the adult male said just loud enough for Callie to hear.

"Who's a baby?" Jason demanded, glaring at his uncle.

"Your uncle is explaining it wrong," Callie said sweetly, taking the spoon and running it along the sides and bottom of the bowl to catch the last of the loose dry ingredients. "A regret is when you do something you *know* you shouldn't have."

"Oh." Jason took back the spoon and stirred some more. "Like when I lie and I know it's wrong, but I do it, anyway, and then I wish I hadn't done it."

"Out of the mouths of babes," Callie repeated softly with great satisfaction.

"I'm *not* a baby," Jason said indignantly.

"No, you're not." She noticed his hand poised and pointing down at the bowl. "And if you stick your finger in that batter, mister, I'll have to throw it all out and make a new batch, and you won't get any."

Jason snatched his hand away.

"Smart fellow." Callie patted him on the head.

"Why do I feel like the bad boy here?" Richard sighed.

"Richard, you're not the bad boy. I'm the bad girl." She certainly didn't want him to feel any regrets. "The regrets are my problem, not yours. You were..." She glanced at Jason and decided what she had to say could be said in front of the boy. "You were wonderful."

Richard smiled bleakly. "I wish I felt that way."

"Well, you should. Just because I'm an idiot isn't a reflection on you, believe me."

"What are you an idiot about?" Jason asked, finally done messing with the batter.

"Everything," Callie replied.

Mark ran into the room and flopped onto Richard's lap.

"Gee, thanks, pal," Richard told Mark in a falsetto voice.

Callie snickered while Jason laughed. If only she could always be a part of this, she thought. But if she let go of her own needs, she would resent Richard and the kids for the rest of her life and theirs.

She couldn't allow that. They all meant too much to her already.

IN THE BATHROOM, Richard had a shower then sat down on the toilet seat cover, exhausted. He'd gotten up too early and eaten too much to counter his jet lag.

The seat cover was cold against his nether regions. He should have frozen them off at about four that morning when he'd found Callie in his bed. Better than being frozen out *after* making love to an earthly angel.

He rubbed his eyes. "Man, talk about screwing things up."

He didn't even grin at his inadvertent double entendre. He'd thought their lovemaking had been a turning point, but it had been a false dawn. How could something so right have so quickly turned wrong?

"Women," he muttered, the thought giving him strength to stand up.

His relationships with women had always been... strange. Never smooth, that was for sure. He should have realized Callie was in the same category the moment he'd awakened to find himself alone in the bed. He should have stayed there and never ventured downstairs to reality.

Not a bad idea, he admitted. In fact, he really should go back to bed for his health. He was very short on sleep. If he did go to bed, Callie would have to stay with the kids....

Richard paused.

He *was* tired. He'd no doubt collapse at any moment, which was no good with a toddler in the house. Amanda could watch Mark, however. No, he thought. She had a life. And there was Jason. At times the boy was almost uncontrollable, and he could get into anything without adult supervision. Callie had promised to stay until the evening, when he'd originally been expected home. So staying now shouldn't be a hardship to her.

His conscience nudged him, the miserable thing. If he were honest, he could cope with the kids for the rest of the day. If his ego were honest, he'd admit he'd taken a blow to his sexual self-esteem and wanted some revenge. And if he were very honest, he hoped to create a second chance with her before the day was out.

Richard brightened. That last was a great reason to indulge his bodily needs today. He pulled on his sleeping shorts and a T-shirt. Stepping out of the master bathroom, he opened the bedroom door and bellowed, "Callie! Come here!"

He raced across the room and leaped into bed. He yanked the covers up to his chin and put a hangdog expression on his face.

"What's wrong, Uncle Richard?" Jason shouted, coming into the room. The boy stopped dead, eyes wide. "You look sick."

Works for me, Richard thought. "Yes, I'm not well. Where's Callie?"

"Right here," she said as she entered. She held Mark on her hip. Amanda followed.

"I'm not feeling well," Richard said, pushing away his pang of guilt about lying to the whole family. Fibs between adults was one thing, but this was something else. He'd have to make it up to the kids in some way.

"It's probably jet lag," Callie said.

"I've had jet lag. This is worse."

She came over to him and put her hand on his forehead. Her fingers were cool against his skin. Mark leaned half-over her, his nose practically in her breast. Lucky Mark.

"You do feel warm," she finally pronounced. "Clammy, too."

He bet. He'd just gotten out of a hot shower. Funny how circumstance could play into one's hands. "I feel sick."

He did in a way. His stomach rumbled queasily, and his head ached. Even his chest felt tight.

Callie straightened. She glanced at the bed as she did. Richard knew she was thinking about their lovemaking. Good. *Very* good.

"Well," she said, "it's fortunate I'm here today, anyway. Okay, everyone out. Let's leave your sicko uncle in peace."

"He...he won't die, will he?" Jason asked, his chin trembling. Amanda looked worried, too.

Richard cursed under his breath. In his scheming to get to Callie's heart, he never once thought how the kids might react, let alone understandably overreact. He flung back the covers, saying, "I'm fine, Jason. It was just—"

"No." Callie put a hand to his chest and pushed him

back in bed. To Jason she said, "Your uncle Richard is *not* going to die. I promise you. He just had too much airplane ride on too little sleep. Once he has a nap, he'll feel much better."

"Callie…" Richard began.

She pushed the covers over him and shooed the kids out. "Don't worry about a thing, Richard, You just rest."

"Callie…"

She waved a hand and disappeared into the hall, closing the bedroom door behind her. He was alone.

"Dammit," he muttered, getting out of bed. He opened the door. His crew was about halfway down the steps. "Callie—"

"See Jason? He's perfectly fine, just tired. He only needs some rest." She looked up at Richard and added, "Relax. You sleep. I'll be here."

She started the kids down the stairs again. Mark held her hand and held the railing on his other side as he negotiated the steps one at a time.

"Callie."

"Go to bed, Richard."

"Callie!"

She turned. "Richard, don't go all macho man on me and try to tough it out. You look like something the cat coughed up on the carpet. Jay's fine now. He knows you're just tired. Amanda's okay and Mark understands the need for naps better than anyone. Now get back in that bed and quit giving me a bunch of grief!"

Richard muttered a curse and followed her orders.

As he crawled back into bed, he wished he'd thought through his little plan. Little it was, because even a pea-brain could have seen what was coming. But no, not him. He should have thought of the kids, but no, his libido had been turned on full force.

He propped up pillows and laid back on them. Staring out the window at nothing, he thought for about five minutes.

"Callie!"

He called again, more loudly when he got no response, then heard feet pounding up the stairs. His door was flung open to reveal Jason.

"What's the matter?" the boy asked, looking untroubled.

Perfect, Richard thought, realizing he could make amends with his nephew. "Jay, I didn't mean to scare you earlier. I'm not sick at all."

"Oh, I know that now." Jason smiled happily. "Callie explained it to me some more. You're only feeling a little bad, like from a cold."

"I don't have a cold or anything wrong, Jay," Richard said firmly.

"Oh. That's real good." Jay came over and hugged him. "I gotta go. I'm playing Race the Waves. Callie brought it over and I wanna beat it before she takes it home with her."

Jason ran out, shutting the door after him.

Richard flopped back against the pillows, disgusted that he hadn't been able to make his nephew listen. "Callie. Please, will you come here!"

Eventually he heard footsteps again in the hallway. The bedroom door opened. Amanda peeked in. "Callie's busy, Uncle Richard, and she says you should be busy sleeping. You okay?"

"Perfectly. I'm not sick."

His niece frowned. "You look funny around the eyes. Callie's right. You need some sleep. Don't worry about us. We know you're not going to die. Even Jay knows it.''

She left, shutting the door against his frustrations.

Richard reached behind him and threw a pillow across the room. It bounced quietly off the wall and onto the floor. He stared at it.

"Callie!"

It took nearly five minutes of calling, but his bedroom door finally opened a third time. The object of his demands stood on the threshold. "What is your problem?"

"I was afraid you'd send Mark this time," he complained.

"Is that all you called me here for?" She began to close the door. "I've got things to do and you need to rest."

"I'm not sick!"

"I know. It's only jet lag. You're worse than Mark."

"It isn't jet lag. I said I was sick to get attention. From you. So you wouldn't leave." There, he thought. He'd come clean in a thorough show of humiliation.

"Of course I'm not leaving. You're wiped out. Anyone can see that. You don't need to get my attention, and I have no clue why you would think I was leaving."

His expression hardened. "This morning you weren't happy that we had sex."

Her expression hardened. "Is that all it was to you? Just sex?"

"No, of course not. We...made love."

"Richard, be honest and admit it was far more just sex than making love." She grimaced. "It's okay. I know I shouldn't expect more and I don't. I truly don't."

"No. It was more. Much more."

"Richard, it really is okay. You don't have to spare my feelings."

"I'm not sparing your feelings!" Once again she wasn't listening to him.

"Shhh. The kids. Look, we'll talk about this later."

"I only said I was ill to get your attention. I'm not ill."

"Richard, you are exhausted," she replied. "And you're half out of it. Now, unless you actually want a drink of water or something, I have to go."

The words hung in the air. "No."

"Get some sleep. You really will feel better."

Richard gave up. He'd tried to do the honest thing, but nobody believed him. He and the boy who cried wolf could cry in their beer together. Soda, in the boy's case.

Maybe it really was jet lag, he thought, closing his eyes. Maybe he was still on the plane coming home, and he'd dreamed the entire thing from the moment he'd walked into the house. He would wake up at any moment and the pilot would be announcing that they were about to land in Philadelphia.

That would be nice.

CALLIE WATCHED Mark's eyes drift closed. The toddler lay on the sofa while Jason played his video game. She knew she ought to put a diaper on Mark before he took this nap, but he'd just used the bathroom.

Decisions, decisions, she thought wryly, deciding she'd wake Mark in an hour. At least decisions distracted her from the man napping upstairs.

What she couldn't decide was whether to be angry or amused by Richard's confession of faking illness. He *had* felt warm, after all. And if he acted a bit like an idiot...well, so had she. Like his youngest nephew, he just needed sleep to straighten him out.

Jay put the game on pause and ran out of the room.

Callie suppressed a smile, knowing his problem. He'd played until nature called—threatened, in fact, at any microsecond.

Her amusement faded. She seemed trapped in the world of what would go into children and what would come out. She'd been there and done that far too often in her teens. Richard's three were charming, but the whole situation reminded her of raising her brothers and sisters. Even now, she wondered about Jason playing so many hours of video games and whether it was good for him or not. He'd been at it all day. He should be playing outside with friends or reading a book. Or maybe his absorption in the game was only a momentary thing for him, since the games were going back with her and he wanted to finish all he could before that happened.

She knew she shouldn't care about Jason's "video or not to video." It was Richard's problem.

"Callie! Amanda won't get out of the bathroom!" Jason wailed.

"Go upstairs, then. Quietly!" she commanded in as loud a voice as she dared. She got up to see what Amanda's problem was. Probably the girl was only giving her little brother a hard time. Callie snorted. Siblings. They loved to torture each other.

She knocked on the powder-room door. "Amanda?"

"Go away!" Amanda cried.

Callie thought she heard tears in the girl's voice, and she frowned. "It's Callie, not Jason. Are you okay? You sound upset."

"I am upset," the girl replied.

"Are you hurt?" Callie asked, turning the doorknob, ready to go in if Amanda let her.

"I don't know. I don't know. There's...there's blood."

"Did you cut yourself?"

"No."

"Let me see—"

"No!"

This time the girl shouted it in total panic. Something clicked into place in Callie's head. She knew exactly what was wrong with Amanda. Womanhood had officially begun. "It's okay, honey. Don't be worried. Every woman has this. It's normal. You'll have it for the next forty years. There's a thrill." Callie made a face at reality.

"They showed us a stupid movie in health class about it, but I didn't know it'd be like this."

Callie sympathized mightily. "Where do you keep the stuff for your time? I'll get them for you."

"I don't *have* anything!"

"Oh, dear." Callie thought. "What about your uncle? Didn't he get you anything for this?"

"He was gonna, but he forgot. I'm stuck in here forever, aren't I?"

Callie clapped a hand over her mouth, afraid she'd laugh out loud. "No, you won't. Hang on."

She got her own personal emergency stash and handed it through the door to Amanda, telling her what to do as she did. She added, "I'll run to the store now for you. I should be back in about fifteen or twenty minutes. Men. They're such ding-dongs at times."

"You bet," Amanda agreed, getting a little spunk back with the rescue. "Except Joey."

"Ah, sweet loyalty," Callie murmured.

She went back in the living room and frowned at Mark sleeping on the sofa. She hated to wake him up just to run to the store. But Jason couldn't watch the toddler, and Amanda might never emerge from the bathroom again.

She'd have to put Mark with Richard.

Callie groaned, not wanting to go back into that bedroom. But she had to, otherwise Amanda *would* be trapped in the bathroom. She wormed her hands under Mark's little body and lifted him. He never stirred, although she half hoped he would so she could take him with her. Now she *had* to put him in with Richard.

She carried Mark upstairs, passing Jason on the way down. The boy was in a hurry to get back to his game. At least one child would be safe enough until she returned from her errand of mercy.

She gently opened the master-bedroom door and peeked in. Richard didn't move. He lay flat on his back, his arms crossed at his waist. Slowly she entered. At the edge of the bed, she stopped and stared down at the sleeping man. Emotions ran through her, warring with each other. She set them aside before any got the upper hand and leaned across Richard, settling Mark on the other side of him in the bed. Finally managing to get Mark down without disrupting either man's or boy's nap, she straightened. She brushed the hair from Mark's forehead as he snuggled against his uncle. Her fingers itched to do the same to Richard. Instead, she stroked Richard's cheek one time with the slightest of touches.

If only things were different…but they weren't.

She left the room on tiptoe. She completed her mission to the store and was back at her estimated time of arrival.

Amanda had come out of the downstairs powder room. Callie found her in her own room, sitting on the bed and looking depressed.

"You okay?" Callie asked, handing over the package she'd bought.

Amanda nodded. "I called Heather. I'm not going to the mall with her today."

"Hey, that's okay. But don't be embarrassed by what happened," Callie said, sitting down next to her on the bed. "You're doing great."

"But I didn't know what to do," Amanda said, her chin trembling.

"Yes, you did. You stayed in the bathroom and told me. You were smart. And you weren't in school like I was."

Amanda's head snapped up. "You were at school when you got yours?"

Callie nodded. "I had no clue what to do, so I didn't do anything. Talk about dumb. I was it." She put her arm around the girl. "Congratulations, Amanda. You are a young woman now, a beautiful young woman. No wonder my nephew has goo-goo eyes around you."

Amanda flushed, but smiled. "Thanks."

The girl had questions and Callie answered them. In fact, she had a good talk with Amanda. She really was a sweet teenager, hurt and confused by her parents' death—and bewildered by adolescence. Unfortunately she had an uncle as bewildered as she by the abrupt changes in both their lives. Once Amanda settled in here with her family, and with school and friends, she would be just fine. Richard, on the other hand, was a real mess. How could he have forgotten Amanda's needs? He'd promised he would take care of it right away that time. Men.

After she left Amanda set to deal with one aspect of her graduation into womanhood, Callie went back to Richard's room. He and Mark lay together in the most innocent of slumbers. Callie's heart melted at the sight of man and child in repose. They looked so sweet together she just wanted to wrap them up in a big hug and forgive Richard his forgetfulness.

"Oh, Lord," she muttered, knowing she was far too sentimental for her own good.

She moved to the bed and reached over Richard to pick up Mark. She was careful not to touch Richard's body in any way. All her awareness was on his face mere inches from hers when her hands encountered wetness.

"Uh-oh," she said, knowing she'd miscalculated Mark's newfound abilities.

"Kiss me," Richard suddenly murmured.

Callie glanced at his face. His eyes were open and focusing sleepily on her face. She was stretched over him, her pelvis nearly touching his hip.

"Hello," she said lamely.

His eyes widened. "Did you pour warm tea on my bed?"

"Apple juice, actually, as filtered by Mark," she replied, hoping to make a joke of the mishap.

Richard bolted upright, knocking her against his legs. "What! Why is Mark in my bed with me? And why doesn't he have a diaper on?"

"I had to go to the store."

Richard frowned and shifted away from his nephew. "I must still be asleep. I was having this wonderful dream that you were rubbing your body all over mine, and then I woke up and you were. I probably needed to get up, but that's not the alarm clock I had in mind."

"I'm sorry," she said.

"Apologize in a minute." Richard climbed out of bed, disentangling his legs from the covers and her. He pulled her upright, bringing her nearly to his body. The heat emanated through his clothes, igniting strong images of their lovemaking. Callie couldn't stand it. She felt faint.

Mark slept on, undisturbed by the events around him.

"So what did your going to the store have to do with putting Mark in my bed?" Richard asked, his deep voice sending an ominous chill up her spine.

"I—" Her voice came out in a squeak. She cleared her throat. "You forgot to get Amanda things for her personal needs, and today was it."

His jaw dropped. "You mean she got her...?"

Callie nodded. "Today."

"Wow." Richard grinned a little. "It's been a momentous twenty-four hours on more than one front. Do I congratulate her or what? What's the adult male–adolescent girl protocol here?"

"I don't know. Maybe very privately say something. She needs to feel good, and if you're matter-of-fact, she'll relax with it. Mark was asleep downstairs and I didn't have the heart to wake him for the fifteen-minute trip to the store. Amanda was occupied. Jason's not old enough, so I put him with you." Callie shook her head. "I'm sorry, Richard. Don't worry. I'll take care of everything, I promise."

"No harm done." Richard stared at his bed. "I think."

"I'll fix it," she vowed, sitting Mark up. The child still slept on in that way kids did when they were flat-out tired.

She stripped bed and child together. Richard helped her, dismayed at the damage done.

"I'm sleeping on the floor tonight," he said.

"Don't be silly," she told him. "I'll have it fixed in no time."

Eventually she had the area cleaned up, and then used

the blow-dryer on it. She walked into her own apartment at about nine that night, officially off her baby-sitting duties. Richard was up and around, although he was still not quite right. No doubt Mark's wake-up call hadn't helped. Richard must think her a complete idiot. She couldn't blame him.

Her apartment was deadly quiet, not even the burp of a drain line to relieve the silence. The place seemed sterile after the small bodies, raucous noise and tribulations of teenagers. And after making love to a man she had badly wanted. A man she still wanted. Here she had nothing. Nothing.

Of her own choice.

Chapter Seven

"Uncle Richard! *Uncle Richard!*"

Richard fought up from some deep depths and managed to pry his eyes open. He felt as if he'd slept on rocks all night long.

Amanda peered down at him, her face wavering around the edges. "You forgot to wake us up for school."

"Oh." Richard became aware of what felt like a blast furnace in the bed with him. "It's hot."

"You look worse than yesterday," his niece said. "Is it still jet lag?"

"Just tired really." A jumble of things swam through his mind. He couldn't quite focus on them, yet they had to do with Callie and demanded urgent attention. Relations were unsettled between them when she had left last night—about as unsettled as his stomach suddenly felt. "I'll take you to school."

He began to push the covers back, sitting up at the same time. Or tried to. His body refused to cooperate, and he could barely raise his head from the pillow. The blast furnace went up a thousand degrees when he did.

"I think I really am sick this time," he muttered, awed by his ability to predict the future.

"You're all white and sweaty," Amanda said. "Like the paste we used in elementary school."

"Get the thermometer from the bathroom," he said with effort. His stomach roiled violently, taking him by surprise. He shot off the bed as if out of a cannon, then staggered past Amanda and into the bathroom. He couldn't wait for the thermometer—only it wasn't the thermometer he needed.

Long minutes later, as he laid his head on the cool porcelain base of the toilet, his stomach temporarily relieved, he decided he was most definitely sick.

"Uncle Richard." Amanda stood in the doorway, looking as shaken as he felt. "What should I do? Should I go to school? I can't get there if you don't take me because the bus left already. Should I stay home? Should I call a doctor or the police or something?"

"Oh, God, no." He pressed his face into the tile floor as his stomach did backflips again. His gut compelled him to repeat his performance of a few minutes ago. He obliged.

By the time he was finished, Amanda was no longer at the bathroom door. He couldn't blame her.

"Amanda?" he called out weakly. When she didn't return, he murmured, "Guess she went to school."

The faces of Jason and Mark flitted briefly across his brain. Heaven only knew what they were doing, and they could tear the house up for all he cared at this point. Eventually he'd be well enough to fix it. He hoped. A third encounter with the inside of the porcelain bowl made him wonder if he'd ever be able to rise above his knees again in this lifetime.

"Wow. You can really puke, Uncle Richard."

From his prone position, Richard opened one eye. Jason stood next to Amanda. Amanda had her hand clapped over her mouth. She looked as if she might join him at any second. Richard hugged the bowl possessively. The kid could find her own toilet. He needed his.

"I'm okay," he finally said. His voice sounded terrible, and it hurt like hell to talk. "I promise, Jay."

"We better stay home," Amanda said. "But you'll have to call the school. We'll get in trouble if we call ourselves."

"Get the phone." Richard struggled against a fourth attack. He won...barely.

A few moments later Jason put the portable phone next to him on the floor. Richard picked it up and tried to discern the numbers on the buttons. His gaze swam. His stomach protested forcefully. He thrust the phone into the boy's hands.

"Jay, you dial."

"I don't know the number."

"Phone book."

Richard lay down on the floor, all his threadbare energy consumed with fighting off a new wave of nausea. He hung on. Eventually he heard Jay punching in phone numbers.

"Here," the boy said, holding out the receiver.

Richard took it and, when the school-office secretary answered, told the woman that Jay wouldn't be in school that day. He had to take another tour at being sick before he was capable of repeating the message to Amanda's school.

When the stomach spasms eased, he moaned at the pounding in his head, the aching in his bones and the jumping in his stomach.

"I think we should call Callie," Jay said.

"I think so, too," Amanda agreed.

"No." Richard croaked the word out. "Imposed too much already. Where's Mark?"

"Still sleeping," Amanda said. "I checked."

"Thank you, honey." Richard closed his eyes, desperate for sleep.

He woke up much later at the sound of new voices. Something covered him although he still lay on the bathroom floor. The kids must have put a blanket over him. They had iced the tiles, though, at some point. The floor was so cold against his skin that his body shook with chills.

The voices drew closer and he realized people were in the bedroom. They were talking about him.

"Richard said he was sick yesterday, then said he wasn't."

Callie's voice. Richard smiled.

"You say he's been vomiting?"

Richard opened one eye at the male voice he'd never heard before.

"All over the place!" Jason replied enthusiastically.

"Have not," Richard muttered in his own defense.

"I'm glad you kids called me... Omigod! Richard!"

Richard smiled at the panic in his angel of mercy's voice. Nothing had ever sounded sweeter than Callie's concern for him. He wanted to kiss her.

Instead, he was violently sick again. Someday he would have a sophisticated lover image, but not today.

Cool feminine hands held his forehead while someone made sympathetic noises.

"Callie, you never could handle anyone being sick in the bathroom. Knock it off before I have two patients."

"Replace me already?" Richard finally whispered as the attack subsided. "He's a peach."

"Not hardly." She kissed the top of his head. "Now

shut up and let my brother Tommy examine you. He's a second-year resident at Thomas Jefferson Hospital."

"The room snooper?"

"No, that's Steve. He's in real estate."

"Oh." Richard concentrated on this brother of Callie's, his relief at the relationship only slightly penetrating his illness. It took a full minute for the realization to sink in that Tommy had the same angelic features as Callie, yet with masculine overtones. The Rossovich siblings he'd met so far were certainly a good-looking bunch.

"Help him onto the floor, Callie," Tommy said, grinning widely. "I'll do an exam here."

"Knew you'd be back," Richard said to her as she eased him to a prone position.

"I'm a bad penny that keeps turning up."

"Love you," he murmured in a wonderful daze. His stomach threatened again, but he was too weak to do more than ignore it.

"You are hallucinating."

Sure hands poked and prodded him, but gently. Finally the hands stopped. Something pressed against his ear for a long moment, then was removed. Richard shivered.

"Temp's up. That's why you've got the chills."

The stethoscope that pressed against his chest was more recognizable than the ear thermometer.

Tommy said, "Nothing more than the flu, kids."

Richard grimaced. He was dying a slow death here, hardly a "nothing more than" situation. A medical guy, his backside. "Go back to school, pal."

"No way!" Jason yelped.

"I think he meant me, not you," Tommy told Jay. To Richard he said, "But you go back to bed, pal. The floor's no place for you, and I don't have to be a doctor to know that.''

Tommy helped him to his feet. Richard groaned and tottered to the bed with both Tommy and Callie's help. Never had he been so grateful to have adults around. He hadn't known how he would be able to handle the kids.

He collapsed onto the bed, happy to be in a warm place under warmer covers. He closed his eyes, wanting nothing more than to shut out the world.

"Could he have gotten sick from all the flying?'' he heard Callie ask.

"No, but it probably exacerbated the condition. If you've got any kind of virus in your system, flying will bring it out in all its nasty forms.''

"I think I might get sick again,'' Richard said, opening his eyes as his stomach began to threaten.

"I'll get a sickie bucket,'' Callie said, hurrying from the room. She hustled the two kids with her.

"Lucky for you, I've got a cure for the sickies,'' Tommy said.

Richard stared at Tommy in horror as the man held up what looked like a large white bullet-shaped pill. He couldn't swallow that, let alone keep it down long enough for it to work.

Tommy took a medical glove from his bag. It looked like Richard wasn't going to have to *swallow* medicine, but rather—

"No-o-o!'' Richard moaned, his nausea forgotten with this new threat.

"It can't go in the normal way,'' Tommy said. "It'll come right back up again. It's either you or me to do it.''

Richard was about to protest again when Callie returned with the bucket. At the sight of it, Richard's nausea hit like a force-ten hurricane. Callie barely made it to the bed in time.

When the spasm finally stopped, Richard held out his hand in defeat. After showing Callie and the rest of the potential audience from the room, Dr. Tommy gave him the equipment for the mission of mercy. Richard didn't know if the medicine worked instantly or whether it was the idea that relief was at hand—or rather, in body—but after about ten minutes he felt better.

He looked at Tommy. "It's a pleasure to meet you, Doctor."

He refused to be embarrassed by the nature of the medicine Tommy had given him. As long as it worked, he was only grateful. If it didn't the man would be lucky if he was breathing, Callie's brother or not.

Tommy grinned. "Not the ordinary way to make an acquaintance, but likewise, I'm sure. Any friend of Callie's is a friend of mine. Although I've got a feeling it's more than friendship here."

"If I had my way, but Callie's way is in control at the moment." Richard paused. "I really only have the flu? I thought I was dying. I still feel like I could at any moment."

"You have the classic symptoms of influenza, strain A." Tommy smiled. "I'm an emergency-room resident at Jeff, and we've been seeing this for several weeks now. It's a violent strain, but short-lived. Expect the kids to get it, unless they've had their flu shots. Heck, expect them to get it, anyway, only not as badly as you seem to have. This thing is tough."

"They've had their shots. I skipped mine. Can you tell? I can."

Tommy laughed. "Oh, I can tell. Big time. Callie's going to stay here until you're better."

Richard shook his head, then stopped when it aggravated his vertigo. "No. We've imposed enough on her."

Tommy laughed again. "No one imposes on my sister unless she wants them to. Callie's the world's best mother hen."

"She's got a job and school. They come first."

"Who told you that? Callie, probably." Tommy made a face. He had Callie's same acerbic expression. "Callie's only been trying to make up for what she perceives is lost time. Don't believe it. She thrives on taking care of others. I keep telling her she should be a nurse or a doctor, but she's got to get past the dry heaves first."

The bedroom door opened. Callie poked her head in. "Is it safe?"

"Oh, yeah." Tommy chuckled. "I'll leave this guy for you to straighten out. You know the drill with fluids. He should be okay in a few days, only a little weak."

"Thanks, Tommy. It was great of you to do this on your day off."

"Anything for my sweet sister." Tommy kissed her on the cheek, then picked up his medical bag. "Besides, you would have made my life miserable if I hadn't come and looked at this guy. I'm no dummy. I know how to stay on my sister's good side."

Tommy left with Callie escorting him out—after she took care of the bucket in the bathroom. Richard lay back against the pillows and closed his eyes. The bed didn't spin, which was a good sign. He listened to Callie and her brother trade affectionate gibes as they walked down the hallway. He wished he had that easy camaraderie with her. With the great sex, of course. But they had a barrier between them that seemed insurmountable.

Tommy revealed something about Callie, however. She enjoyed nurturing. Richard had seen that before with her, but now he understood she was fighting her own nature even more than she was fighting him.

Tommy had also revealed his own callousness about Callie's feelings. If the rest of her family was that way with her about what she wanted from life, no wonder she became so adamant when her goals were threatened. No wonder she left no room for compromise.

Richard understood her better now. His battle for her was all uphill. She was worth the effort—but he didn't see how he could win. He had three kids, whose feelings had to come under consideration, and he had disaster striking every five minutes with Callie, too. This moment was one of them.

Yet she, despite all her protests, had come when he had desperately needed her.

There was something in that.

HERE SHE WAS again.

Callie sighed as she pulled into Richard's driveway for the second time in two hours. This time she was returning from dropping Jason and Amanda off at school, to their dismay. The two had been great when faced with one very sick uncle. But the situation had eased by midmorning, and with her at the house now, the kids had no reason to miss the rest of the schoolday.

"Jason was not a happy camper, was he?" she asked Mark, strapped behind her in his seat.

"I want happy camp!" Mark said.

"I'll buy you one tomorrow," Callie told him.

She turned off the car, took Mark from the back and went into the house. The place was quiet. She found that amazing after the weekend with the kids all over it. In fact, the house seemed empty, as if someone had rubbed the life right out of it.

She helped Mark off with his jacket and shed her own before they climbed the stairs to check on Richard.

He was sound asleep in the bed. His color was better, the pallor under his tanned skin gone, although perspiration beaded his forehead. His fever must be spiking, she thought. She'd get some aspirin in him when he woke up. Right now, he was better off resting. He'd had some morning.

"Unca 'shard seepin," Mark whispered dramatically to her.

"Unca 'shard needs it, honey," she replied, shutting the door behind them as she led Mark to the stairs again.

She'd had some morning, too. She hadn't been at the office long and had been dealing with a report when Amanda had called about Richard. The girl had been panicky but trying to control it. When Callie had heard how often Richard had been sick that morning, she'd called her brother Tommy to meet her at the house.

Her boss, however, had *not* been a happy camper. He had told her in no uncertain terms that she had better be back tomorrow, and she had better have the report done. Callie had argued against both, pointing out that she had time off she hadn't yet taken and was entitled to, as well as the report not being due at state headquarters for another week and a half. She didn't see how she'd be back before Friday, not as sick as Richard sounded. She'd be lucky to be back even then. And she would no doubt wind up with flu herself. She'd be out of work all next week probably. Then she'd be fired. Almost no one got fired from government jobs, but at the rate she was going, she'd make the top-ten list of people who'd been kicked out on their ear.

Guilt assailed her, but not about her growing job woes. She never should have made love to Richard, for his health's sake. If flying brought out the worst in a virus, what did sex do to it? Probably it had had a field day inside Richard's body, while she had had a field day with the outside parts. What a mess she'd made of things.

The telephone rang in Richard's office downstairs. Callie decided to answer it. She could at least explain his illness to his clients, so they would understand why they wouldn't receive a return call for a few days.

"Holiday Imports," she said when she picked up the receiver. A sheet of letterhead in the printer told her the company name.

"Hey, it's Marv at the airport. The big guy finally got a secretary, eh? Well, tell him he's got a shipment down here that's come in from Malaysia. He has to sign off on it before we can send it to the distributors."

"I'm sorry, but Richard's ill with the flu." She watched Mark toddle over to the small sofa. The child climbed up on it, turned around, sat down and looked at her. She blew him a kiss. He grinned back.

"Damn!" Marv said. "He's got to come today. The fruit can't be released until he signs. Hey! This ain't diplomatic stuff—it's just the business side. Since you're his secretary, you can sign this time."

"Ah..." She looked at Mark. No sense explaining the relationship to this guy when she didn't understand it herself. "I have his nephew to watch while Richard's ill. I can't come with the baby."

"Bring old Marky-Mark with you. Richard does all the time. No problem."

"But—"

"Lady, I gotta have this fruit signed. If it ain't, it'll go bad and then Richard makes no money. Neither does the distributor and everyone's ticked off. Now, you can sign for Holiday Imports, so sign."

Callie knew she'd look like an idiot saying she wasn't Richard's secretary after she'd just led Marv to believe she was. She calculated the consequences of going and not going. Going had more positives. The airport was only a half hour away. She could be there and back before Richard even woke up.

"Okay, I'll go. Where are you exactly in the airport complex?"

Marv gave her directions to the commercial hangars where cargo was stored for pickup. After she hung up, Callie peeked in on Richard, who was still sleeping. She bundled Mark back into the car and handed him a cookie she'd taken from the kitchen on the way out.

As she strapped him back in his seat, she said, "What a life, kid."

Mark took a bite of the cookie, then offered what was left to her.

She kissed his free hand. "Thanks, but you just keep that after you've drooled on it. I know a claim when I see it."

Veni, vidi, signi, she decided after finding the warehouse hangar and taking care of Richard's paperwork. She had come. She had seen. She had signed. Think of what Julius Caesar could have conquered with a pen. She'd found Richard's job interesting, but her sister would be disappointed if she saw what Richard really did for a living. Callie vowed to tell her.

When she got home, she'd have to remember to tell Richard that he had hired her while he'd been sleeping.

"Plane go boom!" Mark announced as one landed on a far runway.

"Plane *lands*," she corrected, bustling him into the car. "What are you trying to do? Scare everyone?"

In his special seat, Mark bounced up and down. "Me go boom."

Callie chuckled. "Now the networks can put away their cameras. No film at eleven, folks."

"I almost go boom," she admitted, maneuvering the car up Richard's driveway for the third time in as many hours.

Richard was still asleep when she looked in on him. One miracle had been provided for at least. She made some heavily sweetened tea and brought it to the bedroom. Mark had come with her. He was getting very good with steps.

This time Richard stirred and opened his eyes.

"Hey," she said softly. "How are you feeling?"

"Like a truck hit me."

She held up the mug she carried. "I brought you tea. You're only allowed three sips every fifteen minutes."

"Who made that rule?"

"My brother, the doctor."

"Figures. First body torture and now death by thirst. I hate to think what he'll do to me next."

"It's for your own good," she chided, amused by his complaining. She couldn't blame him, but the three-sips routine worked.

He looked at her, his gaze red-rimmed and hollow. Poor thing, she thought, wanting only to wrap him in a big comforting hug.

"You shouldn't be here," he said. "I was doing okay."

She laughed. "If you had been doing any more okay, you'd be in the hospital. Now drink your tea."

"I've imposed on you enough. Go home. I feel much

better." He tried to sit up, probably to prove his point, but never made it. His head dropped back on the pillow. He looked exhausted.

"Unca 'shard go boom," Mark said.

"Out of the mouth of a real babe," she murmured, helping Richard sit up to drink the tea.

Somehow it felt right to hold him, to help him through this time. She didn't feel put upon or resentful. She felt good...and proud...and home.

She took the cup when he reached for a fourth sip. "Oh, no. Good things come in threes. By the way, you hired me today."

"I did?"

She nodded. "Someone had to sign off on fruit from Malaysia, and Marv decreed I was it."

"I would have gone."

She shook her head. "Richard, you couldn't even walk back to bed by yourself. Don't worry about it. I'll take care of that and some calls piling up in the office, and I'll be official."

"Thanks," he said, producing an anemic smile.

Mark climbed onto the bed and lay down next to Richard.

"He's going to get it," Richard said. "Tommy thinks so."

Callie grinned at his pained tone. "You'll be up and around by then."

"Amanda and Jason will get it, too."

"You'll be able to handle that."

"No, I won't." Richard leaned his head against her shoulder.

"Sure you will." Her voice sounded as breathless as she suddenly felt. For goodness' sake, she thought, the man was sick. How could she be physically responding to their closeness when he was ill?

Because he was still sexy. She couldn't *not* be aware of him as a man.

"You'll get it, too," he said, looking up at her. "Your brother says so."

"Tommy used to put pebbles up his nose just to see if they would get stuck. Don't believe everything he says, trust me."

"I'm sorry, Callie. It was too soon for us to make love."

Callie swallowed. She didn't want to discuss it. They'd done enough already. "It's okay, Richard. It was my choice that night."

"Just don't regret it."

"I don't."

"You do."

"No." She couldn't tell him that she regretted having to walk away from their lovemaking. She'd known she had to or lose everything she worked so hard to achieve.

"I'll make it up to you, Callie." Despite his illness, he looked determined.

She smiled. "I'd like that."

"Can I have more tea now?"

"Only if I hit you over the head with it. Your fifteen minutes aren't up."

"You're tough."

She chuckled. "Mark's fallen asleep on your bed again, sans diapers once more. Now that's tough."

Richard smiled and closed his eyes. "I don't know. Watching you blow-dry the bed had great sexual overtones."

Callie let go of him, but gently. As he slumped back,

she said, "You're not too sick if you can think that, Richard."

Richard grinned wryly. "Don't bet on it."

She had a lot of things she would bet on, but falling for Richard wasn't one of them.

She didn't feel quite so tough at the moment. In fact, she felt almost in...

Callie forced the emotion away. He was sick and she was vulnerable. This wasn't the time to decide on anything.

Chapter Eight

Richard stared at the slender lump huddled under the covers.

"Don't say 'I told you so,'" the lump croaked in misery. "I know I've got it."

He grinned. "Tommy fix you up with his magic bullet?"

"The boy was positively ghoulish about it, the sadistic bastard." Callie looked at Richard with mournful eyes. "You should be home, not here. You're barely out of bed yourself."

"True, but I feel a helluva lot better than you do."

"The world feels a helluva lot better than me."

"I'll help you now," Richard said, grateful Tommy had called him about Callie catching the flu. Richard had gotten a key from Tommy and come over to her apartment to check on her. Jason and Amanda were still at school, so he would pick them up later.

His own flu bout had been short-lived, as Tommy had promised, because by the third day he had been up and about. He hoped that the same would hold for Callie, who'd gotten it right after he had. While he felt better, he was still tired at times. Callie had been so terrific when he'd been sick that he hoped he could reciprocate a little. In one way he could. "I can hold your sickie bucket for you."

"I'm thrilled," she said, sinking more deeply under the covers.

Mark climbed onto Callie's bed and lay down next to her. "Callie thick."

"In the head," Callie muttered, reaching out and stroking Mark's soft hair.

"Yes, she is sick, Mark. But we'll make her better. We hope."

Richard sat down on the bed, partly to be close to her and partly to ensure he didn't suddenly collapse on the floor if his legs decided to turn to rubber without his permission. It'd be a heck of a thing if Mark wound up taking care of both of them.

His hip pressed against hers. Callie's face was almost colorless, and her reddened eyes were rimmed with violet circles. Her hair sprawled every which way on the pillow. She looked ill, yet he couldn't help a moment of physical response to her. His sexual attraction to her overrode everything else.

Of course she'd probably kill him if he acted on his impulse, sick or not.

Her telephone rang.

"Oh, God," Callie muttered, pulling the covers over her head.

"I'll get it," Richard said, rising. He opted for the phone in her living room, so she could rest. "Don't worry about Mark. He's well padded."

Mark had had a slight setback what with Richard's illness and then his trying to cope with getting through the days afterward. Richard had discovered the transition stage in the life-responsibility process wasn't all it was cracked up to be. Potty training was hard work. Either that, or he didn't have Callie's touch.

When he answered the telephone, he discovered Callie's boss on the line. By the time Richard hung up, he was angry.

"You work for an idiot," he announced, coming back into her bedroom. He liked its cheery yellows and whites, but they didn't alter his mood at the moment.

"I know that. He's never happy, but I'm late with a report. It's due in the state offices on Wednesday."

"Doesn't he know you were taking care of a very sick man? Doesn't he have compassion?"

Callie chuckled. "We're talking about my boss here."

"Right. He's also complaining about some guy in the office who's complaining that he's dead when he isn't. He's blaming you. Your boss is, not the guy."

"Me?" She put her hand over her eyes. "I called some people to get that straightened out, and they all said they'd put him back into the system."

"I guess he came right back out again."

Callie made as if to get out of bed. Richard pressed his hand to her shoulder to push her back down.

"Oh, no," he said. "You stay put."

"I'll lose my job if I don't get that report to him," she said, eyes tearing. "It's in my laptop."

"You work for me, remember? So you have a job if you need one." She'd taken care of his phone calls very efficiently while she'd taken care of him. Mail, too. He'd had a minimum to handle yesterday. But she wouldn't lose her job over one little thing. "Maybe a little diplomatic push will help," he said.

"I don't know about this," she replied, dubious.

"Relax. It can't hurt. Now, what's the file name of this report?"

"I better get it." She started to rise again.

And again he pushed her back. "I said I'll take it in for you. Before I do, you'll have your three sips of tea and you'll take a nap. Tommy said you were pretty ill last night."

"Very. And you're getting very bossy." She tried to rise once more, then settled back against the pillows in defeat.

Richard chuckled.

"Okay, so a baby can knock me over with a feather," Callie admitted, sighing.

"All the more reason to stay in bed and take care of yourself." He smiled. "And I'll take care of you, too."

"Richard." Her look told him he was in for another no-relationship lecture.

To forestall it, he added, "It's strictly between friends."

She smiled wanly. "I'm too sick to fight you."

"Good, because I'd probably lose." He reached over and took Mark. "Come on, kid. We'll go break Callie's computer now. You'll like that."

"You're getting good with him," she said around a yawn.

He grinned, pleased with the praise from her. "I had a good teacher. In a lot of things."

He bent down and kissed her forehead. Mark's head klonked against hers.

Callie groaned and rubbed the sore spot. "Gee, thanks. That was about the only place that didn't hurt."

"Sorry about that."

Richard went out and fiddled with her laptop, not having any problem finding the file and printing it on her home printer. She used the same software he did, although hers was an older version. As the finished sheets spit out one by one, he noted she did very nice work.

He and Mark took it to the office. Callie's boss, an unpleasant man, couldn't grasp that she was too sick to come herself. People waited for help, including one stubborn old gentleman who'd accidently been declared dead. Richard couldn't help but like him. Everyone waiting wanted Callie. Richard could see she nurtured people here, too. They, at least, understood her illness and sympathized. Her boss didn't. Richard resisted the urge to punch the guy in the nose. He did pull diplomatic rank a little, and her boss backed down somewhat. Grudgingly, but he did. That he'd saved one thing for her pleased Richard.

When he got back to her apartment, he stretched out across the foot of her bed. The trip had exhausted his still-weakened body.

"I'd say I told you so, but I'm too sick," Callie murmured.

"I think you got it in, anyway." Richard closed his eyes, needing to rest just a moment. Mark had crawled in next to Callie, so he was safe for a while from toddler disasters.

"Having two men in one's bed is supposed to be some women's fantasy. Somehow, I can't see it."

"Mmm," Richard murmured without opening his eyes. "I never thought that my first time in your bed would include my youngest nephew. Freud would have a field day. Take a nap, Callie. You need it."

"Somehow I don't think it's me who does..."

Richard drifted off. Seconds later, it seemed, he was jolted to alertness when a foot nudged him in the chest. Kicked him was more like it. He sat up, disoriented.

"The kids will be home from school in twenty

minutes,'' Callie said, confirming he'd been out for more than twenty himself. Her eyes were still red-rimmed but amused. Mark lay next to her, sound asleep. Everyone had napped except the person who'd been ordered to do so.

"I was out that long?" he asked in disbelief.

"Oh, yeah." Callie grinned at him as if she'd enjoyed his presence in her bed.

Richard wished he'd been awake enough to enjoy it, too. Disgusted, he said, "I'm a fat lot of help, aren't I?"

"You probably saved my job. That's enough for one day."

"But I didn't get you aspirin or fluids every fifteen minutes. That's what I'm supposed to be doing."

"Oh, I did that myself while you were out cold." She tapped a half-full glass on the nightstand. "So far, so good. Go home to the kids, Richard. I'll be fine."

"That's what I said, remember?" He had to admit she looked a little better than he had on his first day. Then an idea hit him, a brilliant idea. "I won't go home unless you go with me."

Her eyes blinked fully open. "What?"

"Sure. You shouldn't be here alone while you're sick. Your brother the doctor wouldn't have called me if he thought you didn't need help. At my house, you'll have a bedroom all to yourself and three servants to wait on you. Me, Amanda and Jason. Mark will entertain you. If you don't come home with me, I'll have to bring Jay and Amanda here. How much rest will you get with all of us crammed in your apartment?"

"I'd get more if you'd go home like you should."

"No, you wouldn't, so that's not an option. I can't let you be here by yourself. I *won't*."

"Richard, you're very sweet. I appreciate your caring. But I'm fine—"

A coughing spasm suddenly overtook her. She sounded horrible and she couldn't stop herself. Richard grabbed the sickie bucket and hovered, just in case it turned into something worse.

Callie waved him away. The spasm passed and she collapsed back against the pillows. "Oh, God, that hurt."

"I didn't have coughing like that," Richard said, worried. "See? That's all the more reason to be sick at my house."

She eyed him sourly. "You're going to bug me to death, aren't you?"

"Yep." He grinned at her. "Where's your coat?"

The move took both their energy reserves, but that Callie saw the sense in it without too much argument gratified Richard. Amanda was just arriving home from school when he pulled the car into the driveway. Jason was usually ten minutes behind her.

She peered in the passenger window, then said as Richard emerged from the driver's side, "She looks bad, Uncle Richard."

"She's got our family flu, lucky girl. Do me a favor and bring Mark into the house. I'll help Callie."

Amanda nodded. Richard came around and opened the passenger-side door.

"I heard her." Callie looked at him hopefully. "I don't look that bad, do I?"

"You look beautiful to me," he said honestly. "Just don't toss your cookies in my car. No offense."

She winced as she stood upright. He held her hand and put his arm around her waist. The wind, cold and brisk, blew harder. He hoped her coat and bathrobe would protect her against it.

As he helped her toward the house, a car stopped at the curb. Joey got out and went to Amanda, helping her with Mark. Callie's sister, Gerri, stood on the driver's side, leaning on the car roof.

"Callie! What's all this?"

"She's got the flu," Richard replied for Callie, not stopping in his quest for the front door. "I brought her home so I could watch over her. She needs it. Your brother said."

"Really?" Gerri pushed her sunglasses to the top of her head. "I'm not sure I like this."

But she didn't add anything more and neither did she volunteer to care for Callie herself.

"Amanda, come on," Richard urged. "You can talk to Joey later, okay? I need your help with Callie and Mark."

"Okay," his niece replied, offering no argument, which surprised the heck out of Richard.

He got Callie inside, Mark and Amanda bringing up the rear. He turned and waved to Callie's sister, but she was already in her car. Joey waved back. Nice kid, Richard thought.

Callie muttered under her breath as the door shut behind them all.

"I'm sorry, honey," Richard said, bending over her. "I didn't hear that."

"It's about my sister and it's unrepeatable," Callie replied. She looked at the stairs and groaned. "I can't climb them. Not yet."

Richard looked at the stairs, daunted by their length and height. "I'll carry you."

"The heck you will. You look as pale as I feel."

He couldn't deny it. His body was already urging him to sit down before he fell down.

"Put me on that little couch in your office," Callie ordered. "I'll be fine there for a while."

That he could handle.

Callie practically fell onto the couch when he got her there, her face white as a sheet from the exertion. Richard wanted to collapse with her, but resisted. He was supposed to be the healthy one…well, the healthier one, at any rate.

Amanda, wise child, came in with an afghan. Mark followed, dragging a throw pillow behind him. They got Callie settled with both.

"I feel awful," Amanda said, momentarily scaring Richard until she added, "If I hadn't called you to come over when Uncle Richard got sick, you wouldn't have gotten sick, either."

"Neither of us would have been sick if we'd had our flu shots," Richard said, stroking Amanda's hair.

Callie reached out and patted Amanda's hand. "You did absolutely the right thing. Don't ever think otherwise."

"Callie would have gotten sick, anyway, whether you called or not," Richard added. "So would I. The flu's going around, and like Callie said, we're vulnerable. Hopefully you three won't get it at all."

"So far, so good," Callie commented. She shivered.

Unfortunately the look she gave Richard said what he was thinking. The kids were bound to get the flu. Oh, maybe not yet and maybe they'd get light doses, but they *had* to get it. Even Dr. Tommy expected them to.

"I'll find another blanket for you," Amanda volunteered when she saw Callie's shivering bout. She went off in search of one.

"Spray that antibacterial stuff *everywhere*," Callie said. She coughed, but didn't have a spasm. "You ought to take me right over to that ridiculous sister of mine and dump me on her doorstep. I can't believe she didn't say a word."

"Actually she did," Richard replied, sitting down on the arm of the sofa. He needed support for his body. "She said she didn't think she approved of my help."

"Who is she to approve or not?" Callie griped. Her words would have packed more punch if her voice didn't sound as though it could be coming from the back end of a wind tunnel.

"Never mind." Richard took her hand and held it. "You're in the best place you can be. With me."

"Mmm." She looked sick, but pleased. "Don't forget to wash your hands with the antibacterial soap after touching me."

HERE SHE WAS yet again.

Callie drifted in and out of sleep, her dozes interrupted by heat waves and shivers as the flu did its worst. Every time she roused from unconsciousness, she thought of how she had walked out of Richard's door two days ago only to be dragged back in again.

It was like being caught in a spider's web. Oh, she could struggle and even walk a pace or two away, but she could never escape. Still, what a sweet web it was. What a sweet man. How could she resist a guy barely out of his own sickbed who insisted on helping her in hers.

She couldn't resist. She truly couldn't.

Callie sighed. She'd kill her brother Tommy for calling in Richard's help. She could have managed by herself; she'd been sick before. Gerri was going down, too, for not taking her big sister in, which would have kept Callie out of Richard's reach.

Gerri's lack of help didn't surprise Callie. Gerri had always put herself first. Maybe she was selfish now because she'd had to share everything with siblings for years. Who knew? But that didn't excuse Gerri's behavior.

Richard's office phone rang. Thinking that if she could reach it she could go home, Callie struggled to sit up. She barely lifted her head before it was spinning. Heat boiled through her body at the movement. She lay back down on the sofa and closed her eyes, panting for breath . Her mouth felt dry and strange, too.

"I'll get it," Richard said as he strode into the room. Clearly he had seen her attempt to rise.

"Good, 'cause I can't," Callie muttered without looking at him.

She heard little feet toddle over to her. A body thumped against the side of the sofa. It leaned into her, small elbows digging brutally into her arm. The odor of milk, chicken and a miss in the bathroom wafted through her senses, nearly gagging her.

Callie stretched away and opened one eye.

Mark grinned at her around his thumb. Dark curls brushed his collar and framed his devil-may-care expression. He pulled his thumb from his mouth and announced, "I go, Callie."

"I never would have guessed."

"You sick," was his next statement. He managed to put the *s* on the beginning of the word this time.

"Never would have guessed that, either," she said, adding, "I bet you're next, the way you're hanging all over me. But I'm too tired to put you at a proper distance. Promise me that when you're sick with this, you'll make your uncle Richard crazy and toss your cookies all over my brother the doctor. There's money in it if you do.''

''Money,'' Mark said in a dreamy voice, and began to play with the little chenille nubs on her robe.

''*Big* money,'' Callie said, almost smiling at the thought.

''Callie, did you bring Go-Karts 2000 with you?''

Jason's voice sounded hopeful. Callie glanced over at the boy. He must have come home from school while she'd been in la-la land.

''Somehow I don't think I'm up for games.''

He shrugged. ''I thought maybe you'd bring it for me to use.''

He looked as if he expected her to get off the sofa and go home for the game.

''I was too busy being as sick as your uncle.''

''No one's as sick as him,'' Jay scoffed.

''Now, there's a recommendation,'' Richard said, after hanging up the phone and catching the last of the conversation. ''Okay, guys, out of here. Dinner in fifteen minutes. Let Callie rest.''

Richard helped Mark toward the door, while Jason dragged his feet sulkily. Clearly he thought the Go-Karts 2000 question was still unsettled.

When the kids were gone, Richard said, ''That boy is going to hear about his attitude.''

Callie tried to smile again, but it hurt. ''He'll look past himself eventually. All kids do.''

Except her sister.

''I'm sorry about the phone.''

''That's okay. I was lying here awake, thinking about going home.''

Richard was silent for a long moment. ''I hope you

didn't think too hard, because it was a dumb thought. To quote a wise woman—you look like something the cat dragged in and coughed up on the carpet.''

"I must be looking better than I feel, then." Callie flushed from more than the fever. She pushed some stray ends of hair behind her ears in a futile attempt to tidy herself. "I seem to remember you saying I looked beautiful."

"You always look beautiful. Objectively speaking, however, you're more on a par with hell freezing over."

"Be still my heart."

"You think you can handle being moved to a nice bed upstairs?"

Callie couldn't stretch out properly on the small couch she currently occupied. Her neck ached from being on the armrest's permanent tilt, and the leather covering felt cold against her overly sensitive skin. "I don't think I can handle moving my pinky finger, let alone my body all the way upstairs. I'll stay here."

"But my phone's got to be bothering you."

"Not nearly enough to make me want to move. Am I keeping you from your work in here? Believe me, not much penetrates the flu fog."

"I can take my laptop out if I need to. I'm concerned for you."

"I'm concerned for *you*." She'd move if she absolutely had to, although she would die afterward.

He grinned and came to her. His fingers stroked her hair from her cheek. "You must be really sick."

"Probably."

Callie closed her eyes as his hand pushed back her hair. He caressed her with a feather-light touch that soothed her and yet filled her with emotion. She allowed herself to be lulled by him. It just felt so good. She was almost asleep when his voice penetrated.

"Why are you always so tough, Callie?"

She almost answered, but let it go. What could she say that hadn't been said already? Besides, she didn't want to argue now. The moment was too sweet for her. She loved the pampering he was giving her. Never had a man stroked her so gently nor been this concerned with her health. In fact, she couldn't remember the last time anyone had done this for her.

A suspicious lump grew in her throat. She pushed back the unshed tears, deciding she was becoming maudlin only because she was sick. Reserves went down and emotions went up. Still, it was nice. So nice…

She awoke sometime later to the sound of yelling.

"I did *not* break the plate."

"Yes, you did, *dweeb*."

"You stink!"

"You stink worse!"

"Hey! Callie's sick in the next room and I just put your brother to bed."

"She broke the plate, Uncle Richard."

"Liar! I did not!"

There was the sound of pounding feet, as if someone was being chased. Then came a loud crash, which had to be a chair falling to the floor. Richard shouted ineffectively as the chase resumed.

Callie pulled herself off the sofa and managed to stumble across the room. She felt light-headed but not as bad as she had earlier.

"Hey!" Richard bellowed just as she opened the office door.

Everyone froze and stared at her.

"Hey," she returned calmly. "You want to keep it

down to Civil War volume? I'm trying to be sick in here."

"Callie!" Richard admonished, coming toward her. "You better lie down."

He looked pale and tired. The day had been eventful enough for him without the kiddie-fireworks ending. Jason and Amanda both looked embarrassed yet mulish. The broken-dish scandal was hardly over.

"*He* broke the dish," Amanda said.

"Did not!" Jason yelped. "It dropped when *she* handed it to me to put in the dishwasher."

"That's enough!" Richard commanded in a voice that could penetrate iron. "Just clean the pieces up, both of you."

"But I had nothing to do with it!" Amanda wailed righteously, throwing down her dishcloth rather like a gauntlet.

"Yes, she did! Yes, she did!" Jason countered, hopping up and down in rhythm to his words.

Callie looked at Richard in commiseration, then waved her hand, not caring what happened next. She decided that since she was upright, she'd head for the refuge of the upstairs guest room. She needed some peace and quiet.

She made it as far as the steps themselves when a wave of nausea overcame her. The vertigo was unstoppable, and she sat down on the steps, too weak and tired to go farther until the attack passed. Her stomach gnawed at her, demanding sustenance. She tried to think of the last time she'd eaten or drunk anything. Maybe it was better not to, she thought, fearing it was a false call.

What a life, she thought. Her job was in jeopardy, Richard's gallantry notwithstanding. She had a test in English literature at the college Monday evening, and she hadn't even started reading *Far from the Madding Crowd.* Her other classes were shot, too, for the week. And she was ill with the flu in a place that reminded her all too much of the chaotic household in which she'd grown up. Things couldn't have been worse.

Richard's front doorbell rang.

"This joint is Grand Central," she muttered in disgust. Even with Richard and the kids at *her* place, they couldn't have made any more noise than here.

Being just a few feet away and needing something to get her moving upstairs again, she forced herself upright and answered the door.

Her sister, Gerri, stood on the threshold. The brisk October night air swirled around and through Callie's chenille robe as if it was only a skimpy bikini.

"Good, I'm glad it's you," Gerri said, thrusting her chin out. Her face held an expression that said she would not be brooked. "You've imposed enough on Richard, and I think you should be ashamed. I think you should leave now before you embarrass yourself and me further in front of my neighbors and friends."

"Your timing's impeccable, Gerri," Callie said.

And putting action to word, she proceeded to throw up all over her sister's two-hundred-dollar Angolini loafers.

Chapter Nine

"That was some statement you made to your sister."

Richard grinned at Callie, who looked much better after three days of rest in bed. His guest bed rather than his bed, maybe, but things happened in slow steps. Right now, she was ready to talk about her "discussion" with Gerri the other night.

"She'll probably never speak to me again," Callie said, sighing.

He wondered if that wasn't a good thing. Gerri had had some big brass ones to come to his house and berate his patient, amazing when you considered she was Callie's sister. "I wouldn't worry about it, honey. She was completely wrong. You just told her so in a unique way."

"*Very* unique." Callie grinned reluctantly, but the pink hue in her cheeks and the sparkle in her eyes showed her amusement.

"I never heard anybody squawk so much like a chicken before," Richard mused.

"Now that was unique," Callie admitted, giving in to a fit of giggles. "I was bad."

"She owes you an apology," Richard said.

"I'll never get it. Gerri doesn't give apologies."

"She should."

Callie smiled at him from across the living-room sofa. The Sunday paper was spread all around her. Today was her first day out of bed. She was freshly scrubbed from her shower, and she wore an old pair of his sweatpants and a sweatshirt. She looked great in his clothes, in his house.

"How do you feel?" she asked.

"Good." He meant it. His exhaustion had eased as the weekend progressed. Amanda had helped him out with Mark. So had Callie's nephew. Joey could have been Callie's son, he mirrored her in attitude and caring. A good boy, he decided, having begun to relax a little where Amanda was concerned. Barely, but that was another story. "I feel ready to fly to Java again."

"Please." She waved a hand. "I can't afford more time off from work or school."

Richard took her hand. "You have been terrific."

"No. You have," Callie said, squeezing his fingers. "You took in a sick woman you barely knew."

Nothing had been more satisfying than caring for Callie during her illness. As a man, he hadn't given such things much consideration in the past. Now he found watching over a person you cared about gratified the heart.

He kissed her palm. "You took in a family you barely knew."

Emotions swirled in her gaze. Richard couldn't resist. He leaned forward and kissed her. The newspaper crinkled under his hip but he didn't care. Her lips were warm, soft and willing. Her tongue mated leisurely with his—

"I feel sick."

They broke apart to see Jason standing in the living room doorway, a dismal expression on his face.

Callie pushed the paper aside and got up, saying to Richard, "You get the sickie bucket. I'll get him to bed."

"Right." The inevitable had happened. The kids were coming down with the flu. "This thing is like a freight train going through here."

"It's life. Unglamorous, unromantic and unrewarding."

"I don't know. It has its moments."

Callie blushed.

Richard grinned at her.

Callie felt Jason's forehead. "He doesn't feel warm."

Richard's grin turned to a frown. "That's odd. We were burning up right from the beginning."

Callie already had the boy in bed and a thermometer in his mouth when Richard bounded up the stairs into the boy's room. He removed the thermometer.

"Hey! It's not done yet," she protested.

"My nephew is." Richard glared at the boy. "Jason, where is the rest of your Halloween candy? You had a half a bowl of it yesterday."

Jay glanced away. "I dunno."

"I do. It's in your belly right now, giving you a stomachache. No wonder you feel sick."

Jason firmed his lips, refusing to answer. No kid ratted on himself if he could help it, and Jason was clearly subscribing to that theory.

"Jay, you are only supposed to eat one piece of candy a day," Richard snapped, angry with the boy for his disobedience. "What did you think? That you could take advantage of me and Callie being ill and no one would notice? How fair is that?"

"Not very," Jason admitted.

"You're supposed to eat fruit for snacks—"

"I hate fruit."

"You'll learn to like it," Richard told him sternly, "Because that's *all* the snacks you're getting for the next two months. You're flagged, boy."

He set the bucket down by the bed and ushered Callie from the room.

Outside, he said, "Can you believe that kid? We've got the flu and he goes out and gives himself a candy bellyache."

Callie chuckled. "He's a pistol. A hungry pistol, obviously, whose eyes and stomach aren't on the same wavelength."

Richard shook his head. "Great. I've got a kid with something that's not even on our expected sick list. He's going to have candy belly, and then he's going to have the real thing. It's only a half hour after he had lunch. How could he even be hungry?"

"He's a kid," Callie said as they went downstairs. "All he had to see was that candy, and his brain went into chocolate shock. My little brother, Jamie, had the same problem at Jay's age. They see it. They must eat it. They must be sick afterward."

"He took advantage of our being in the living room, and Amanda and Joey's taking Mark for a walk," Richard said. "That's how he got into the bowl without being stopped."

"I'd watch that," she said.

"Damn straight I'll watch Jay's candy intake."

"I meant Joey and Amanda taking Mark for a walk."

They resumed their seats on the sofa. Jason, by mutual unspoken agreement, would be fending for himself until his chocolate attack eased. You play, you pay, Richard thought unsympathetically.

"What do you mean about taking Mark for walks?" he asked, puzzled by her comment.

"Just that you should always know where they're walking Mark to," she said. "Tommy used to take Jamie out all the time. I thought it was big-brother love. It was, in a way. Tommy was more interested in fooling around with Mindy Schuller behind the old gas station on the corner while Jamie played in the weeds. Jamie got poison ivy before Tommy could get to home plate with Mindy."

Richard cursed. "This is never ending, isn't it?"

"It's called the teenage years. I caught hell from my mom because I didn't watch over Tommy better. The bum was fifteen. *He* should have known better. He did know better."

"And they let him be a doctor?" Richard asked, astonished.

"Where do you think my brother got his inspiration from?" But Callie grinned, clearly forgiving Tommy for his checkered past.

"So you're telling me Joey's like Tommy," Richard said, getting the point. Unfortunately the point scared the hell out of him, just as he was relaxing with the boy. Joey and Amanda were only thirteen. Too young, both of them. Surely. He wondered if chastity belts came in Amanda's size.

"I'm not telling you Joey's like Tommy. My nephew is a sweet boy. I'm just saying it doesn't hurt to keep your eyes open and your mind objective. It's good practice for later."

"Oh."

She chuckled as he finally got the actual point. It was

great to have her back to normal and giving him guidance. Her being ill had frightened him nearly as much as the potential Amanda had for getting in trouble. He reached across the space separating them and caressed her hair. The blond strands pulled back tightly and then falling loose in a ponytail fascinated him.

Callie turned to look at him, her eyes wide and wary as a doe's. But she didn't pull away from his touch.

"Did you kiss anyone behind the gas station?" he asked, not sure if he was jealous or curious. Jealous won. This was Callie, after all.

"No."

"Why not? Were you such a good girl?"

"No one ever asked me."

"I would have asked you," he said softly. "I would have done more than kiss you."

She said nothing. He knew he would kiss her now. So did she. He leaned toward her and she met him halfway in a blistering kiss. Their mouths opened so their tongues could meet—

The front door opened.

They pulled apart. Richard cursed under his breath as Mark ran into the room. He didn't begrudge his nephew's presence. He just begrudged the interruption.

Mark's solid little body was bundled in a hat and jacket, but he brought the brisk air in with him as he flung himself at Richard and Callie.

"Bird fly!" Mark said happily. "Bird fly to Grandma's!"

"Better them than me," Richard said, after figuring out that Mark meant the geese flying south, probably to Florida. Amanda and Joey must have explained migration to the child.

"You look better, Aunt Callie," Joey said.

"I feel a lot better," Callie replied. "How's your mother? Is it safe to get within a hundred yards of her? Or will she take me out?"

Joey looked heavenward. "I'd stay here for a while longer, Aunt Callie."

"Thanks for the warning."

Richard stared at his niece, looking for signs that Amanda had joined the gas-station club. Her cheeks were rosy, but that could have been from the cold November day. Her eyes were a limpid brown, but then, they were always that way. Her lips did not look freshly kissed. Now *that* was good, he thought, relieved.

Joey looked charmingly gawky, not knowingly mature. Not trying to play doctor because he wanted to grow up to be one.

Then Richard wondered if one could tell. The idea of a chastity belt looked better and better. For Pete's sake, he thought, disgusted with himself. He was worrying for nothing. He had to be. Amanda and Joey were only kids. At thirteen he hadn't had enough nerve to hold a girl's hand in private, let alone in public. Joey shouldn't be any different—except for the evidence of Fast Uncle Tommy.

"Can I stick my head in the sand on this one?" he asked seriously.

Callie looked amused as she shook her head. "Nope. You've got to hang in there with it."

She could have been talking about herself, for she certainly tried hard to stick her head in the sand about their relationship. Being sick had its advantages; they hadn't been able to ignore each other and indulge hurt feelings. Instead, they'd been with each other. Not in a sexual way, but it helped. And maybe it was better.

Richard's brain took a right turn and he wondered if

he should encourage her to hang in there with him. Maybe if she could see that a relationship between them was no threat to her needs, she would be open to him.

He spotted an article of interest in the newspaper section she currently held. In fact, the piece seemed to leap off the page to get his attention.

Richard pointed to the article. "See that? There, on the society page? That's Marcia Ortega. She's a local, a bank vice president who just got appointed the Philadelphia consul for Argentina."

"I take it you know her?" Callie asked, looking at the picture of the older woman.

"Sure. We all know one another. She's at the docks more than the airport. That's how Argentina ships most of their fruit to the States. She was vice consul for Chile for three years before the new hitch."

"How'd she get the Argentine post if she's from Chile?"

Richard grinned. "She's not from Chile. She's from Chester, Pennsylvania. Her mother's Chilean and her dad's Argentinean. Family connections are as good as telephone-system donations. There's a ball being held in her honor next week. Would you like to go with me?"

"Me?" Callie's eyes widened at the invitation.

Richard laughed. He hadn't planned on going, but the spur-of-the-moment idea had taken fruit. He pardoned himself for the pun. But he liked seeing the usually unruffled Callie look surprised as hell. He felt in control. "Yes, you. It's formal, very fancy, but lots of fun. We do it up right, trust me. And you and I deserve it. After the drudge of the flu, we need a break. This'll be a great one."

"Who'll watch the kids?" she asked. "Or will we take them?"

"Hell, no!" He shuddered at the thought of Jason and Mark in formal surroundings. Slyly he said, "I'll ask your sister Gerri to baby-sit."

Callie burst into laughter. "I'd love to see that."

"Then say yes and watch me."

"But I don't have anything formal to wear." She paused. "Well, I've got a couple of awful bridesmaid dresses. I refuse to wear them."

She was obviously very tempted to accept. That was good. Richard replied with logic, "Borrow a dress. Or rent one. No one will know but me, and I'm renting my tux. Since that's settled, you're going."

"Is that a statement or a question?" she asked, eyeing him narrowly.

"A question if you want. A statement if you need the push. I am a diplomat, after all."

She snorted. "You're the fruit guy, Richard. I know, because I was the fruit girl for you."

"Sounds kinky, so it works for me. We'll go and be fruity together." He held out his hand. "Pass over the sports section. I want to see the individual matchups for the Eagles-Cowboys game today."

"Philadelphia fan?"

"Dallas."

She passed the section he requested, whacking him over the head with it as she did. "I'm an Eagles fan, you crumb."

"Love those signs of affection," he murmured.

"I've FORGIVEN YOU," Callie said to her sister, breezing into Gerri's house on her way home from class Tuesday night. "Now, do you have a formal I can borrow?"

"Wh-what?" Gerri squawked.

Callie smiled sweetly at her sister. "I said I forgive you."

"You were sick all over my shoes!" Gerri yelped.

"Then you can forgive me, and we're even," Callie told her. She'd said yes to the ball, and now Cinderella needed a dress. Gerri had a number of dresses for formal occasions. Callie would humble herself only so far to get one—but she'd humble herself enough. Better to let each other's rude behavior pass.

"My shoes were ruined!" Gerri said. Clearly letting things pass was a foreign concept to Gerri. "And you've been living over there, haven't you? My neighbors have noticed. Callie, how could you?"

"I was *baby-sitting* while he took a soccer player home to Indonesia," Callie replied, now not inclined to allow anything to pass. "Then he got sick, and I got sick. We're *friends*." She skipped their lapse into intimacy and focused on where the relationship needed to be. "It's no big deal—although if you thought it was, you should have taken me into your house while I was sick. I don't believe I heard any offer from you to do so, but maybe I was too out of it and missed it."

Gerri's expression grew less outraged and more furtive. "I was busy with the children, always running with their activities. It's never ending, Callie, but you wouldn't know that. You should have been at Mom's or something. Not Richard Holiday's."

"You know Mom has a heart condition, and she can't afford to get ill. She certainly hasn't the strength to care for someone."

Gerri would never change, Callie thought. Her sister would always be critical of others while being the "not me" girl about the same thing.

"What do you need a formal for?" Gerri asked, turning the conversation elsewhere now that she was on the defensive.

Callie smiled, knowing this would be good. "Richard's asked me to a diplomats' ball."

"What!" Gerri's eyes bulged with astonishment. Then her face hardened. "You didn't wheedle the invitation out of him while you were there, did you?"

Callie froze for one long moment at the insult. Then she moved close to Gerri, practically leaning into her, forcing Gerri to step back in intimidation. Callie said, "It's lucky you're my sister, otherwise you'd be wishing you'd never said that. Now stop being a self-centered idiot and let me borrow a dress."

"I didn't mean to insult you," Gerri said, recovering a little dignity. "It's just that Richard Holiday is an important man. I'm sure he has a lot of beautiful women throwing themselves at him. I don't want to see you hurt. I just didn't word my concerns right."

Gerri hadn't worded this any better, Callie thought, toying with the idea of rubbing her sister's nose in the potted tree. She couldn't have implied in clearer fashion that she thought Callie wasn't good enough for Richard. However, Gerri was right in one respect: Callie was hurt. But by someone in her own family, not Richard. Following Gerri upstairs, she murmured, "I should have rented a dress."

Fortunately revenge worked its subtle way—in Gerri's dress going to the diplomats' ball with Callie's body in it. Cinderella had never had it so good. Callie would deal with Gerri later.

Cinderella was downright cheated by having to leave at midnight, Callie acknowledged as she walked into the ballroom at the Wyndam-Franklin Plaza Hotel in downtown Philadelphia. Callie had no such restrictions. She held her breath against the joy in her heart as she looked on in wonder.

Crystal chandeliers hung like glorious stalactites from the tall ceilings, their light illuminating the gold brocade wallpaper. A small string orchestra played on an elevated stage that was decorated in autumn mums and carnations. Men wore tuxes and women glittered in jewels and floor-length silks.

And I'm one of them, Callie thought in awe as she held Richard's elbow with one hand and surreptitiously nudged up the strapless bodice of her hunter green chiffon gown with the other. It figured that Gerri was bigger in the bust than she.

"This beats the airport warehouse, doesn't it?" Richard said, leaning over to whisper in her ear.

She chuckled. "This is fairyland. How often do you do this?"

"When someone gets promoted or appointed. It gives us a great excuse to party in a pale mirror of the Washington-corps balls."

"This mirror's bright enough for me," she said. "If it was any brighter, I'd be blind as a bat."

Richard laughed. He looked terrific in a tux. Certainly he looked a world away from the harried Batman she'd met a few short weeks ago. Tonight the kids had been left in Gerri's care. Gerri would complain later, but she hadn't said no to Richard. Callie would have loved to have been a fly on the wall when Richard had asked her sister to baby-sit.

She'd almost wished that the kids would get the flu bug on Gerri, but that was truly unfair. So far none of them had, and Jay, beyond a rumbly belly, had had nothing more than a candy gut last week. She'd even caught up with her work and her school classes and so was free as a bird tonight to enjoy herself. She intended to do it in a big way.

A part of her brain warned her this night would be dangerous for her. It was the kind of evening that caused women to fall in love. She'd have to be careful, very careful, to keep her emotions in check.

"Do you think your sister will ever forgive me for getting her to baby-sit?" Richard asked with a chuckle.

"You're the star of the neighborhood. How could she say no?" Callie smiled. "Knowing Gerri, she'll be thrilled that you asked her and not another neighbor. And here I thought you were only kidding."

"I never kid," he said. "Let's dance."

The ball lost a little of its glamorous luster as everyone gyrated to a string version of the Rolling Stones' "Satisfaction." But Callie felt a little more down-to-earth and that was good. She'd been feeling rather overwhelmed by the affair.

"Callie, this is the consul for Panama, Ira Gorstein," Richard said, waving to the gentleman boogying next to them. "Ira, this is Callie Rossovich."

Callie shook hands, then the man spun her around in a circle.

"Beautiful," he said in a pure Philadelphia accent. He could have been from the old neighborhood. *"Boo-tee-full!"*

When she was back with Richard, and Ira had moved off to boogie in a different direction, she commented, "He's got business connections to Panama, right?"

"Family. His grandfather was some big politician there before the son came to Philly years and years ago. Are you having fun yet?"

"Absolutely." Callie grinned. "It's strange without the kids, though."

"No bickering. No broken dishes. No 'To bathroom or not to bathroom, that is the question.'" Richard sighed happily and swiveled his hips in time to the music. "I love the kids, but it's *great* to be alone with you."

"Hey! Richard. Richard Holiday!"

Callie turned with Richard to find a handsome man grinning at them and dancing with a very pretty woman. Richard laughed. "My God. Jared. What are you doing here?"

"The Chilean consul was one of my first clients when I opened my own law practice, so Allison and I got invited," the man replied. "I thought I might see you here, since I know you're connected somehow. You remember my wife, Allison."

"Of course." Richard took Allison's hand and suavely kissed it. He touched Callie's waist, adding, "This is Callie Rossovich, woman extraordinaire. Callie, meet my cousin Jared Holiday and his wife, Allison."

Greetings were exchanged as the song ended and Callie found herself bussed on the cheek by the Holidays. This must be one of the elusive cousins Richard had talked about.

"She is extraordinary," Jared agreed.

"Hardly," Callie said ruefully.

"Don't listen to her," Richard said dismissively.

"We won't," Allison promised, grinning at Callie.

"I just realized how much time has passed since we saw you at your brother's funeral," Jared said seriously. "I feel badly, Richard. We meant to keep in touch better than we have."

"I know. I've been swamped with the kids and moving, so I haven't been much better."

"How are the children?"

Richard chuckled. "Adjusting."

They chatted with Jared and Allison a little longer, the men catching up, until a new song started and people began dancing around them.

Callie smiled as she and Richard were crushed together by the dance crowd. If this was Richard's idea of being alone, he must barely feel crammed when in New York City rush-hour traffic. Jared and Allison danced away.

The music slowed. Richard pulled her closer and swirled her in time to the music. He didn't ask her to dance; he just assumed. She couldn't find it in her heart to tell him he might have assumed wrongly. The evening held so much promise she wanted nothing to ruin it. She *wanted* to dance with him and that was all that mattered. He just hadn't asked first. The man was entitled to get away with machismo once in a while.

She melted against him as the lights dimmed. Their thighs brushed together. One of his hands rode low on her hip, his fingers just above the curve of her derriere. His other hand cuddled hers to his chest. Their cheeks touched.

Callie smiled to herself as his cologne, sharp with sandalwood, teased her senses. She couldn't remember the last time she'd danced intimately with a man. She felt pretty and pampered and incredibly feminine. She felt desire and desired. When was the last time she'd felt that way with any man?

She couldn't answer. She had this response to Richard, and that was all that mattered. She would take this night and keep it in a mental memory book, already filled with images and sensations of him. She would take out the remembrances to make her smile and feel loved, even if for just a moment, long after her midnight hour struck. Even though she wasn't Cinderella with a time clock to punch, a midnight of sorts would eventually arrive. A darker midnight from which she would never return.

But not yet, she thought, snuggling closer to Richard as "Sitting on the Dock of the Bay" played out to the end.

Later, she and Richard caught up with Jared and Allison again and had a longer talk. Callie liked them both, Jared reminding her of Richard. Allison was indulgent of her husband and very kind to her. But mostly Callie indulged herself with Richard and loved every minute of it. They splurged on every item the endless buffet table held. They laughed over trying to do the macarena and the matchups of amateur diplomats to their respective countries. They sipped shared champagne.

Callie was floating by the time they left the ball. She swore her feet hadn't touched the ground since the second round of champagne. Richard was the ultimate escort: attentive, witty and sexy. She had been with a wonderful man in a sensational setting and her top had stayed up all evening. What more could a girl ask?

"One thing," she murmured aloud as Richard walked her to her door.

"One thing what?" he asked, smiling and taking her hand.

"Oh, nothing really." She smiled at him. "I was just thinking this was a great evening. A perfect evening."

They stopped at her door. "You are a wonderful woman, Callie."

She chuckled. "You are a great suck-up."

He grinned. "Keep thinking that. I don't mind a bit."

He leaned down and grazed the corner of her mouth with his lips. Callie's breath caught in her throat. He touched the other corner with a second butterfly kiss. Her head spun from the sensations.

Wanting a full kiss, Callie sought his mouth with her own. He eluded her, still giving the barest of kisses on her face. He ran his hands down her arms, sending shivers of awareness through her.

She had warned herself to indulge in the fantasy only so far. She had made it a point to join the fun without causing repercussions. But somewhere the lines had blurred, and now she wanted more than indulgence and fun. She wanted reality and emotions. She couldn't use the excuse that this was a dream and she didn't try.

"Come in for coffee," she said in a low voice, knowing the invitation included more.

He raised his head. "Are you sure you want me to?"

"Oh, absolutely."

She put her hands to his face and pulled him into her kiss.

Chapter Ten

Richard looked at the breakfast mess and muttered, "Back to reality."

Had last night happened? Everything seemed in a haze. And yet he could easily see Callie again, so beautiful in that gown, laughing and sensuous. He could feel her moving slowly against him, every inch of her body swaying in time to the music. He could also feel her naked body moving urgently once again with his, taking him inside her, making love in a way that scored his heart.

He wished he'd been able to stay with her until morning. A week ago she'd been practically living with him. Due to illness, maybe, but he didn't care. His house seemed empty without her. It seemed even emptier to have left her behind in her own bed.

What was she thinking right now? What was she regretting yet again? If only he hadn't had to leave after making love—but it had been late and the kids were with Gerri, not the best of situations to allow him to indulge himself and Callie further.

Commitments. He had them, and Callie had shed them.

Richard cursed, hating his thoughts.

"I didn't do it," Jason said, having overheard his uncle as he entered the kitchen.

I did, Richard thought. "I was just thinking out loud."

"About what?" Jay dumped a used cup in the kitchen sink.

"I don't know." Richard sighed, knowing very well. "I was thinking about Callie."

"Oh." Jason scratched his nose. "You like her, don'tcha?"

"Yes, I do." It was a relief to admit it to somebody, even a seven-year-old boy.

"She's more fun than Joey's mom." Jay made a face. "She made us watch a dumb movie called *Little Women* because it was…'lightning.'"

"Enlightening." Richard smothered a smile. Jason's movie tastes ran to *Space Jam* and *Casper.* "Enlightening" was hardly his style.

"She wouldn't let me play video games, either," Jay complained further. "She said it was childish. I *am* a child!"

Richard laughed helplessly.

"It's not funny, Uncle Richard," Jason said. "Can we have Callie back?"

"I wish." He wanted Callie in so many ways.

"Why don't you just go get her?"

Kids were to the point even when they missed it, Richard thought. The truth was, he was afraid to seek her out after making love. If he did, the Pandora's box of emotions was bound to open. He couldn't face that, so what he didn't know wouldn't hurt him.

As the day wore on, however, a bright Sunday that invited walks in the woods, long drives down country roads and warm cider before fireplaces, Richard tried to concentrate on loading dishwashers and clothes dryers and faxing buyers' needs to his contacts in the Far East. The work week on the other side of the world would be starting in a few short hours. He wished his had started already, just so he could get past the agonizing Sunday.

By five o'clock he could stand the uncertainty no longer, and he dialed her number from his office phone. She answered on the second ring.

"Hello?" Her voice sounded strong and sure.

"Hi," he said.

He could feel the charged pulse of sensuality between them over the telephone line.

"Richard."

"I wanted to thank you for coming with me last night," he said, and immediately hated the lame words. He cleared his throat and got to the point. "I wanted to see how you were after last night. After making love."

He glanced around his office, just in case one of the kids had snuck into the room. Well, Mark was playing blocks on the floor, but he didn't count.

"I...I don't know."

"Really?" This was progress. At least she wasn't regretting it and rejecting him as he'd feared. "I wish I could have stayed. I wanted to."

"Don't apologize for that. You had to go home to the kids. How did they do with my sister?"

"She enlightened them with *Little Women* and no video games."

Callie chuckled. "I'm surprised they didn't tie her up and torture her."

He refused to be deterred from the subject of their lovemaking. "Last night was special for me. I hope for you, too."

"Yes." Her voice was low.

Richard straightened. This really was progress. "Callie...have you changed your mind?"

"Oh, Lord." She sighed heavily. "No. Yes. I don't know. I'm confused."

"I'll come to you." Mark knocked his blocks over, drawing Richard's attention. His budding plan deflated faster than a popped balloon. "No, I can't. I have the kids. You come here."

"No. I'd rather do this over the phone."

"That sounds ominous. Let me—"

"No, no. Unless you're sending me Girl Scout cookies, stay where you are. I need some space. Or a swift kick in the pants. I'm all over the place emotionally."

"Okay. Let's back up the truck and start again," he said, wanting to head her in the right direction. She was halfway there. He hoped. "You're no longer sure our lovemaking was a mistake. And you're confused about that."

"It never should have happened a second time. I'd like to think it was fancy clothes and too much champagne, but I think popcorn and jeans would have made no difference. I guess I'm lonely and needy."

"Jeez, you're not a bag lady."

"Bag lady!" Mark repeated happily.

"Is that Mark?" Callie chuckled, then said, "You only want me because you need a mother for the children."

"What!" Progress shot out the window like Superman racing a speeding bullet. "Where did that nonsense come from?"

"It's obvious. Never-been-married-before male becomes guardian to three young children and immediately starts telling women they mean something more to him than a sex partner."

Richard's jaw dropped. Her pronouncement of his motives astonished him. "You make me sound like some calculating male who wants to offload his responsibilities. How can you even think that?"

"I don't think that! How can *you* even think I would think that?"

Her voice sounded as angry as he felt. "Because you just said that."

"I said your urge to settle down is based on your desire to find a mother for the kids. You'd have this reaction to any female without a criminal record. Someone decent and nice who likes children will do for you. It's the wrong reason for us to get involved."

"You're taking a psychology course, aren't you?" he demanded to know. "You have to be to come up with such crazy ulterior motives for me wanting you. It's simple, Callie. I like you. I'm attracted to you. I think we have a foundation to pursue a relationship between *us*. Just us. That you've been helpful with the kids is incidental."

"It could be," Callie conceded. "But I don't think so."

"Okay, let's analyze you, because I'll be damned if I'm on that couch by myself." He gripped the receiver tightly. "You're a woman who's looking for kids to mother and a man in her bed and none of the responsibilities that go with either. You use your career goals like a shield to keep a man away and then huff and puff about *him* crossing the line while you're reaching over and yanking him in with both hands."

"That's nonsense!" Callie yelped indignantly.

"It's the same nonsense you spouted about me but from the opposite direction, Callie."

"Callie!" Mark's head snapped up from his blocks.

He got up and raced over, flopping against Richard's legs. "Callie! Callie!"

Richard grimaced as Mark reached for the phone. "No, you can't talk to Callie now."

"Want Callie!"

Richard knew how his nephew felt.

"Put him on," Callie said.

Great, he thought. Little Mark would get the sweet Callie while he got the... Never mind what he got, he decided. Reluctantly he put the receiver against Mark's ear. He could hear Callie saying, "Hello, Mark," several times but the boy only grinned. Richard fumed. Damn, but she could tick him off good when she wanted.

He tried to take the receiver back, but Mark dodged him for a few critical moments. Finally he got the instrument away from the toddler and put it to his own ear.

"Callie?"

She didn't answer. The line was dead.

"Callie go bye-bye," Mark said, racing around the room with his arms out. The little twerp was thrilled that Callie had said bye-bye to him.

Richard knew she had taken advantage of Mark's interruption to get off the line. "Stinker."

He glanced at Mark. "Not you."

Mark ran happily toward the couch. Richard sighed and hung up the phone.

SHE HAD BEEN a coward.

Callie groaned as she carried her sister's dress up the driveway to Gerri's front door, wishing she'd faced up to her confusion about Richard with Richard.

Instead, she'd spouted psychobabble—and had it thrown back in her face very adeptly. Even Mark hadn't talked to her. She'd hung up the telephone after a few minutes of awkwardly trying to coax a word out of the boy. In truth, she'd made sure she'd hung up before Richard got back on the line.

She needed to sort this out herself first. Or else she was a coward. She leaned toward the latter. It made more sense.

"Hi, Aunt Callie," Joey said with a welcoming grin when he answered the door.

She bussed his cheek. "Hi, kid. How's school?"

"Good. But we lost the soccer playoffs. One and out." Joey made a face. "Amanda's school is going into the semifinals for South Jersey."

Callie smiled. "Talk to your mom and dad."

Joey looked heavenward. "Dad does whatever Mom says. I'll never get on a good team."

"There are other things than soccer teams," Gerri said, having overheard the gist of the conversation while coming out of the kitchen.

"There's college-scholarship money in soccer, Gerri," Callie said. "If Joey's on a good team, maybe he can get recognized for his talent."

"He's in a very good school," Gerri countered, looking like she'd swallowed lemons. "That will count for more in the type of college Joey can go to. He needs Harvard or Yale."

"I do?" Joey asked, wide-eyed.

"Yes, you do," Gerri said firmly. "Your aunt Callie would know that if she ever stopped playing mother hen and had children of her own."

"Well, I've been properly spanked," Callie quipped, ready to do the same to her superior-minded sister. But she set the annoyance with Gerri aside. Gerri would never learn, anyway.

Joey, obviously knowing when a good retreat was needed, waved goodbye to Callie and disappeared upstairs.

Callie smiled at Gerri, to show she wasn't too annoyed with her. She held out the garment she carried. "I brought back your dress. I had it dry-cleaned—"

Gerri snatched it out of Callie's hands. "Oh, no!"

"—at a one-hour service," Callie finished lamely. "Why? What's wrong?"

"A cheap dry cleaner could ruin the dress," Gerri said, flipping up the filmy plastic bag. She examined the dress closely. "Thank God! It's okay."

"Oh, too bad," Callie muttered under her breath. If she were to be hung for a lamb, she might as well have ruined the dress and be hung for a lion. More loudly she said, "Thanks for baby-sitting the other night for Richard."

"What choice did I have?" Gerri asked. "I couldn't very well refuse him. He's a diplomat and shouldn't be offended. But I know you put him up to it, Callie, even if he didn't."

"Me!" Callie gasped.

"Oh, don't act the innocent," Gerri said, looking vexed. "You've been shameless with Richard. It's embarrassing for me and the children. All the neighbors have noticed and they've made comments. Callie, I hate to bring this to your attention, but why would a man like Richard, with his position, have a relationship with you for any reason but one? He's not going to stay with you, you know. A man like that wouldn't."

Callie looked at her sister, ready to strangle her. Only the penalty stopped her.

"Oh, don't give me that look." Gerri sniffed dramatically. "You were always above yourself. Mom should have reeled you in, instead of letting you lord it over the rest of us. The others in the family can kowtow to you, but I certainly won't. I don't care if you make a fool of yourself over a man. Just don't do it so blatantly in front of *my* friends."

"Gerri, you're nuts!" Callie exclaimed, finding her voice at last. "I don't know what your problem is, but back off!"

Callie stalked out of the house, afraid if she stayed longer, she really would do physical harm to her spoiled-rotten sister. She couldn't believe how Gerri had attacked her. It was all nonsense, but it hurt. Hurtful words. Gerri had always been good at that. Still, the notion that she was somehow beneath Richard gnawed at her. She'd never seen him act superior about anything or anyone. He was no snob. She was certain of that.

Yet, she didn't feel she measured up. Maybe that was a reason she wanted her distance. Yes, she needed to get a degree before she considered anything with a man and family. But she did have feelings of inadequacy. Callie shook the notion off. Gerri was nuts, plain and simple.

As she drove out of the area, she passed by Richard's house. Making an instant decision, she turned the car around and parked in front.

When she climbed out, she glanced around the houses, then made a rude gesture. "Take that, you bunch of nosy nasties. If you think I was crude before, just watch out."

She smiled to herself, feeling instantly better. She walked up the walk and knocked on Richard's door.

Amanda opened it. The teenager grinned widely when she saw who it was. "Callie! Hi! Thank God you're here. Uncle Richard's got to make a squirrel costume for Jason. By tomorrow."

Callie chuckled ruefully. "I think I'll leave now."

"Oh, no. We need help." Amanda gripped her arm and pulled her into the house.

Richard was in the kitchen with the squirrel-to-be. Jason stood on the table. He wore brown pants and a brown shirt. On his head was a Mickey Mouse cap with the famous ears. Sticking out the back of Jay's pants was a feather duster dyed a mottled dun color. Mark was trying to climb onto the table and not yet succeeding because his uncle shooed him off.

"It hurts, Uncle Richard," Jay whined, tugging at his tail.

"Leave it alone," Richard commanded, pushing the boy's hand away. "I've got to see it before I can fix it."

"Guess who I found," Amanda announced, grinning triumphantly as she led Callie farther into the kitchen.

"Callie!" Mark shouted, and stopped trying to get on the table with his older brother.

He ran to Callie and hugged her legs. She reached down and picked the boy up. Mark's arms wrapped around her neck, and Callie hugged him back, kissing his hair, grateful the boy didn't act as if she was beneath him in the social stratosphere.

"It hurts, Callie," Jason whined by way of greeting.

Callie grinned at him. "You look like an ostrich with a gland problem, Jay."

"See?" the boy said to the room.

She turned to Richard. He stood there, grinning like a fool, obviously very pleased to see her. And not because she could turn Jason from lousy ostrich to good-looking squirrel better than he could. His smile held a hint of knowing intimacy, as if he and she were the only two people in the world.

She remembered their conversation and the way she had scooted off the telephone. He'd dared her to take a risk with him and see where their relationship would go. After Gerri's performance tonight, she wanted nothing more than to accept that challenge.

"Hi, stranger," he said.

She smiled, feeling more welcome here than she did anywhere else. "Hi. I was in the neighborhood and thought I'd stop by."

"I appreciate that…just for myself—" his grin widened "—but if you have any advice on how to improve the squirrel costume, I won't say no."

"Throw it out and start over," she suggested.

"Yeah!" Jay cheered, and yanked the feather duster out of the back of his pants.

"I didn't mean the tail," Callie said. "That was the best part."

Richard laughed heartily. "I thought so."

"Why is he in brown?" she asked, frowning. "Squirrels are gray…or is he supposed to be one who rolled around in the mud for three days?"

"I'm s'pose to be a squirrel who doesn't want to store nuts for the winter," Jay said, making a face of disgust. "It's a dumb play we're doing for the kindergartners about autumn."

"I forgot we had to put a costume together tonight," Richard said. "The play's tomorrow."

"You've been a little busy," Callie said, excusing him on his own behalf. "But a squirrel rolling around in the mud isn't a bad idea. It shows he's playing, instead of working hard like he should be."

"You mean I have the body of it solved?" Richard asked, his tone excited.

"I think we could get away with it." She set Mark on the table and said, "Now don't fall off, big guy," before turning to Jay. She pursed her lips. "The mouse ears have to go."

Jay flung the hat across the room. "Yippee!"

"We'll make whiskers, instead, from a brown paper bag, and he can tape them on his upper lip."

"I'll get the bag," Amanda said, going into the utility room where they were stored.

"He still needs a tail," Richard said. "And this one hurts."

"He does... Mark, no." Callie snatched the toddler up as he tried to get down from the table.

"I knew he'd do that," Richard said, shaking his head. "That's why I didn't let him up there in the first place."

"Oh, I knew he'd get bored and want to get down," Callie said, then planted a kiss on the toddler's belly. Mark squealed with laughter. "I was waiting for it. This way he's discovered it isn't as much fun as he thought and he won't be trying to get on the table all the time like before."

Richard bowed. "The master at work once again."

"The lording-it-over-everyone-else at work again," Callie said.

Richard frowned. "Where did that come from?"

"An *un*wise woman." She waved her hand in dismissal.

At least she knew Gerri was an unwise woman, even if what she said hung on like the last tree leaf. She turned her attention to Jason.

Within twenty minutes they had whiskers on the boy and a tail that didn't hurt. Callie reminded Jay to tell his teacher he was Ding-Dong, the squirrel who played in the mud, rather than gathered nuts. Jason actually liked the notion.

After Amanda went to her room, Jason hit the shower and Mark was put to bed. All the kids were content with having solved a family crisis together. Richard looked very happy. Callie felt a satisfaction she didn't find anywhere else.

That gave her pause.

Richard ushered her into the living room, where they could be alone. "I know you didn't come over to help with a squirrel costume."

"I came to apologize for what I said the other night on the phone." She knew she'd been too harsh in her assessment of his interest in her—even if, deep inside, she believed it.

"But you still think it's true," he guessed shrewdly.

Callie sighed. "Yes, but you don't. That's what matters."

"Callie, why do you think everything will be taken from you if you find yourself involved with someone? Someone like me with a ready-made family?" His voice was earnest, his gaze even more so.

Callie glanced away, unable to look at him directly. "Because it would. Because I would allow it."

"Then why can't you look me in the eye when you say it?"

She glanced back involuntarily, startled by his words.

"Maybe it's something you don't truly believe, either," Richard said. He cupped her cheek. "I'm not after you for the kids. I promise you that. I'll muddle through like I would have tonight."

"Jason would have been a dirty squirrel with a bad butt," she replied, chuckling, although his words about what she believed bothered her.

"So he would have muddled through, too." Richard

kissed her mouth lightly. "I should be annoyed with you for what you're thinking. But I understand it."

"I don't." Her sister's disapproval flitted through her mind. Instead of weakening her resolve, it strengthened it. "Maybe we could try a dinner together."

He smiled and kissed her again. She melted against him, the hard wall of his chest crushing her breasts. Her nipples grew hard in response. Desire flowed through her veins, heating her body.

He raised his head. "Dinner would be great."

"Just don't use my sister as a baby-sitter. Ever."

"Why? Did she complain?"

Callie snorted. "She always complains."

"No problem." He traced his finger down her cheek, sending shivers of delight along her nerve endings. "Stay awhile."

"The neighbors will talk," she murmured, stretching up to kiss his cheek, his forehead, then his mouth.

"I don't give a rat's behind about the neighbors."

"That's wonderful to know," she murmured happily.

He pulled her closer. She knew she should stop things, but she didn't care. She felt as though a door long closed had been opened finally. A door she needed to have opened by Richard.

RICHARD WAS CONTEMPLATING suicide when his telephone rang.

It was an idle thought, he admitted to himself. He had no clue where to get a baby-sitter now that Gerri was off the A list. He'd find one before he turned eighty. The trick was, would Callie wait that long? He finally picked up the receiver. "Hello?"

"Richard? It's Jared—your cousin Jared Holiday. We ran into each other at the ball—"

"Of course." Richard grinned. "Hey, it's great to hear from you."

"I'll bet you didn't think it would be this soon. I want to keep in touch, believe me. This family has ties so loose the bow falls right out of it."

Richard chuckled. "No kidding."

"How are the kids?"

"Good." He thought about Jason's turn as a lazy muddy squirrel. The kid had had a ball with the part, despite his complaining the night before. "Very good, as a matter of fact. Two are at school at the moment, and Mr. Mark is down for his nap. It's a great moment in a man's life. How are you doing?"

"Not as good as you obviously. Cousin Michael talks a lot about when his kids are off with projects or friends. He lives for those moments, I think, which scares the heck out of me about having children. I suppose I'd be thrilled for a few spare moments if I had six like he does."

Although Richard had only half that amount, he commiserated. "I know where he's coming from."

"I bet. Listen, Allison is hosting the family Christmas party this year. We want you and the kids to come, to be part of the newly reorganized Holiday clan. Peter, Michael, Raymond and I have gotten pretty close since we found wives. I know everyone wants to see you again—and especially the kids, under better circumstances than the last time."

"We'd like that." Richard shook his head while thinking of all four cousins giving up bachelorhood in the same year. "This early, I've got every night free, so just tell me when."

"That's why Allison wanted me to call you now. How about December twelfth?"

"Sounds fine to me," Richard said, flipping up the wall calendar near the telephone. He marked off the date. Most of his other days were free, too, as he'd surmised.

"Bring that pretty lady of yours," Jared added. "Allison thought she was terrific. So did I."

Richard smiled, pleased that his long-lost cousin had liked Callie. "I think she's terrific, too." He paused for a moment. "Jared, you're married... Can I ask you something?"

"Sure."

"Do you understand women?"

Jared roared with laughter. "Hell, no. That's the fun of it. Why? Is Callie confusing you?"

"Does the sun rise every day?" Richard countered.

"Man, have I been there. I can see you need help. Let me make a few phone calls and I'll ring you back."

"Okay." Richard hung up. Jared was a busy man now that he'd launched his own practice. That was good. He thought of his mystery-of-life question regarding women. The creatures *were* confusing. At least he knew he wasn't the only one confused, which was a relief. Maybe he shouldn't question why Callie had reversed herself and was not willing to pursue a relationship. Maybe he ought to just concentrate on convincing her that her fears were unfounded.

But first he had to get a baby-sitter.

When the telephone rang again, Jared was on the other end.

"I talked to the guys," he said. "We'll be over this evening. Early. Raymond's got to get to bed before nine."

"What guys? What bed?" Richard asked, totally confused.

Jared snorted with amusement. "You need help, my

friend, about women. Trust me on this. A little moral support among males keeps us from being total idiots when it comes to the opposite sex. Ray's got a wake-up call for four in the morning because his radio show starts at six. That's the bed part. We'll see you later. We're looking forward to it.''

At seven that evening Richard found himself surrounded by moral support in the form of his four cousins, whom he hadn't seen in years, except briefly at his brother's funeral. To say he was confused was an understatement, but he liked the four men seated at his kitchen table. The deep satisfaction he sensed in his cousins—as if each had found the core of himself—intrigued him.

''Jared says you're confused about a woman,'' Michael began after they were all settled with beers. ''We're here to see you through it.''

''Jared is kind to do th—'' Richard began.

''Jared's an attorney,'' Raymond interrupted. ''He's never kind.''

''Thanks,'' Jared muttered, shooting his cousin a dark look. ''And to think I like you.''

Raymond just grinned.

''Listen, love is easy,'' Peter said. ''There's no cure for it. I know. I've tried.''

''Just keep a little perspective on the situation,'' Michael said. ''But not too much. I think I went into shock when I met my wife, because I went way too far the other way. Thank God, Janice is sensible.''

''Callie's sensible, but I don't know about love,'' Richard replied, pondering the emotion. Maybe Peter was closer to the mark than Richard had ever considered when it came to Callie. Could he be in love with her?

Or could he be in love with the way she'd helped him out? Was there a difference?

"None of us knows about love," Raymond said. "Either you are in love or you aren't. Just don't fight it, whichever way you are."

"Now there he makes a point," Jared observed.

"I think my situation's different," Richard said, confused.

The four cousins laughed.

Now thoroughly confused, he said, "No. Really."

He explained about Callie's having to raise her younger siblings and how she feared falling back into that and being kept from meeting her goals.

"No difference from ours, trust me," Peter said when Richard was finished. The others nodded, knowing expressions on their faces.

Richard gaped at their assuredness.

"Women are...unique," Michael said. "But their concerns are the same as ours."

"I'd love to study women's physiological chemistry," Peter said. "I bet it's all over the place."

"I made a list of my wife's quirks," Jared mused. "She threw it out."

"Don't even get me started about Holly," Raymond said of his bride. "You have no clue how unique she can be."

Richard wanted to dispute that. The man had never met Callie. "Well, it may all be a moot point. I can't even get a baby-sitter so I can take her out to dinner."

"Bring the kids to my house anytime," Michael volunteered. "Six or nine makes no difference, believe me."

"Thanks," Richard said, grateful for the offer.

"What we're saying, Richard," Michael finished, "is

don't worry about where you're going with a woman. If she's unsure but worth fighting for, then fight for her for all you're worth. If it's love, you won't have to fight. It'll work out in the end. Just hang in there for the duration.''

The others chimed in with advice.

''Fighting love is totally useless.''

''Just lie down like a lamb to the slaughter. It'll save you a lot of aggravation.''

''It's our family motto.''

''Ah...guys,'' Richard said hesitantly. ''What you're basically telling me is that despite being married, none of you has a clue about women.''

''That's about the size of it,'' Jared replied.

He spoke for the group.

Chapter Eleven

"I'm still dead."

Callie knew the voice before she saw the face. Lester Jones. She'd been so absorbed in creating her latest statistical spreadsheet that she hadn't heard him enter her office.

"You can't be," she said. "I fixed it. Twice."

"You didn't fix it good enough, girly, 'cause my bank still says I ain't among the living."

"But I talked to them," she protested, outraged. "Sit down and I'll get this straightened out with them once and for all."

As he sat in a visitor's chair, she looked up the information card she'd made for him. She dialed his bank. When she got hold of the manager, she reminded the woman of their previous conversation.

"Yes, I remember," the woman said. "I took care of that."

"Lester says he's still dead to the bank," Callie replied. "He's sitting in my office right now, I assure you. And spitting nails. Could you check for me? I'll hold."

The woman agreed. When she came back on the line, she said in a puzzled voice, "I don't know what happened, but he wasn't corrected in our computer system. I know I did it. Oh, well. It's fixed now.''

"Thank you," Callie said, hanging up. To Lester she said, "Okay. You're fixed."

"Ha!" the man scoffed. She couldn't blame him for being dubious. He added, "What about the rest of my life, honey? You fix that as good as the bank?"

Callie sighed, wondering herself if the other agencies she'd dealt with on his behalf had done as they'd promised. "I'll check and call you tomorrow."

"I'll just wait here until you do." Lester wiggled his butt further into the chair, looking as though he wouldn't be moving anytime soon.

Callie eyed him and frowned. He frowned and eyed her back. His stubbornness was almost palpable. She knew she'd lose the staring contest and conceded. "I'll try to get an answer today."

But she had her own call to make first.

When Richard answered his telephone, she said, "Hi. I have bad news."

"You're not canceling on me, are you?" he asked grimly. "I'll drag you out on this date if I have to, Callie."

She chuckled, liking his determination. At least one of them didn't have doubts. "What did you do? Take a caveman pill?"

"Not yet, but I have a feeling I'll have to with you."

She smiled, not able to help herself. It was nice to have a man go primitive. "Actually I called to say I'll be late, so why don't I come straight to your house, instead of you picking me up?"

She was still leery about the idea of exploring a relationship with him, but felt she'd be ultimately better off getting Richard out of her system, rather than wondering for the rest of her life if she'd made a mistake.

"What's wrong? Why will you be late?"

"Nothing's wrong. I just need to finish a few things here that can't be put off."

Lester cackled, his expression pleased.

"Okay," Richard said. "What time will you be here?"

"I'm not sure. That's why I want to go to your house. I hope it doesn't mess up reservations."

"The place I have in mind is flexible."

"Good." Lester motioned for her to hurry up with the call. Callie grimaced but asked Richard, "By the way, when I was sick, didn't you call someone you knew in the government to have my friend Lester Jones brought back to life?"

"The Lazarus guy? Sure. They promised to take care of it. Why?"

"I was just checking, because his bank messed up and didn't correct the situation."

"Is he why you're still at the office?"

"Yep."

"Is he planted there with you?"

"Yep."

"Wanna take him on the date, too?"

"We might have to."

"Just get here as fast as you can—without Mr. Jones."

"My thoughts exactly."

She hung up.

"Got a hot date, honey?" Lester asked.

"You just mind your own business," Callie said, "or your bank *won't* be making a mistake, okay?"

Lester sniffed indignantly. "No need to get huffy. I

was just asking. He's a nice young fella. Doubt he could find his way out of a paper bag, but nice and polite.''

"Yes, he is," Callie agreed.

She admitted she liked Richard's eagerness to see her. He was good-looking, virile and intelligent, and he wanted her. All tempting lures she found less and less strength to resist.

She straightened out Lester's problem as far as she could while offices were still open, disgusted to discover his pension agency had somehow erred and he was still off their records. The veterans' administration had messed up, too, on his disability. She didn't hold out much hope for the others, but Lester was temporarily satisfied and willing to go home.

After he left, Callie freshened her makeup. She decided her pink satin blouse with the Chinese collar and black suit she'd worn all day would see her through the evening. She resisted the urge to rush home and dress in her fanciest clothes for Richard. The less she preened, the more simple the date would be. She needed simple, for she was nervous, skeptical that officially seeing him was right for her. Wishing she could blame her shift in attitude on her sister's comments, she admitted she couldn't. A part of her was eager for this date, to try for the impossible.

When Richard answered his door, she nearly ran back to her car. He looked so good in his gray suit and dark shirt that she didn't trust herself to get through the evening without falling into bed with him. His maroon paisley tie drew her gaze to the hard wall of his chest. Her blood slowed and heated, throbbing in her veins.

"Hi," he said innocently, yet sending a shiver of pleasure down her spine. "You look terrific."

She found her voice. "You do, too."

"Come in for a minute while I get my keys."

She stepped inside. He closed the door just as she realized the house was silent. "Where are the kids?"

"At my cousin Michael's," he replied, taking his keys from the catchall bowl on the foyer table. "Remember meeting Jared at the ball? He put me in touch with my other cousins. They're…different, I'll say that. Michael married a woman with six kids."

"God help her oldest," Callie said automatically.

"I think the situation there is different from yours," Richard replied. "Janice, Michael's wife, is an accountant who works out of home. Anyway, the kids are over there this evening. Heather, the oldest, is a teenager, too. She and Amanda seemed to like each other. They were talking about school."

Callie smiled. "Good."

"The triplets are about the same age as Jay."

"Oh, Lord." The thought of four Jasons chilled her—and she *liked* Jason.

"Little Amy took Mark under her wing. She's a charmer." He grinned. "I actually found a baby-sitter, Callie. That's a major victory for me."

"For tonight." She wanted to be with him alone and deliberately stepped to the door, opening it. "I hope we're going somewhere with dinner in it. I'm starved. If not, just hit a fast-food drive-through, and I'll be a happy woman."

He laughed. "Fortunately I planned well for dinner, so you'll actually get a meal without a wait. I hope."

"That's what I hope, too."

The restaurant was Italian, with dark cozy corners, marvelous food and enough space between tables to encourage intimate exchanges. Callie tried not to succumb to the ambience. She was off the hook for the moment since Richard preferred to talk about the kids rather than sex.

"Richard," she said when he finished his tale of Jason's latest prank. "I love your family but this date should be a test to see where *we're* going. We need to focus on ourselves. The kids just suck me in—they're my weakness. I think we should make a rule that we won't talk about them for the rest of the night."

Richard raised his eyebrows. "You don't want to talk about the kids?"

"No, I do," she said. "That's the problem. We need to talk about us. What you're doing. What I'm doing. What we like and dislike. What our dreams are...."

"I know yours." He nodded. "Okay, you may be right about the kids. So how's school?"

"It's going well, now that I'm caught up with my work." She stopped, having nothing else to say on the subject.

"How long do you have before you graduate?"

"Another eight credits." She smiled, having something else to say on said subject.

"Wow." He looked impressed. He should, she thought. It had taken her years to get to this point. "You could earn that in one year."

"If I were going to school full-time," she replied. "It'll probably take me another two with night school. I can only carry one course during a semester, two if I'm lucky."

He leaned forward. "Have you considered scaling back on your workload or finding a job with more flexible hours so you can attend school full-time? It would be worth the sacrifice."

"I'm sacrificing now." He had no idea how consuming work and school could be without piling on more.

"I have to be able to eat, Richard. The job I have now pays extremely well. It allows me to be on my own, something I'm not willing to give up even for school."

He smiled slyly. "You know you still work for me, and I'm a very flexible boss."

"That was a technicality while you were sick." Lord, she thought, trying to imagine working in the same room with him for hours at a time and *not* making love. It couldn't be done. Right now, even though their conversation wasn't meshing, she wanted nothing more than to shut him up with a kiss. He'd be dinner for her—and dessert. Who needed food? Pulling her thoughts back, she said, "What does my working for you for those few days have to do with anything?"

He shrugged a little too nonchalantly. "I was thinking that if we made it permanent, you could go to school full-time. I probably can't pay what you're used to—after all, you work for the government—but I'd be *extremely* flexible. Night hours, for example…"

Unfortunately night hours appealed more than he would ever know. The offer of work was sweet; she had no doubt he meant it. No one in her family had ever suggested they would be willing to support her while she went to school. "Thank you, but no. The object of college is only to finish school, not finish in record time."

"Too bad." He grinned. "I liked having a secretary."

"You were so out of it you didn't even know you had a secretary until I told you you did." She grinned back at him. "My turn for questions. How did you get into the export business?"

"My roommate in college was from Fiji. Ronnie Uvatu. His dad brought over Fijian art for collectors when he visited. I fell into the business through him, then began importing more commercial items, like fruit, toys and such. Everything grew so fast from there that I left college to handle the business full-time. I bought out Ronnie's dad, and the rest is Holiday Imports.''

"So you just point to something and say, 'I'll import that'?''

He chuckled. "Sort of. It's guessing at trends, believe me. I bombed with the electric kettle. That was my foray into the big time.''

"An electric kettle?''

He nodded. "Micronesian countries use them like crazy, so I thought well, hell, if they're big in the tropics, they'll be big here. They weren't. They still aren't, even though I see them in catalogs sometimes. I took a bath on 30,000 for this area alone. A hot bath.''

She groaned. "Bad joke.''

"No kidding. I stuck with past success and bounced back with the Australian fascination. Americans love Crocodile Dundee. And frozen New Zealand lamb.''

"You import that?'' she asked, surprised.

"I'm the paperwork man for a food distributor here in Philadelphia.''

"No wonder my food bill's so horrendous. I had no idea such layers existed in getting a lamb chop.'' Clearly he was aggressive and thrived on working for himself. She admired that. "How are you doing with the job and suddenly having to raise three kids?''

"Can't tell you. Your rules.''

She stared at him for a full moment, nonplussed by his refusal. Then she realized what he meant. "Oh, that's okay. You can answer.''

He shook his head. "Rephrase the question.''

She groaned. "When did you get a law degree?''

"I was a big 'L.A. Law' fan. Actually I was taking

pre-law for my college major. Come on, you can ask the question in a different way.''

"All right. How is it going with your current situation?''

"Barely managing.''

"Oh.'' She felt bad. He had two overwhelming tasks and was trying to handle them simultaneously. "Can I help?''

"No.''

His tone held a finality that offended her, as if she wasn't good enough to touch either his business or his kids. "Pardon me for offering.''

He laughed. "You sound like I just told you that your dress clashes with your shoes. I said no because your life is busy enough, too busy. And you've already been a tremendous help. Don't worry, I'll manage. I think I'm beginning to get the hang of it.''

She looked heavenward. "Richard, you are hanging on by your fingertips. Amanda's very fragile emotionally, and she's a teen. No other recipe for possible disaster is necessary. She could erupt at any moment. Jason's a bundle of energy with no place to put it, and Mark has fallen backward in the toilet-training department. You need help.''

"Yeah, but we can't talk about it at dinner.'' He smiled smugly.

Callie eyed him, resisting the urge to strangle him for throwing her own words back at her. "We can now. I just decreed it.''

"Actually I was enjoying getting to know what you're doing with school. We haven't even talked about your major yet. What is it?''

She waved a hand in dismissal. "Forget me. I'm not interesting.''

"I think you are."

"Richard, you need help with the kids. Now why don't you just admit it?"

"I may need help, but you won't be the helper. You have other things to do. But I do find it interesting that your offer to help is automatic. Think about it, Callie."

"I…" She paused, recognizing he was right. Despite her adamant order to speak only about themselves, *she* had brought up the children. She found them more important to talk about than her courses or her job, or his. Worse, she now argued to allow her help with the kids.

Maybe she needed to look further inside herself, find out what was really in there.

"I FEEL GUILTY about the kids."

Richard glanced up from his after-dinner coffee, surprised by Callie's admission.

She set her coffee cup down and sighed. "It's not right for us to be out having a nice dinner without them."

She had been quiet after their discussion about whether or not she could help with the kids. He'd won that battle, but now it was clear her concerns had coalesced in another fashion. What a romantic date.

"They're probably having a great time getting to know their second cousins," he replied. "We're supposed to be here, getting to know each other."

"I know, I know. But what if they're not having a good time?" she asked logically, her gaze earnest. "Amanda's all over the place emotionally when she's at home, let alone when she's stressed out. Jason could barely let you be sick without panicking. And Mark's only two. Enough said there. We've just about finished dinner. Let's go get them."

"You make it sound like they're Little Orphan Annies at Miss Flanagan's." Richard grimaced. "First, you don't want to talk about them, then you want to talk about them, then you feel guilty about not taking them to dinner."

"I know, I know," she repeated, then sighed. "Don't you feel the least guilty leaving them with strangers?"

Richard thought about it for a second. "No."

"Richard! How can you say that?"

"Because they're with family. Granted, I haven't seen Michael in years, but he offered the other day, and I felt it was right. I know my brother saw Michael occasionally, the others, too, and he liked them. Michael's got six stepkids. He never would have offered to watch mine for a night if he didn't like kids, now would he? Stop sweating it."

"This must be a man thing," she said in disgust.

"What's a man thing?"

"Anything that women don't understand."

"Maybe, Callie, you ought to rethink yourself," he said, feeling pressured because he didn't feel guilty. "Why are you worried about the kids when they're not even yours?"

"I know they're not mine." Her voice trembled with anger. "I never thought you would say something like that."

He reached across the table and took her hand. "I didn't mean to offend you. I love it that you care about the kids. I know they love it, too. I also know you're afraid of ties that keep you from your goals. What I was saying so poorly was that you shouldn't have to feel guilty, because they're not your responsibility. Right now I'm feeling guilty because you feel guilty, and yet I don't feel guilty. Boy, are we screwed up."

She laughed. "I think you're right."

"So why exactly do you feel guilty?"

She made a face.

He gazed at her sternly. "We've had two fights and a veal parmigiana."

"We didn't fight. Not really. We just disagreed."

He chuckled. "You really are confused. Finish your coffee and we'll go get the kids. Knowing you, you'll hound me until we do."

Her relieved smile almost had him laughing. Still, he wondered what her contradictions meant. Hope, an emotion he wanted to believe, said the contradictions meant she cared, possibly cared deeply, for him and his family. Despair said they meant she didn't find him interesting enough for one evening without his niece and nephews. Common sense told him her state of mind might be good or it might not.

Richard set aside his thoughts, since they might confuse *him*, and finished his coffee. He kept the conversation light on the ride to Michael's. Callie seemed more animated, as if she was looking forward to seeing the kids. That wouldn't surprise him after what her brother had told him regarding her need to nurture. If his hope was right, then he had seen it refuse to be tamped down tonight, no matter how much she tried to force it back.

Michael and Janice said nothing when he and Callie arrived earlier than anticipated. The kids were busy with their cousins, to his relief. Although he'd said differently, he had been a little worried about the arrangements. Probably he'd fed off Callie's guilt.

"Do we have to go?" Jay moaned, watching his older cousin David play a video game. "David's going to show me *The Legend of the Five Fingers*."

He was flanked by three lookalikes, two males and one female, who seemed ready to block his departure.

"Amy!" Mark shouted, running around the foyer. "Amy! Amy! Amy!"

"Mark! Mark! Mark!" a cute-as-a-button dark-haired girl shouted while running ahead of him in circles.

Amanda didn't say a word. She was too busy upstairs with her cousin Heather.

"Now why did I feel guilty?" Callie murmured.

"Damned if I know," Richard replied, pleased that his charges were so content with the arrangements that they didn't want to leave.

Eventually they got Richard's three Holidays moving out the door and into the car.

"That's a lot of kids," Richard said as he backed down the driveway.

"They were fun," Amanda said. "Heather's going to ask me to her next sleepover so I can meet her friends."

"They have sleepovers with more children?" Richard asked, trying to envision wall-to-wall teenage girls in Michael's house. His brain refused to create the image. He couldn't blame it.

"Heather has them all the time," Amanda said, laughing.

"Me love Amy," Mark announced. "Me love Pooh. Poopies!"

"We got you out of there in the nick of time," Richard said, grinning.

"Chris, C.J. and Cat showed me their rooms," Jay said, adding his two cents to the praises of the cousins. "They have bunk beds in Chris and C.J.'s. Cat sleeps with Amy in another room. Uncle Richard, they taped the room right down the middle! Amy's side is all girly.

Cat's is way cool. And David lent me *Five Fingers*. He's way cool, too."

"The Jason seal of approval." Richard smiled as he drove, happy this part of the night had worked out. "I guess you liked your cousins."

"Yes!" Amanda and Jay said together. Richard assumed Mark felt the same since the little boy happily shouted, "Car!" whenever one passed them.

When Richard turned into the neighborhood, he realized that Callie had been very quiet all the way home.

"You okay?" he asked, glancing over at her when he pulled the car to a stop in his driveway.

She came out of her reverie and smiled slightly. "I'm fine."

She looked distracted to him. Fortunately Mark insisted on Callie carrying him into the house and then putting him to bed. Richard hustled Jason along the bedtime process, sensing Callie would leave if he wasn't at the door to stop her. He knew Amanda would go to bed on her own and simply kissed her good-night.

He snuck into Mark's room as Callie kissed the child good-night and was able to escort her out after giving Mark his own good-night kiss. Something inside him, however, noted the moment, and he felt like part of a family. Callie's presence made the difference between him and the children being distant strangers. It wasn't that he needed a woman to give the sensation a traditional value. She had taught him how to reach inside himself and open up to the kids, something he and Callie desperately needed themselves.

When they were alone downstairs, Richard said, "How about some coffee?"

"I should be getting home," Callie said.

"I believe I forgot to mention *my* rules for this date.

You and I must have a nice after-dinner coffee and conversation," he said with a grim smile.

"We did that at the restaurant."

"Rules revision. You and I must have an after-dinner coffee and conversation at my place." He wasn't about to get caught on a technicality.

She smiled wryly. "That's nice, but I have to go."

"You want to tell me what's going on here?" he demanded, dropping all pretenses. "You won't let me pick you up, using the excuse of being late, and then we can't talk about the kids. Then you feel guilty about the kids, even though we're not talking about them. So we bring them home early and it's bedtime, and now you're up and leaving. *You* wanted a regular date and yet do everything to sabotage it when you get it."

She sighed and sat down on the hall steps. "Richard, I have been a terrible date, and I know it. I'm so sorry."

He sat down next to her. "You're the best terrible date I've ever had, but you want to tell me why?"

She blinked, as if trying to see for herself. "Fear. Confusion. Do you know what threw me the most this evening?"

"No, but you better tell me."

"Seeing that household of six kids. Nine of them, with your three. The place wasn't trashed, and no one was screaming at anybody else, and the parents seemed to be in charge. The oldest girl, Heather, had Amanda up in her room. She wasn't downstairs supervising the younger kids. I tried to remember when I had a friend over to my house when I was her age, and I couldn't. I always had to watch the younger kids. I *never* had a sleepover. Oh, I realize the circumstances were different. Michael and his wife are more affluent for one thing. They probably have more help with the kids, too. But I

was bothered by the comparison with my life." She
shook herself. "It's silly, I know, and I'm sorry to take
it out on you."

He cupped her face and turned her to him, giving her
a tender kiss. Her lips parted. His tongue met hers, swirling in a gentleness that sent sensual shock waves through
his body. He would have thought only an unstoppable
fire of sexuality would create such a desire in him. But
this was more, tying his emotions together in so many
ways. All he knew was, Callie was hurting and he
wanted to do everything in his power to heal her.

He kissed her again and again, little kisses that promised much. Finally he whispered, "Let it go, honey.
You're so much more than whatever you might have
lost."

She sighed and combed her fingers through his hair.
He loved the feel of her hands on him. Soothing…coaxing…tempting…

"Am I?" she asked softly. "Then why can't I let it
go?"

"Maybe because you haven't tried."

He kissed her once more. Heat flared between them
this time, suddenly, shockingly. Callie pressed her
breasts against his chest, and her hands gripped his
shoulders as her mouth ran wild on his.

They were both panting for air and each other when
the kiss ended.

"I don't know that I've tried that," she murmured,
resting her forehead against his.

"Stay and I'll let you try more," he murmured back,
kissing the corner of her mouth.

She kissed him in return.

Discussion was over for the moment. Maybe that
wasn't a bad thing.

Chapter Twelve

"Do you think we'll ever have a normal date?"

Callie chuckled wryly at Richard's question. She stretched fully against him, naked flesh to naked flesh. "It's five in the morning and I'm in your bed. What do you think?"

"Nope, and I am eternally grateful we won't." He snuggled closer. "Normal dates are for wimps."

"Normal dates are for normal people. What does that make us?"

The question, or rather, general thoughts of normalcy, had rattled around under the surface of Callie's mind since last night. She'd managed to thoroughly confuse herself and Richard. Now it was five in the morning and she was lying in Richard's bed, naked and sated and more confused about what she wanted than ever before. Thank God, he was a patient man.

He kissed her cheek. "Normal people are wimps, too. Now aren't you glad we're not?"

"Yes."

She freely admitted it. She wanted to be in his bed. From the moment she'd agreed to dinner, she knew their lovemaking was inevitable. She could no longer deny it.

"I really should get up. I shouldn't be here when the kids wake up."

"I don't think the kids would be surprised at all to find you here," he said against her hair. "I bet they'll be as delighted as me." He pressed his hardening body to her softer one. "Nope, nope, I'm wrong. *No one* is as delighted as me that you're here. If I were more delighted, I'd be stone."

"Richard!" She turned into him, even as she protested his bawdiness. "I really should go."

"You really should do something, but *going* isn't it."

"You are a dirty old man."

He pressed his hand between her legs, pushing them apart. "You bet."

She smiled when he stroked her intimately, then caught her nipple with eager lips and tongue. Callie shuddered as her body heated. Everything inside her seemed to turn to hot thick liquid. She gripped him closer, her body demanding more. She should be sore and not able to even think of making love after they had eventually made their way upstairs last night. First they had been frantic for each other, then tender, then challenging. But she could not get enough of him.

She wrapped her legs around his hips, pulling him inside her. They held each other still, unmoving, taking pleasure in being one and letting the wanting build until they could stand it no longer. Richard's thrusts were forceful, and she met each one with no shame and no regret. Her satisfaction came almost instantly, yet rippled deeply within her, touching the core of her with gentle pain.

"You make me feel whole," he said when he found his voice.

"This isn't good for the children," she said, thinking

about any of the three catching them in such a compromising position. She risked too much spending the night with him, yet she wanted him so badly she was unable to resist. No amount of warnings about what she was doing mattered. She'd only known Richard a short time and already needed him on many many levels.

"Of course it's not good for the kids. They're too damned young for sex. You should know that." His voice held amusement.

She ran her hands down his back, loving the warmth of his skin against her palm. She loved the way his flesh moved under her touch. "You're Mr. Comedian, aren't you?"

"I'm in bed with a beautiful woman I care a great deal about, and we've just made love. Why shouldn't I be happy? You worry too much." He kissed her temple. "I like that about you."

Callie smiled.

"Actually—" Richard nuzzled her neck, his breath warm on her flesh "—I love that about you. Callie, I love you."

Callie tensed, the words hanging in the air between them.

Richard raised his head. His gaze searched hers. "You have a problem with that."

"God, yes." She saw the hurt in his eyes. "I didn't mean it like that."

Richard rolled off her. He stared at the ceiling. "How did you mean it? And it better be good because it'll take some fast talking to get me past what I'm thinking."

"I'm confused," she said. "Look, every time I take a baby step forward in this relationship, you take ten giant steps away and say, 'Come here, Callie. This is where you need to be.' I'm just not ready for it. That's no reflection on you. It's me.''

"Why did you think we were having sex?" he asked.

She chuckled. She couldn't help it. "I think that's the woman's line. Don't men want just sex from women?"

"Sometimes. Not this time. You knew that." He glanced at her. "I feel used."

Callie put her hands over her face, feeling as if she'd entered some sort of surreal life. Through her fingers she said, "I'm not using you. I wouldn't know how to use a man."

"It feels like you do." He pulled her hands away. "And look at me while you're doing it."

Callie lowered her hands and glared at him. "I'm *not* doing it. That's the point."

"Then what are you doing? I say I love you, and you say you have a problem with that."

Callie groaned. It was far too early in the morning to deal with the normal havoc Richard caused inside her, let alone this. Love! Truly, the word exhilarated and frightened her. She just wasn't ready yet for love. She wasn't ready for any deep relationship.

"Richard, calm down and look at it from my perspective. I'm trying to get my life together. How can I be ready for love? So many responsibilities go with the emotion I don't know if I ever *will* be ready for it."

"As long as you think of love as a series of responsibilities, you won't," he replied, thrusting out his jaw.

"Love *is* responsibility."

"It's an emotional state. You do things because you want to. The person who loves you understands why you can't when you can't. You work on it together—because you love each other."

She wanted to believe him, but she couldn't afford to.

She wished she could trust that his emotion stemmed from physical attraction and mental meshing, but she couldn't. "Richard, it's too soon for you to even know if you're in love—or in love because you need a partner to help you with the kids."

"I know how I feel."

"Do you really?" Suddenly she felt on firmer ground. "You need to have some perspective, too. You're a single man who's just acquired three kids to raise. God knows you have a right to be confused about how you feel—"

"Uncle Richard!"

Jason's voice gave a second's alarm before the bedroom door swung open. Callie yelped and dived under the covers. She held no hope that she hadn't been spotted.

"I heard voices," Jason said from a distance. His voice was muffled by the covers over her ears.

Callie strained to hear, trying not to be aware or distracted by the solid wall of Richard's chest against her cheek. Heat poured off him. Despite their crossroads, she only wanted to reach out and touch the silky pelt of hair that arrowed down his stomach.

"Voice?" Richard echoed. "Oh, I had my radio on."

Jason didn't ask how it had suddenly turned off. Instead, he asked something right out of left field. "Is Mark going with us today?"

"I don't know. Where are we going?"

"Duh! My class trip to New York City." Jay's tone rose with enthusiasm.

Richard cursed. "Damn! Is that today?"

"'Course it's today. What'd ya think? It was tomorrow?" Jason didn't wait for a reply. "I'm real excited.

Do you think Mark'll puke when we get to the top of the Empire State Building?''

"No, but I will."

Jay laughed.

"Jay, it's early. Why don't you go back to bed for a while?"

"Oh, I'm not tired."

"Well, I need my sleep, son. You go on. Okay?"

"Okay. Callie's going with us, isn't she? You said she would."

Callie poked Richard's chest, but not in desire—in revenge. Damn him! How could he volunteer her for a class trip and never say a word?

Richard yelped, then brushed her hand away. "No, Jay. She has to work."

"But her car's here."

"Ah…she had car trouble. I drove her home."

"Oh. Okay. See ya later." The door closed.

The second Callie heard it click shut, she yanked the covers down and whispered fiercely, "How could you volunteer me to go to New York and never say a word?"

Richard looked innocent. "I told him you couldn't."

"After you told him I would."

"I meant to ask you because I thought I would need help with Mark and they were short on chaperons. The trip would have been canceled if I hadn't volunteered. A lot of parents work and can't go."

"I work! I can't go! And I'm not a parent!" She couldn't believe he'd done this to her.

"That part didn't matter. You only have to sign a form saying you're willing to chaperon." He smiled sheepishly. "I felt bad about that, and frankly, that was at the point when Jay was acting up. I thought if he saw that I was willing to do things with him, for him, that he and I would be closer. They gave me special permission to bring Mark, because of my situation. I thought you might be willing to help with the kids, too. You seemed to like them. But we all got sick and I forgot to talk to you about the trip. Don't worry about it. It wasn't fair to you at all, and I'm sure they've got enough adults by now.''

"Don't bet on it." Callie thought she would explode with anger. "And Jay *expected* me to go. How's he going to feel when not only do I not show up, but the trip gets canceled because I don't? He'll never trust an adult again. Especially not you."

Richard shook his head. "You're seeing this all out of proportion. Jay will understand when I explain it to him. And you're diverting the subject away from our real problem. Us."

Callie closed her eyes in despair. Within fifteen minutes she'd run the gamut of emotions from tenderness to panic to outrage, all caused by Richard. No wonder she was confused by the man.

"I shouldn't go. I really can't."

"I know."

"I care about you, Richard."

"That's all I ask."

"It's too soon. Maybe it will always be." Just thinking of his declaration opened a chasm inside her, one she was terrified to peer into.

"It's not too soon, but it's too inconvenient for you," he countered. "I know that. But it doesn't change a thing."

"You can't be sure how you feel yet."

"I can."

"You can't. Trust me."

"I do. But you have to trust me on this."

"I…" She realized anything she said would be patronizing or hurtful. She closed her mouth.

Richard pushed back the covers. "I'm getting up. I have to, anyway. And you need to go to work."

"I can't." she said.

He paused, one foot halfway to the floor. He glanced over his shoulder, pulling her gaze from the muscled expanse of his back. How many times last night had she run her hands over those muscles? Enough to know their every nuance.

"What do you mean, you can't go?" he asked. "You couldn't wait to get out of this bed earlier."

"Jason will hear me if I leave now. I don't want to explain that and neither should you. And if I did somehow manage to escape, how do you explain my car suddenly being gone after you told him it was broke?"

"The tow truck came?"

"And a seven-year-old boy missed that event?" She shook her head. "Not likely. They're like sharks at feeding time whenever emergency trucks, any trucks, are around."

He gave a shrug that affirmed his agreement rather than his indifference. "True. They love trucks more than cowboys do."

"Right. And I have to go on this trip."

His expression changed. "No, you don't. I was wrong, I'll tell them—"

"No," she said, shaking her head. "I would never forgive myself if I didn't go. Not when they're short of chaperons and the trip could be canceled. That's not fair to the kids."

"What about the parents of those kids? They said no. Granted, they work, or that's the reason I was given. But they could lose a day as easily as you. More easily. It's for their kids."

She shook her head. "I'm a little more cynical than you about parents. Jason's had enough trauma in his life without another adult not being there for him and maybe humiliating him in front of his class. I will not, however, speak to you again."

Richard smiled. "You are the most wonderful woman. I do love you."

Callie grimaced. "Go take your shower, Richard. Before I find a gun and shoot you. If you hadn't done this for Jason's sake, I'd find that gun."

He rose from the bed. Her ire dulled at the sight of his body, lean and naked and gleaming in the pale dawn light. He padded unashamed into the bathroom, as if to give her a prolonged view of what she was about to throw away. Despite the emotional turmoil he'd created, Callie still felt a jolt of remembered joining. He and her as one. It had been so right. It made her want more, made her almost willing to throw everything away and fall madly in love with him.

Why did he have to say he loved her and push her into the whirlpool again? Why couldn't he understand she wasn't ready to even hear the words? She might never be. She had doubts, too, about his feelings. She couldn't shake the notion that his love was tied up with the kids needing a mother figure, as well as a father one. Nearly any woman would do for that purpose, and she was afraid he'd eventually realize that.

Worse, she was responding to Jason's needs, too. She ought not to care if the class trip was canceled because Richard forgot to ask her to chaperon. She cared all too much and hadn't been able to say no. That was danger-ous because it meant she was falling right back into putting others' needs before her own. Even last night, when she should have been happy without the kids, she hadn't been. She didn't even want to think about what her boss would say when she took time off from work yet again, so she didn't think about it.

Richard emerged from the bathroom, wrapped only in a towel. She pulled the bedclothes back over her head so she wouldn't see him dress. When he went downstairs, she still left the covers over her head, hoping that would help block her thoughts. But she could smell his scent on the sheets. She could still feel his body heat.

She heard the kids getting up. She heard their chatter and their laughter. Every fiber of her being wanted to be a part of their day. Every day. Richard's deep voice made her so aware of what she didn't have—and wanted.

At some point she became aware of the house noises diminishing, the front door opening and closing several times. When that stopped, she knew she was alone. She scrambled out of the bed she'd shared with Richard and raced to dress. If she was to make the trip, she would have to hustle home and change. She refused to wear her clothes from last night all day today. And she would shower at home.

She was out of Richard's house in record time, although she wondered if Jason or Amanda had noticed her coat and purse in the living room and asked questions. She hoped not. The two had enough to handle without explaining the sex life of two adults.

The *more-than-sex* life of two adults. She could deny a lot of things, but she couldn't deny it was more than sex with Richard. It was.

Callie pushed the notions out of her head. Right now she needed to stay practical and angry with Richard. The latter was self-preservation. She opened her car door—

"Callie! This goes too far!"

"The voice of doom," Callie muttered, not turning to face her sister, Gerri. More loudly she said, "Out of the way, girl. I've got to be on a bus to New York pronto."

One problem sidestepped, she thought as she backed her car past her sister's shocked face. An odd notion hit her, and she smiled wryly.

She and Richard still hadn't had a normal date.

HOLDING THE HANDLE of Mark's stroller, Richard hovered near the elevators at the top of the Empire State Building. He watched Callie shepherding Jason and some other boys at the high fencing around the stone terrace wall. All of them were trying to peek over the edge down to the street. Way, way down to the street. He could get on airplanes, but wide-open heights like this bothered him.

He called out, "Guys, get away from there. Please."

Jay turned around and grinned. "We're okay, Uncle Richard."

Callie didn't turn at all. She hadn't spoken to him, either, during the entire trip. Well, she hadn't spoken to him unless she absolutely had to. Nothing was worse than a two-hour ride on a school bus next to a woman who looked straight ahead—especially when she had been insatiable for him just a few hours before.

Despite the fifty-degree temperature and crisp breeze, sweat broke out on Richard's forehead as the kids stood on tiptoe to see below. "Jay, you may be okay, but I'm not. Now, step back from the edge. Why don't you use the binocular stand? Maybe you can see across the city to Jersey. Here, I've got money."

The herd of boys he chaperoned pounded over to him

at the promise of cash. They gathered around him, hands out and palms up, as he fished coins from his pocket.

He passed the money out, saying, "Now you guys understand that this is a bribe to stay away from the edge."

The boys laughed. They had been rambunctious but well behaved enough during their tour of Ellis Island and lunch at the Fulton Fish Market. Certainly they were unaware of the tension between him and Callie. Most of the trip participants hadn't noticed, either. Jay's teacher had gushed all over Callie for coming along, since she made up the requisite number of adults. At least one thing had turned out okay this morning, but, man, did he wish he hadn't gotten out of bed today, not with Callie still in it!

He sent the boys off to view New Jersey. Callie, he noticed, still stood at the fence, gazing out over the city. He desperately wanted to call her back, but knew she probably stayed over there just to irritate him. She was doing a good job of it.

Sitting down heavily on a bench, he admitted to being wearier than he'd been in a long time. He had only himself to blame for the cause. Not only had he had very little sleep, but he'd forgotten he'd volunteered to chaperon and also added the trauma of declaring his love to Callie. Then he had compounded all that by forgetting to ask her about helping today and putting her in an untenable position.

"Sky!" Mark shouted, nearly standing in his stroller. The child reached his hand up to try to touch the white puffy clouds. The day was glorious, one of those great moments November produced in the Northeast.

"Let me tell you, son, being this close isn't a thrill when you're old," Richard said, grinning wryly. Maybe falling off a cliff in another life had given him this feeling now. "Are you having fun with the big kids?"

Mark stopped reaching. He leaned almost out of the stroller. "Yeah!"

Richard laughed. "I'm glad someone is."

He lifted Mark the rest of the way out, holding the boy on his lap. He wanted Mark to see the city, but not as close as Jay had. It was time to check on his charges, anyway, who'd seemed to scatter to every corner of the observation terrace.

He walked past Callie, debating whether to stop and attempt conversation. Her back was to him, although she had to be aware of his presence. Okay, she was ticked off. She had a right to be. Maybe he was better off *not* speaking to her.

He went around the terrace area made famous by *An Affair to Remember* and *Sleepless in Seattle*. The place *would* have to be romantic, he thought in disgust. He and Callie should be strolling arm in arm, looking deeply into each other's eyes. Instead, she was in a furious funk over at the potential suicide ledge, and he was chasing down a gaggle of seven- and eight-year-old boys. Cupid had missed *his* backside big time.

"It must be old age," he muttered to himself. To Mark he said, "Men are idiots. It's a curse, kid. You have it. I have it. Jay has it. Maybe Tom Hanks doesn't have it, but he's the only one."

"Ding-dong," Mark said aptly. "Want a cookie."

He wasn't sure whether Mark was demanding or offering. "In a minute."

He found the boys taking turns viewing the city from a pair of standing binoculars. Their aim, evidently, was to look through every viewer on the terrace. Richard wondered whether they would run out of coins or time first. He silently bet on the latter. They were set to leave the building in about ten minutes.

"Are the kids okay?"

Richard whirled around at Callie's voice. Unfortunately she looked as though she'd spit out nails, instead of words. But she had asked *him*.

"Callie!" Mark shouted, leaning toward her with outstretched arms.

She smiled and took him automatically. Her hands brushed Richard's arms during the exchange. His had brushed her breasts. He refused to think about it.

"You didn't have to take him," Richard said.

"I don't mind." She cuddled Mark to her.

Richard frowned, something in the scene bothering him. Not jealousy. Heck, he'd be happy with jealousy. Suddenly he knew. "You took him because he wanted your attention."

"Do you have a problem with that?" The way she eyed him, he knew he was on dangerous ground.

"No, but you do."

Her eyebrows shot up.

"You're not putting your needs first when you need to." He swallowed. "Boy, I hope I'm explaining this right, because I have a feeling you're about to slug me."

"I've been about to slug you since five this morning," she countered. "So what else is new? All right, tell me why I am not putting my needs first when I take Mark because he wants to be held by me. And don't tell me I'm not good enough now."

"Hell, no," Richard exclaimed, realizing he'd opened something unexpected.

"Hello, no!" Mark shouted.

Richard chuckled. Callie even grinned. Then she sobered. Richard knew he was back in trouble. "I could have held him, Callie. I was happy to. I'm capable of it, I think. You need to say no sometimes. That's all I meant."

"You rope me into this trip without a thought to my needs and then worry about my holding Mark." She looked around. "Anybody see the irony here? Anybody? Anybody?"

"I am sorry, and I apologized earlier for this. I would have taken responsibility for my failure today if you hadn't come. Jason would have gotten over it. I would have learned a lesson I wouldn't have forgotten. I might even have found a replacement and none of this would be happening."

"In other words, you're saying I'm responsible for my being angry with you."

He looked heavenward. "No, I'm saying you had every right to refuse this morning to chaperon. You have nothing to feel guilty about or pressured into doing. I tried to say this earlier. I did say it. Maybe I shouldn't have depended on you like I did in the beginning. Or brought the kids on dates. Or done things the way I did. I set you up today, and I was wrong."

"You're mixing a lot of things in there."

He smiled slightly. "Yeah, I am."

"Ding-dong."

"Thank you, Mark." The kid was right, Richard thought, although he felt better now that he'd said the things he needed to say to her. Maybe the romantic atmosphere helped.

"I accept your apology for volunteering me without telling me first," Callie said. "I don't accept that I could have walked away from the job."

"I'm still in trouble about that, then."

"Absolutely. Now, can I hold Mark because I want to?" she asked.

"Of course. But only because you want to."

"I do."

He drew in a deep breath. "Callie, about this morning—"

She raised a hand. "We've talked enough, okay?"

They hadn't, but he recognized he was pressing her. But he did love her. He had no doubt. Just for her, just for moments like this when her goodness came through. "Okay."

"I think I'll take Mark over to look down at the street. He'll like the cars being like tiny ants."

Richard's stomach crawled. "You're doing this to punish me."

She smiled. "You'll never know for sure, will you? Want to join us?"

"No way."

She smiled broadly. "I thought not."

"You're no Meg Ryan, Callie."

She laughed. "I'm just showing Mark the city, Richard. This is the trip of a lifetime for him. Me, too. Relax."

He watched her take Mark to the fencing. Callie actually pressed her forehead against the chain link and pointed down at the cars on the streets. Perspiration trickled down his back. She was a wicked wicked woman. But she was speaking to him again.

"Uncle Richard! Time to go," Jay called out.

"Thank you," Richard murmured, sending up a prayer for his rescue.

Chapter Thirteen

"You're fired."

Callie stared at her boss, stunned. He glared back, his weaselly expression triumphant. He'd always been fussy and curt with her, but she never realized before how much he personally disliked her. She wondered how long he'd been looking for an excuse to terminate her. At last she found her voice.

"You can't fire me just because I took a day for personal business yesterday," she said. "I still have days left in—"

"Oh, yes, I can. You've been out of the office too much lately, and the work's not getting done. I'm firing you for poor job performance."

Callie felt her face burn as anger boiled up inside her. She refused to give it an outlet—and give this clown more ammunition. "I've done my work at home *and* kept up with my voice mail. There's very little behind here in the office—"

"That's not the point. You're out. Now."

"Fine. I'm entitled to one month's severance, full unemployment and a hearing, because I'm filing a protest. You gave me a great evaluation on the last quarterly performance ratings, so there's bound to be a big question about your suddenly firing me.'' She leaned forward. ''You don't know the half of what I do around here that covers your butt and makes you look good. Have fun, pal.''

She picked up her coat and purse and walked out the door, just as Lester Jones walked in.

Callie opened the door wider to let the older man pass. ''Come on in, Lester. It's so good to see you again. Now step right over to that gentleman, and I use the term loosely. He'll be happy to help you with whatever you need today.''

''Hey, Callie! Where you going?'' Lester demanded.

''I've been canned, as they say in the sardine world.'' She grinned, although she felt no amusement. ''I'm off to see the job wizard.''

''You can't go. I'm finally back among the living, thanks to you,'' Lester said, looking bewildered rather than belligerent. ''Got my notice yesterday that I'm back with my bank. Who's the idiot who fired you? That clown over there?''

He pointed to Callie's former boss.

Callie kissed Lester soundly on the cheek. ''You're a terrific person, Lester. Take care.''

She raced out of the office. When she got in her car, her lip trembled. She refused to cry. That would give the idiot in there satisfaction—if he knew. Darn, she thought, dashing away a few escapee tears with the back of her hand. She couldn't give in just because her world was crashing all around her. Going with the kids on their trip yesterday had been the right thing to do; she would never feel otherwise. In fact, she'd had so much fun with the kids, she'd gone to bed last night reassessing her life in general and her convictions in particular. But with no job, how would she pay for school and have a place to live and eat, too?

She drove around for a while, aimlessly, just letting the fiasco of the morning sink in. As she did, an urge arose in her to go to Richard. Never had she needed a hug more, and she wanted it from him. How could she feel this way when it was her involvement with his family that had caused her to be away from her desk so much and given her boss this opening?

But she did want to be held and to talk to Richard. She couldn't fight the need to confide in him, even when she was still angry with him for committing her to the trip and then forgetting to tell her. She was ready to half blame him for today, although she recognized that her boss would have found an opening somewhere else to remove her from the job. What happened wasn't Richard's fault; nor was her going on the trip yesterday. He was right—she had made the choice to go. Now she must live with the consequences of it. But above all else in their relationship, Richard had become a friend. A very good friend. That was why she needed to see him now.

She pulled into Richard's driveway, already feeling better. Richard looked surprised when he answered the door.

"Callie! What are you doing here?"

He also looked disheveled. His hair was tousled and he wore a sweatshirt with the sleeves cut short, their raggedy edges fraying. Mark peeked out from around his legs, thumb in mouth.

"Hi," she said. "Got any more school trips you might have forgotten to tell me about? I'm a free bird at the moment, so let's chaperon away."

To her horror, tears began to roll down her face.

"Callie!" Richard exclaimed. Mark stared, round-eyed, at her.

"Just leaky plumbing," she said, sniffing back more tears. "I'm sorry. I'll go."

"No you won't." He took her arm and dragged her into the house, shutting the door behind her.

His arms enfolded her in a strong protective embrace. Callie melted against him and had herself a good little cry, simply because she couldn't remember the last time someone had held her for a good little cry. She couldn't remember a man ever doing it for her.

Nothing felt more secure, more deep-down satisfying than to have a man's arms around her in compassion. She really needed this. All modern notions aside, it must hark back to the ancient pact between men and women when men shielded women and women nurtured children. Mark wrapped his little arms around her legs from behind and laid his head on the back of her thighs.

"Callie have boo-boo," Mark said.

Callie patted the little boy's head. "Just a little one. I'm okay, honey. Honest."

"What happened?" Richard asked. "Did you have an accident? Did someone...die?"

Callie laughed and hiccuped at the same time. "Nope. Even our friend Lester is back among the bank accounts. Nothing too tragic, although I feel like I got hit by a ten-ton truck. I got fired this morning."

"What!" Richard held her at arm's length and gaped at her.

She nodded and smiled. "Thanks for the hug. I needed it."

"This is about yesterday, isn't it?" he said. "And all the other things you've done for me that have taken you away from your job. That son of a—"

"Watch it," Callie interrupted, pointing to Mark who was gazing intently up at both of them.

"Your boss can't get away with this. I'll get dressed, go down there and ream him out until he gives you the job back. Who does he think he is? Simon Legree?"

"I believe that's the picture on the wall in his office," Callie said. "But you're not going down there. I'm calling the state offices and lodging a protest against him."

"Good." Richard grinned. "It's also good to see you get some of your spunk back. I'll come and testify on your behalf. I'll get Lester to testify. He'll be great."

She chuckled. "A diplomat and a crank at an employee adjudication hearing. I can't wait to see that."

"Diplomacy's going right out the window, honey." He sobered. "Seriously, what can I do to get you your job back?"

"I don't know." More tears clogged her eye ducts and her throat. "I had no idea he disliked me so much."

"The guy's an idiot."

"Lester said that."

"Was he there?" Richard laughed. "Two minutes with Lester, and the guy will be begging you to come back. Let's go into the kitchen. You can make some calls, have some coffee and decide what to do."

She knew she probably shouldn't, but she needed this togetherness. All her life she had served up sympathy to others and their needs, and it was nice to have some come her way from a man who cared. Okay, so he'd caused a lot of this turmoil in her life, had left her confused and now jobless, but he also managed to make her feel better when she needed it most.

"Poopies!" Mark said suddenly, running into the bathroom.

Richard laughed. "The kid can put life in perspective, can't he?"

"I'm more impressed that he went straight to the source," Callie said. "He's more than ready to be a big boy, Richard."

"Me, too."

After Mark was seen to, they went into the kitchen. Richard served up coffee and a couple of oatmeal cookies, while Callie made her necessary phone calls. When she was finished, she took a sip of coffee. The hot liquid soothed her frayed nerves. Mark sat on her lap, his head back against her chest as he sucked his thumb, content to give her comfort. He didn't even try to reach for the coffee mug—a good thing.

"I feel badly about this," Richard said, watching her from behind the cooking island. "It's my fault, all of it. I depended on you too much, Callie, without concern for your needs."

Callie shrugged. "It's not your fault. You couldn't help getting sick or having to escort that soccer player home or my getting sick—"

"I gave it to you."

"A technicality. You could have told me about the school trip, but the truth is, I would have gone, anyway, because the kids needed me. Your coming into my life and the events that took place only gave my boss the ammunition he needed to fire me, that's all. I know now he was looking for anything he could."

"It only makes it worse that I was the one who supplied him." Richard let out his breath in a rush. "I never meant this to happen, Callie."

"Oh, no," she said. "Don't you start blaming yourself, otherwise I'll never forgive *myself* for telling you."

"Tellin' you, Callie," Mark said, pulling his thumb

from his mouth to make the pronouncement. He poked it back in again.

Richard smiled ruefully. "I'll blame myself a little, okay? But I do have a solution. Work for me here at the import business."

"No," Callie said automatically.

"No," Mark repeated.

"Yes," Richard said.

"Yes," Mark repeated.

"Look," Richard added, "I'm swamped here and you know it. You've seen my life. If you took care of a lot of the work in the office, I'd be freed up to take care of the kids' needs. It's not rocket science, and you're bright. You'll catch on in a day or two. I can't pay what you're worth right now because business is way down since I haven't been able to keep up with it. But we can help each other out."

"This is very dangerous," Callie murmured, thinking of how much time she'd be spending with him nearly alone in this house. She was confused enough about him without adding her daylight hours to the time spent in close proximity to his lovely body. And heart.

"You don't have to worry about me firing you if you chaperon a class trip," he added by way of incentive. "You can be sick all you want, too."

Callie chuckled. She couldn't help herself.

"And I'll pay for your school."

"What!"

Richard came around the cooking island and bent down, his fingers playing with her hair. "I'll pay for you to go to school. Lots of businesses do it now for employees. You can even take day classes if you want. I consider it an investment."

Callie closed her eyes. He was offering heaven to her,

and it was wrapped up in a sexy body and knowledge-able mind she couldn't resist. "No. It's not right."

He stroked her hair more. "Yes, it is. It feels right to me."

"I barely know you. You barely know me."

"We know each other well enough, Callie. Very well where it counts. Time is relative."

She was very tempted to take up his offer. But would it solve her problems? Yet, it was a skewed version of her goals. She was determined to recapture her missing youth, to do for herself at last, to have that college degree, to cater to no one but herself. Now someone, a wonderful someone, was offering to give her what she wanted.

"It wouldn't work, Richard. Knights don't ride in on white chargers to rescue maidens in distress. That's fiction."

"Actually it's love, honey. That's why I want to do it."

"Oh, God." Tears sprang up into her eyes again. Callie wiped them away with her fingertips. "I can't accept. I…I'm confused. I don't know how I feel. I don't know how I want to feel or how I will feel in the future about you, about us. I'm being so unfair to you. I'm sorry. I hate myself for it."

Richard chuckled. "You do guilt well, girl."

Callie couldn't suppress a laugh.

"You're always telling me I'm ten steps ahead of you," he said, "and I realize I've done it again. How about if we table the college deal and stick with the job offer for now? When you catch up, we can move on. Callie, just so you know, I really do need the help here. In fact, you should know it better than anyone else."

She smiled. This felt better to her sensibilities than the

other. "It's strictly a business offer. I work for you from nine until five and you pay me...how much?"

He named a figure close to what she'd been earning. Callie snorted in disgust. "Who are you kidding? They didn't pay Iacocca that much when he ran Chrysler."

"That's what an assistant's worth to me. But if I know you, you'll be too stubborn to accept it." He pursed his lips. "Okay, I'll pay you two-thirds of that, but give you a two percent commission on everything we import and sell. That means you'll have to hustle to get a decent salary."

Callie grinned. "Deal. But just until I get my old job back."

Richard kissed her soundly on the lips. "Deal."

"And it's pure business," Callie added, lest there be no mistake in their relationship.

"Purely." He kissed her again.

His mouth was hot and she yielded to it, instinctively needing to taste him. Their tongues melded. Callie forgot everything about pure business. Caught up in the kiss, she plain forgot everything.

Mark began to shift in her lap, finally bringing her back to consciousness and common sense. Her lips felt bruised—and the rest of her felt wanton. "This isn't going to work, Richard."

He grinned. "Sure it will. Just watch."

"ALL THE BILLING is done, and I've gotten those replies out that have been sitting around since the time I did them when you were sick. And your e-mail is caught up, too. Oh, I've also talked to Singapore. That was cool."

Richard grinned at Callie's happy expression. She'd been on the job for two days, and she was clearly having fun. Better, his business was running up to speed—and moving forward. Even better, he felt more rested and able to deal with the kids now that he had help with the workload. But best of all, Callie was here for hours at a time. He loved that.

"I wish I'd had you when I was in Center City," he said. "You would have had the business on the Fortune 1000 list. You look good behind my desk, too. Can I kiss you now?"

"No. I have to go to the airport for that flower shipment from Malaysia and handle the quarantine papers." She rose from the chair, setting a few envelopes aside as she did.

He came around the desk and kissed her, anyway, taking her by surprise. Callie really did stick to a pure-business attitude. This was the first time he'd been able to kiss her since she'd begun the job.

"Mark's asleep," he said. "Let's go upstairs and take a nap, too. You've got a few minutes."

Callie leaned back in his embrace. "This is sexual harassment."

Richard let her go. "I don't even want to mess with that."

She smiled. "I'm being flip and I shouldn't. This is sexual *confusion.*"

"Oh, in that case..." He reached for her but she eluded him by ducking under his arm.

"Richard, I *have* to go. One of us does. You or me, pal. Which one?"

He groaned. "You're making it tough for a lecherous man."

"You didn't hire me to be lecherous. You hired me to work."

"You're no fun." He sighed. "Jason has a Cub Scout

meeting, and I agreed to take a few kids who need rides. You go to the airport, I suppose.''

She smiled. "Life is tough, my friend.''

"I'm in the car with five boys. That's tough.''

"It could be worse. You could be in the car with Amanda and four of her friends.''

Richard shuddered. "No thank you.''

"Chicken.''

"Speaking of chickens, we have to work on you and I soon.''

"Mmm.''

"Noncommittal. I like that,'' he said. "It's a step sideways from confused.''

Callie shook her head. "You're a pain in the tush, you know that?''

"Yes. When it comes to you. But I won't push.''

She laughed. "I'm in your house, in your life, all because you've wheedled me into it in record time. And you complain.''

Richard made a face. "I didn't wheedle. Cary Grant never wheedled. He enticed.''

"Oh, yeah. You're Cary the sequel.''

"Not with diapers up to my ears,'' he said ruefully. "Go to the airport before I wheedle you up the stairs.''

"Okay.'' As she walked out of the room, she said, "I'm expecting a call from the state employees union about that protest I filed. Be sure to get the name of an actual person I can call back.''

"Okay.''

"Don't forget that Amanda is going to Joey's first basketball practice this afternoon right after school.''

"Right.''

"And you said earlier to remind you that Mark has

those funky diaper pants on. You better check him when he gets up.''

''Gotcha.'' Richard sighed as he helped her into her coat. ''Cary Grant, I ain't.''

Callie chuckled and turned to him. ''You have a charm all your own.''

He smiled. ''I think you're coming around.''

She kissed him lightly on the mouth. ''Maybe.''

When she was gone, Richard realized that hiring her had been the best idea he'd had. Life was so much easier with her around. The kids were happier, and he was extremely happy. What more could he want?

Everything, he admitted. But Callie wasn't ready to hear that. Hell, he could barely sweet-talk a kiss out of her. Her life had been turned upside down, so her hesitation was understandable. At least, he was trying to understand it. Time was on his side now, however. With a little more of it she would relax and realize she cared for him. He truly believed she did.

Unfortunately all hell broke loose while she was gone.

''What do you mean, I have to give a talk?'' Richard demanded as Jason's fellow Cub Scouts scooted out of the car and onto the driveway of their leader's house.

Jason turned away. ''I forgot to tell you, I guess.''

''You forgot your head, Jay.'' Richard frowned at his nephew. ''Look at me when I'm annoyed with you, okay? You owe me that much.''

Jason turned to him, his expression contrite. ''I'm sorry, Uncle Richard.''

Well, Richard thought. A sincere apology certainly took the wind out of his sails as far as righteous anger went. Who was he to yell, anyway? He'd done the same thing to Callie, but on a grander scale. And the consequences had been more dire for her. In his own case, he'd just lose an hour. But his nephew needed to learn not to do it again. "I'll bail you out this one time, but never again commit me to doing anything that you haven't talked with me about first, Jason. It's irresponsible."

"Okay."

Jason jumped out of the car, his body language jaunty. Richard wondered if his little lecture had sunk in at all. He unbuckled Mark from the car seat and went into the "den" to give his talk, which turned out to be about trailblazing. Richard knew nothing about trailblazing, which annoyed the den mother. Worse, Mark kept wandering around the woman's house and getting into things while Richard talked.

At home later he discovered Callie's important call on the answering machine, but the message was garbled and naturally the most crucial parts missing. Like the name and number of the person on the line. Callie would kill him. And Amanda wasn't home yet. Richard frowned, glancing at the kitchen clock after settling Jason at the table with homework and Mark with a snack.

"She should have been home by now," he grumbled to himself.

Callie came in first. Mark ran to her and she picked him up, giving him a hug. She looked radiant with the boy. Never had a hiring felt so right, Richard thought proudly. Now if only he could get her on board more permanently...

"Boy, a milk-and-cookie kiss," she said. "I'm so thrilled."

Jason laughed. "I won't kiss you!"

"Now, I'm really thrilled." She ruffled his hair.

"I will," Richard said, catching her at the waist and kissing her soundly. When he was finished, he couldn't tell who wore a sillier grin—Jason or Callie. "No milk-and-cookie kiss, I know."

"It'll do." Callie blushed. "You're sucking me into all this. You know that."

"My game plan." He didn't have any doubts about it. Maybe the kids were wrapped up in this somewhere, but they were a minor consideration when it came to how he felt about her. Now was the worst time to give her bad news. "Callie, that call came for you...."

"Oh, good," she said brightly. "Where's the name and number? I'll probably have to call tomorrow, won't I? It's after five."

"The message was garbled on the answering machine. I couldn't make out the name and number."

Her face fell. "You've got to be kidding!"

"I was out with Jason, who committed me to a talk he forgot to tell me about." Richard glared at Jay, who looked positively innocent.

"Like uncle, like nephew," Callie said. "Jay, that video game is going home with me today."

"But, Callie, I didn't even play it yet!"

"I'm sorry about that, but no video games from me for three days. You need to remember to ask people about doing things before you say yes for them. Your uncle hasn't learned the lesson yet, but you still have a chance, my friend, and I intend to help you."

"I learned today," Richard muttered. "I learned before, too."

"Right."

"Yes...well..." He decided they had digressed enough. "Unfortunately I wasn't here to take the call personally, but the machine should have taken care of it. I'm sorry there was a problem."

"I needed that call."

"I need da call," Mark repeated.

Jason smiled. Callie didn't.

"Call back and talk to whoever it was you talked to in the first place," Richard said. "They can track down who's handling your case."

"I guess I'll have to." Callie drew in a deep breath and let it out slowly. "This wasn't anyone's fault. Maybe God is telling me I shouldn't get my old job back."

"I could have told you that." Richard put his arm around Callie. "I'm truly sorry."

"I feel like Lester," she said. "I'm dead and nobody told me."

The front door opened and closed. Amanda came into the kitchen, smiling happily. "Hi."

"Hi, yourself," Richard said. "You're kind of late, aren't you?"

Amanda glanced at the clock. "Only forty-five minutes. Joey's coach drove us home and treated us to dinner first."

Richard felt his blood pressure shoot up. "You've already had dinner?"

Amanda nodded. "Uh-huh."

"Then that's the last practice of Joey's you'll go to."

His niece's jaw dropped. "What!"

Richard said sternly, "Practice was supposed to be over by four and you were supposed to be home by four-thirty. That's what time you told me. And you didn't even have the courtesy to call. You've lost the privilege of going to Joey's practices."

"No!" Amanda shrieked.

"Ha-ha-ha," Jason sneered.

Amanda shrieked again, yanked off her beret and threw it at her brother. Jason shot out of the chair and went after her. Richard, feeling like a lion tamer in a cage, quickly wedged himself between the children. He caught both by the arm and sat them down at the table.

"Stop it," he said. "I will have some order in this house, and if you don't like it, too bad. Jason, you're in trouble already, so don't make it worse for yourself. Amanda, courtesy starts at home, and you will adhere to it. I expect you here directly after school. You will do your homework, and you will obey the rules of the house. If you show me you understand them and will abide by them, I'll change my decision about your attending things at Joey's school. You made a choice. You screwed up. You do have the ability to be paroled early for good behavior, okay? But you do this again, and you won't see the outside of your room until you're out of college. You, too, Jay. Do you both understand?"

The children nodded.

"Okay," Richard said, nodding back. "Jay, finish your homework and get ready for dinner. Amanda, go up to your room and do yours. I'll look at it after we eat."

The kids dispersed on their appointed tasks. Richard puffed his chest out, feeling more in control than ever. The things a little extra sleep and a little less chaos could do.

Callie gazed at him thoughtfully.

Richard smiled at her. "Not bad, eh?"

"Not at all."

"Just remember, I don't need you for this. I need you for *this*."

He kissed her thoroughly.

"Poopies!" Mark yelled.

Chapter Fourteen

"Mark's out like a light."

Callie chuckled at Richard's leer. She knew she shouldn't, but somehow Mark's afternoon nap time was rapidly becoming let's-fool-around time for the adults.

"I have three letters to write and fax for you," she murmured, then sucked in her breath when he lifted her hair and kissed the nape of her neck. Who knew napes were so sensitive? Especially hers. She needed to concentrate on business. It was improving, but they had to stay on top of it. "They're regarding those bids, which are due in Hong Kong today."

"Write 'em tomorrow, I don't care."

He pulled her from behind his desk and into his arms. He fitted his mouth to hers in a perfect kiss. Callie's head spun, the sensations pushing her out of control.

"How am I supposed to resist this?" she asked when he turned his attention to her throat and chest.

"You're not." He grinned against her skin, having already unbuttoned the top of her blouse. She had no clue when he had done it.

"I should. I really should." She meant it only half-heartedly. "I am supposed to be *working* for you."

"You are, and you're doing a marvelous job." He

gave her another breathless kiss. "This is break time—
and you're doing a marvelous job there, too."

This is confusion time, she thought. Her feelings for
him confused her more and more, especially being with
him like this.

When they went upstairs—on tiptoe past Mark's
closed door—her heart led the way. Her soul made love
with his, just as their bodies came together as one. He
was exquisite, everything she needed or wanted, and not
just in making love.

Spending long hours in his household had shown her
that people could share responsibility. Richard entrusted
her to run the core of his business, giving her direction
and then letting her get on with it. He spent his time
caring for his niece and nephews, going to her only for
advice on discipline. She involved herself as much as
she wanted, and she wanted to much more than she
needed to. She also loved the job and, truth be told,
didn't want to go back to her old one. One of the best
changes in this quick change of her life was that she'd
found the time to get caught up in her college courses.
All thanks to Richard.

As she lay with him in the aftermath of their lovemaking, replete, she admitted what her heart had known
almost from the first moment they'd met. She loved him.
How could she not? He was a caring man, a sexy man,
a strong man and a tender man. Her fierce need to protect
her dreams and goals was easing because they seemed
as much a priority to him as to her. Maybe, in the right
situation, she could have it all. Maybe this was the right
situation. Maybe it didn't matter whether it was right or
not, because she loved him.

"What are you thinking?" Richard asked, stroking
her arm and kissing her hair.

"That you are a marvelous man."

He smiled, his eyes closed. "You're sweet-talking me, woman."

"You deserve it."

He laughed. His fingers traveled down her spine and over the curve of her derriere. He cupped her flesh, his palms kneading. Warm liquid pooled deep within her.

"You're going to kiss me, too," she added in a whisper. "And I will die a happy woman."

"Good." He opened his eyes and gazed at her. "I know you aren't ready to hear it, but I have to say it. I love you, Callie."

Callie swallowed, knowing that if she told him the same she would be taking a big step toward trusting him. "I love you, too."

He turned to her, his lion's eyes wide. "Callie."

She kissed him softly. "I have for a long time and it scared me. Maybe I'm not so scared anymore. Well, I am, but I love you more than I'm scared."

He pulled her on top of him and brushed her hair back from her face. "I don't know what I did to make you come around, but I am so glad you did."

"You did nothing and everything." She kissed his nose. "You yelled at me, harangued me and basically shamed me into loving you, I think."

"Now there's a strong recommendation," he said ruefully.

She kissed him again. "I think I needed it. I do have to let the past go, just as you said. But, Richard, please don't take ten steps forward because I've taken this one, okay? Wait until I'm there with you."

He laughed. "Right." He pressed her hips closer to his. "I'm here, ready, willing and sort of able."

She giggled. "Let me be the bearer of bad news. The

kids are due home from school in twenty minutes. And Mark will be awake at any time. Besides, I have those faxes to type and send.''

''All we do is work, work, work.''

She reached between them and stroked him, emboldened into playfulness. ''Complaints from the peanut gallery?''

''Who you calling a peanut?''

They were laughing when they finally got out of bed, Callie only slightly regretful about pointing out reality to him. Her body ached so sweetly, so lovingly, that she never wanted reality to intrude again.

In the hallway he kissed her deeply, expressing his emotions without words. Callie melted against him. When he raised his head finally, he said, ''I won't hurt you, Callie. I promise. I need you and love you just for me.''

She hoped so, aware of the concession she was making in her life.

''Thanksgiving's in a few days,'' he said. ''It's a time for family. Will you come be with me and the kids as part of our family?''

Callie burst out laughing. ''Richard, you just took ten giant steps again.''

''I did?'' He looked genuinely puzzled before he smiled. ''Oh, well, if you've got it, flaunt it. Will you come? I promise to make everything.''

''This I've got to see.'' Even though her sister Gerri had the holiday dinner at her place every year and Callie cooked the turkey, she couldn't resist Richard's invitation. In truth, she wanted to be with him and the children, a baby step for which she was ready. ''Yes, I'll come.''

''Great.''

Gerri could cook the turkey herself for once, she thought, although she dreaded telling her sister.

The business phone rang downstairs, just as she heard Mark calling from his crib in his room.

Richard grimaced. "Not a moment too soon. I'll get Mark. You get to work."

"No, I'll get Mark," she said. "You go talk to adults, and I'll talk to the resident toddler. You've got some other local callbacks you have to make, anyway. Better do them before the end of business today."

He left her with a last kiss, after which she went in and saw another of the men in her life. Mark grinned at her.

"Want potty, Callie."

"Good Lord, child," she said. "You're going right into superhero territory, aren't you? You and your uncle. Come on, kid, we'll go make superhero history."

As Callie helped the miniature Holiday through his paces in the bathroom, her mind held fast to the real Holiday man in the family and what he offered.

She was on board a train she no longer wanted to stop.

"Wow. AN A on that algebra test. Way to go, Amanda!"

Richard gazed at the paper his niece had proudly presented to him. Amanda had worked hard in the past few days on the math chapter after a quiz showed she had a few gaps in her knowledge. Richard had worked with her, Callie's presence in the office alleviating lack of time and business worries for him. He was proud of his niece for her accomplishment and told her so.

He was also proud of Callie for loving him. He knew she was taking a chance that he and the kids wouldn't overwhelm her needs. He just had to make sure that didn't happen. Right now things were working. He worried a little about how they would handle the first bump in the road, but not enough to let it diminish what they'd achieved so far. His life was on an upswing, and he'd be damned if he'd send it in the wrong direction again.

"I've asked Callie to Thanksgiving dinner," he said to Amanda. They were in his office. Callie had been right. It had been good to talk to adults about business. He wondered how she was doing with the resident toddler, who was out with her for a walk. "I've done some shopping already and I'm going to make the turkey and all the trimmings, because I don't want Callie to do any more than be our guest. How about helping me with the dinner? Do a good job, and I'll let you go to one of Joey's basketball practices. If Thanksgiving goes well and you have no slipups about getting home on time from the practice, then maybe we can talk about when true parole can begin. Think of this as a good-behavior test."

"Okay." Amanda frowned. "I'll do whatever you want...but I won't have to stick my hands in the dead turkey, will I? It's disgusting."

Richard laughed. "No. There's plenty more to do than that. I'll be the disgusting one, no fear."

"What's disgusting?" Jay asked, wandering in.

"We're talking about Thanksgiving dinner. I'm making it, including stuffing the bird, which your sister finds disgusting to touch because it's dead, although she likes to eat it."

"Ooh. Can I help?"

Richard grinned lopsidedly. "One girl's disgust is one boy's delight. Sure—if you wash your hands thoroughly first."

Jay made a face. "You guys always make me do that. What else are we having?"

Richard brainstormed with the two on the rest of the meal. They split up the chores, too. Learning to make things fun for the children actually made it fun for him. He had to admit that marshaling his troops felt good. He looked forward to Thanksgiving now, having held out a carrot to Amanda to get her cooperation and with Jay just being Jay. He'd probably have to hose Jay down after they stuffed the bird just to keep the kid near the health street's straight and narrow. Callie would be in for a big surprise—and another lesson in Richard Holiday's brand of love. His cousins had been right. Just go with the flow. Helping it along didn't hurt, either.

The front door slammed, drawing his attention. Amanda and Jay jumped, startled by the sudden noise.

"For once it's not you, Jay," Richard said, frowning. "Don't tell me Mark's started now."

"I'll go see," Jay volunteered. The boy raced from the room, then shouted, "It's Callie and Mark."

"Like I couldn't figure that out," Richard muttered, shrugging. Amanda giggled and left him to his work, sorting through another of the files Callie had updated. The woman was good. Too bad she'd filed that protest about her old job and finally talked with the person who'd called her—they'd tracked the woman down eventually. Richard wondered if he could up the business ante as Callie furthered their personal relationship. At the rate she was going, she would make his business a lot of money. Herself even more. If nothing else, he'd learned he'd gone in the wrong direction by hiring nannies, au pairs and housekeepers for the kids. He should have been hiring a business assistant, instead, while dealing with the kids himself.

"Ah, the woman of the hour," he said cheerfully when she entered the office.

"Tell that to my sister," she said between clenched teeth.

"Now what?" Richard asked, although he could make a good guess. "She's not after you again about being here, is she?"

"Are there craters on the moon?" Callie practically ripped her coat down her arms. "She stopped me on the street while I was walking with Mark to give me a lecture on propriety."

"Good thing she didn't see us at nap time," he said, grinning at her.

"I'd love to shove nap time under her nose." Callie shivered. "I'm sorry, Richard, that my sister is such a...prude. I don't know what's wrong with her."

"Your sister's problem is hers, not mine. Or yours. Ignore her. You're here for many legitimate purposes, not the least of which is just being with me. In fact, that's the best part."

Callie's brow furrowed. "I don't know. Richard, what if she's right about the neighbors' gossiping? I don't want to cause you, or especially the kids, who are innocent, any problems."

"Hush." He rose from his chair and put his arms around her. "That's enough of that nonsense. Nobody gives a damn about me and you and the kids being together all day or all night. And if they did, then you can have them. We're happy and the kids are happy. I love you, Callie, and that's all that matters."

"I know. But I don't want to make trouble for you," Callie said.

He would have kissed the words away, but the doorbell rang. A second later Jason yelled out, "It's Joey's mom, Uncle Richard!"

Callie broke away from Richard's embrace. "Now what?"

"Let's find out." He took her hand and led her into the foyer.

Gerri stood just inside the door. Her hair and makeup were impeccable, her casual suede jacket sinfully expensive and her expression daunting. The grim line of her mouth said she was an angry unhappy woman. Not even the pouty peach lipstick she wore erased the impression.

"Good," Gerri said crisply. "I think Callie needs to hear the truth, so I'm glad she's here. I recognize, Richard, that you are a diplomat, a man with beautiful manners. I know that you don't want to hurt my sister's feelings in what must be an increasingly intolerable situation for you. You've been very kind about this. Far too kind. But she's been here far too much, annoying you, so I'm sure—"

"Callie does not annoy me," Richard broke in, his blood pressure rising swiftly. Callie stood next to him, surprisingly silent.

"Maybe not." Gerri smiled archly at him. "My sister can be charming when she wants to be. But people around here are noticing her presence and saying less than acceptable things about it. It's reflecting on her. It's reflecting on me. And on you, something I'm sure you don't want. I've tried to tell her several times that she's behaving foolishly, but she won't listen. Now she's wormed her way from being a nanny for you into this job, or whatever she now claims she's doing here. I know there's a…convenience in this situation. You're a man. I understand that. A very kind man. I know Callie is not the kind of woman with whom you'd form a long-term relationship, but it seems you're far too polite to tell her that yourself. I don't want to see her hurt, but it's become ludicrous for all of us. I think now if you just tell her the truth…''

The more she spoke, the more Richard gaped. He could feel his jaw dropping farther and farther in astonishment. Finally he found his voice and roared, *''Are you nuts?''*

Gerri's eyebrows shot up, and she backed away a step. ''I…I…''

''You have to be,'' he said, stopping her stammering. ''How you can think that load of nonsense is beyond me. I love your sister. *Love*. She's here because I want her here. *Want*. I don't give a damn what you or anyone else thinks in this neighborhood. If you've got nothing else to do with your life than be jealous of Callie, then too bad, only, butt out of my business.''

Gerri stared at him, wide-eyed.

''Your sister sacrificed herself for her family. You had it easier than she did. Far easier, but you don't give her a break. Did you know she lost her job?''

''Mom said something about it—''

''And did you offer her any help whatsoever?''

''Well, no.'' Gerri looked helplessly at Callie.

Callie said, ''Richard, it's okay.''

''No, it's not okay,'' he said to her. ''Your sister ought to be ashamed of herself, coming in here and accusing you of a bunch of crap like that. They usually shovel it out from under an elephant's backside.'' He hardly sounded diplomatic, but he didn't give a rat's behind. To Gerri he said, ''All I've got to say to you and any of the other people around here is, get a life and stay out of mine. Got that?''

Gerri nodded. Suddenly she burst into tears.

''Jeez,'' Richard said, totally disgusted.

Gerri wailed even louder, then turned and ran out the door.

Richard grinned. "Good, now she knows."

"Knows what?" Callie asked, glaring at him.

Richard stared at her in shock, realizing she was angry with him. "Callie, you can't tell me you were buying into those tears. Or anything else."

"You didn't have to be so...harsh to Gerri."

"Harsh? Callie, she shredded you like a cabbage for coleslaw. Stop making excuses for her."

"I'm not making excuses. Yes, what she said was stupid, but you should have let me handle it in my way. I better go after her."

Callie started toward the door. Richard put his hand on her arm, stopping her.

"And what way is your way?" he asked, growing nearly as angry with her as he was with her sister. "Running after her like you're her mommy to sooth her hurts? Someone starts minding my business, and she's going to be told to knock it off, especially when she's attacking someone I love. I don't care who she's related to. That was all nonsense, anyway. No one in this neighborhood gives a hoot about me or my family. Or you. Not even Gerri."

"Clearly Gerri believes they do. I know she's self-centered, but she means well."

"She means well? Your sister means well like a cobra about to strike means well. She's selfish and nasty. I'm sorry, but she is. This tirade of hers was all about hurting you, not what people are saying. I can't believe you're still making excuses for her."

"I'm not, Richard."

"Sounds like it to me. No wonder you're the way you are. Your family's got you wrapped around their finger.

They insult you, and you're ready to forgive and forget.''

"It's not that...."

"Then what is it? Because it sure sounds that way to me. I love you, but I'm not fighting with your family for you. Not when you're letting them walk all over you."

"I'm not letting Gerri walk all over me."

"Right." Richard let her arm go. "Go on. Get the mother hen out of your system."

Callie's eyes shimmered with unshed tears. "Please understand, Richard."

He thrust out his jaw, refusing to speak because he understood all too well. She was choosing family over him. He had lost a brother and a beloved sister-in-law, leaving him to know better than most how important family was. But Gerri's behavior was inexcusable, and Callie shouldn't be talking like this. Not after he had been defending *her* to the woman. The notion infuriated him.

Callie headed into his office. She came out with her coat. Richard's heart sank, but he refused to allow it to show.

"Don't be mad at me, Richard," she said. "I *have* to talk to Gerri."

"I'm not mad," he replied. "I'm disappointed."

Callie shook her head. She opened the door, closing it behind her as she left. The house felt as if all its vibrancy had left with her.

"Uncle Richard." Amanda's voice sounded small and faraway.

Richard sighed and faced his niece, who stood in the doorway to the kitchen. Mark and Jason stood next to her, both wide-eyed.

"It's okay, kids," he said. "Don't worry about it."

They didn't need to. He would.

LATE THANKSGIVING afternoon, Callie parked her car in front of her sister's house and sat there, completely exhausted.

And completely miserable.

She hadn't slept well since her fight with Richard. Soothing Gerri after leaving Richard to talk to her had been far more difficult than she'd imagined. It seemed she'd made every excuse in the book to herself for Gerri, and even wound up making a spoken apology, which Gerri ungraciously accepted. Richard's behavior had been proper, while Gerri's hadn't. The whole thing had left ashes in Callie's mouth ever since.

Worse, Gerri's contriteness vanished immediately afterward, replaced by a slightly righteous attitude. Callie let it go in the interest of peace. In the further interest of peace, she had called Richard and told him she thought she ought to go to her family's dinner as a goodwill gesture. He had been curt and cold.

That had hurt more than she ever thought anything would, because she felt as if she'd let him down. Mostly she felt wrong. Just plain old done Richard wrong. Every fiber of her being yearned to drive farther down the street to his house, park in his driveway and prostrate herself before him to ask for forgiveness.

Yet she dragged herself from the car, feeling as though she had to get one problem solved before she dealt with the next. She opened her trunk and cursed heartily when she saw the turkey juice that had dripped onto the once-immaculate rug covering. She'd wrapped the pan containing the now fully-cooked stuffed turkey in about ten layers of foil. But somehow the juice had found a weak spot and leaked out, probably when she'd made that hard stop at a light.

Her contribution to Thanksgiving was another exhaustion factor. She'd been up since dawn stuffing and cooking the turkey.

"Contribution, my fanny," she grumbled. She remembered Gerri's words when she said she was coming to dinner, after all. *I'm not as adept as you are, Callie, at making a turkey. Besides, you always make it. I just love the smell of it when you come in the door.*

Yeah, she thought, wrestling the still-hot twenty-pound pan out of the trunk with clumsy hot pads. She always made and then smelled like the bird, and this year clearly wasn't going to be different. She always bought the turkey and stuffing materials, too, and that wasn't different this year, either, despite her being out of work. Technically out of work, that is; she wasn't sure where she stood with her old job right now, or with Richard and his import business. The family always insisted on a fresh, not frozen turkey. She'd driven over half of Jersey last night, trying to get one from a local poultry farmer. Didn't anyone know what went into making a turkey like this? Didn't anyone care?

No one came out to help her, although her brother Tommy opened the door and waved. "Thank God you're here, Callie. It's a mess."

Callie struggled with the heavy pan. "Here, you idiot. Take this before I drop it."

"Oh." Tommy leaped to help her at last. He took hold of the turkey pan, then snatched his hand back. "Ooowww! It's hot."

"I hope your patients get that right-on-the-money diagnosis." She helped him make a better transfer with the hot pads, then noticed a dark shadow on her best blazer. "Oh, no! The juice got on my clothes."

"That's nothing," Tommy said. "All hell's broken loose in here."

"What do you mean, this is nothing?" she demanded, swiping fruitlessly at the greasy stain. "It's my best jacket."

Tommy nudged her with his elbow and called out, "Callie's here!"

"Callie!"

She practically backed outside again when Gerri hurried toward her with a face blotchy from crying. Gerri threw her arms around Callie and burst into an explosion of weeping. "Get in! Get in before anyone sees me! I can't face them. Oh, it's horrible. We're bankrupt! And Joe's left me, just gone."

Callie's heart thumped, half from her sister's news and half from the slew of little nieces and nephews racing toward her for hugs. And candy. Callie immediately dug in her pocket for lollipops, although Gerri clung like an octopus. The kids disappeared as soon as they got their treat. Callie felt as though she'd just handed out bribes for love. Probably the kids didn't want to miss their treats, but didn't want to come too near their aunt Gerri, with her bewildering behavior. At least Callie hoped so, but it gave her a bad feeling, especially after having Mark's hugs for nothing.

Her parents sat at the kitchen table, hangdog looks on their faces. Her sister Helena frowned at her husband, Andy, while her brother Steve sat on the other side of the room from his wife, Bobbi. Her youngest brother, Jamie, a first-year student at Penn State, sat on a stool at the counter flipping cashews in the air and catching them with his mouth.

Young Joey huddled in the back of the kitchen, his expression stone-faced. Callie's heart went out to him. She disentangled herself from Gerri and gave him a hug. "It'll be okay."

Joey just nodded and put his arm around her. Callie sensed that he needed reassurance. Poor guy. His sister Kristen, one of the horde of kids now watching a movie in the den, had obviously taken her father's disappearance better than Joey had. But then, despite her young age, Kristen had always been independent and self-possessed.

"Gerri's such a wreck she hasn't even started dinner," Helena said. "I'll do some, but I'm not doing it all. You'll have to do more, Callie."

Gerri gasped. "I have a right to be upset!"

"I'm upset, too, but you don't see me acting like a screaming meamie." Helena sniffed a few tears of her own. "Andy's company restructured and he's had to take a pay cut. I'll have to go back to work. Callie, I'm going to need your help with some baby-sitting."

Callie gaped at Helena, who seemed oblivious to what she'd asked of her oldest sister.

"She can't," Gerri said. "I need her help here. Everything's gone, don't you understand? Joe said *I* spent every penny we have! This morning I got up and he was gone, just walked out on me. What am I supposed to do? We've got no money in the bank. Nothing. How am I going to pay the bills? Poor Joey and Kristen will have to go to public school this semester."

Joey's head came up. He grinned. "I gotta call Amanda."

Callie smiled as her nephew sped out of the room. Someone was happy at least. She couldn't find a whole lot of sympathy for her sister. Gerri had needed to curb her spending for years. But although she understood her brother-in-law's disgust, it wasn't fair of Joe to skip out on his family like that. She knew now why Gerri had been acting the way she had. She'd been under enormous stress, and so anything that seemed untoward made her frantic to control, including Callie's relationship with Richard.

Tommy broke into Gerri's tears. "Get a grip. You'll just have to live like the rest of us—on Poor Street. It won't kill you. What's Callie supposed to do for you, anyway?"

Callie smiled at her brother coming to her defense. She hadn't been overjoyed to hear her sisters blithely demand her services. Usually Helena was more sensible, but Callie realized she'd set both sisters up to expect her to bail them out because she always had before.

"Besides, I've got a wallpaper project I want Callie's help with," Tommy added. "If she's helping you, she can't help me."

Callie glared at him while her sisters protested strongly. And here she thought he was on her side.

"Knock it off," her middle brother, Steve, said. "You aren't the only ones with problems. I might as well tell them, Rose." He glanced at his wife. "Rose and I are getting a divorce after Christmas. If anyone needs Callie's baby-sitting services, it's me."

The squabbling rose higher and higher, yet Callie didn't care. It felt as if she were looking at herself from the outside, a stranger in this household of people making demands of her. She realized they expected her just to drop everything and make their life better. But what about her own needs? Never was it clearer to her that she was the family drudge. Yet she felt less like a family member than ever.

Suddenly she knew that her family, the family she needed, lived down the street. The man she loved was only a few hundred feet away, and she'd nearly walked out on him. On them all.

"What an idiot I am," she said out loud.

Everyone stopped bickering and stared at her. She looked at each one, then said to her mother and father, "Why don't you two say something? Tell them what they should do. It's not my job."

"You always thought it was," her mother said. "You were such a good little mother that even if I tried to do it, you just took it out of my hands. I guess we all got used to it."

"Well, I don't want it anymore. Everyone," she announced, "I'm sorry for all your troubles, but it's time you take responsibility for your lives. I have my own life to live, so Gerri, Helena, Steve, Tommy, Jamie…good luck and God bless. I hope you get your lives back together, but I can't help you any longer. Go see Mom and Dad."

"Yeah!" Jamie said, clapping his hands. "About time, Callie. I'm the youngest, and I could see you wearing yourself out with these clowns, including me."

Tommy burst out laughing. "My God, but Jamie's right. Go for it, girl, and leave us dopes to ourselves. I'll happily paper my own house. Happy typical Thanksgiving. Everyone's miserable."

"I'm not. You guys have your turkey, and it's the last one from me," Callie said. "I'm going to Richard's. By the way, I'll be there quite a lot because I love him. If anyone's got a problem with that, too bad."

She strode from the kitchen and out of the house, leaving a bunch of gaping mouths and two applauding brothers behind her. The sun shone brightly, warming her skin. The breeze, though brisk, lifted her hair and gave her hope. She left her car parked where it was and walked down the street to Richard's. With each step she felt more confident and yet apprehensive. She was confident in her love for Richard, in her belief that she would reach all her goals and have a family, too, with his help. She was apprehensive about whether Richard would accept her. He had been very angry with her after their fight about family.

"Dope," she said, meaning herself.

She took a deep breath, a steadying breath, then knocked on Richard's door. Jason opened it.

"Callie!" he shouted happily, hugging her.

"Thank God I left my hearing aids at home," she said wryly, hugging him back. "I'd have no eardrums left."

"Do you still like my uncle Richard?" he asked hopefully.

"I love him. You, too. Okay?"

Jay grinned. "Okay."

She walked in behind Jason, who launched himself into the house to shout that she'd shown up. She noticed the dining-room table through the doorway on the right. It was beautifully set for four people. She prayed it had room for five.

Amanda came to the top of the stairs, her portable telephone in her hand. Grinning, she waved at Callie and said, "I'm on with Joey. Is it really true? He's going to my school soon?"

"He's not going to his for long, that's for sure," Callie replied.

"Can he come over for dinner here?" Amanda asked.

Callie was touched that Amanda thought that she, Callie, was the one with the answers. "If it's all right with his mother and with your uncle Richard, it's okay with me.''

What the heck, she thought. Might as well make two kids happy today.

''Great!'' Amanda whooped. ''Uncle Richard will be glad to see you—''

''Turkey for me, Callie!'' Mark called out as he toddled into sight. He wrapped his arms around her legs. ''Turkey for me!''

''Yeah, but who's the turkey, pal?'' she asked, rubbing his back.

Suddenly Richard was at the doorway between the kitchen and the foyer. He looked wonderful in a sweatshirt and jeans. His hair fell across his forehead, and a little flour streaked his jaw, but that only added to his charm. His expression, however, was shuttered, giving nothing away.

Callie straightened, feeling more apprehensive than confident. ''Is there room for one more at the table? I'd like to have Thanksgiving dinner with *my* family.''

Richard slowly grinned. He moved toward her.

''You are my family,'' she whispered when he took her in his arms. ''I hope you'll forgive me for being an idiot the other day.''

''Honey, I was one, too. I should have hog-tied you to the sofa.''

''I like your diplomacy,'' she said, smiling. ''And you're a little kinky, too.''

''I'm a lot kinky, given the chance.'' He sobered. ''Are you here to stay?''

''For as long as you want me. And I'll work and I'll finish college and I'll be happy as a clam changing Mark's diapers.''

''No need. He's in major training now.''

"Joy of joys."

Richard kissed her, a mind-boggling kiss that melded her to him and left her dizzy with love. Never had she been happier. Never had she known such joy of joys as she had with him.

"I'll help you in the kitchen," she murmured against his lips.

"It's all done."

She leaned her head back, her eyes wide with surprise. "All of it?"

"Yes. Let's go have Thanksgiving dinner with our family," he said when he finally raised his head.

RICHARD SET the beautifully browned turkey on the dinner table. Its fragrant aroma combined with the yeasty odor of rolls and the sweet smell of candied yams. He'd done it all himself, with a little help from Jason, and even Mark. Amanda had set a beautiful table and taken care of all the cleaning and other sundry jobs that added to the pleasure of eye, nose and eventually mouth.

Callie sat at the other end of the table, looking serene and absolutely perfect. Her nephew Joey sat next to Amanda. Richard decided not to worry about young love for the time being. His love was having its well-deserved day.

"Before we eat," he said, "let's each of us tell what we're thankful for. Jay, you go first."

"I'm thankful to eat turkey and stuffing," Jay said promptly.

Everyone chuckled.

"I'm thankful to be *here*," Joey said next.

Callie giggled while Joey grinned lopsidedly. Richard had heard the story of what had happened over at

Gerri's. He felt badly for the boy and his mother—and proud of Callie for putting herself first.

"I'm thankful to be here, too," Amanda said. "With you, Uncle Richard, and everyone…"

Her voice trailed away, but not her sentiment. Jason nodded in agreement. "I'm very glad you're here, too," he said.

"And I'm thankful to have opened Gerri's door on Halloween," Callie said. "Finding Hercules, a goddess, Robin and Batman was the best thing that ever happened to me. I'm thankful that here I'm needed for *me*, and not to make a dinner or wash clothes or anything else. I'm thankful I have a job somewhere and a formal protest pending over another." She grinned. "And I'm glad I have dreams and you understand them."

"How about a Christmas wedding?" Richard asked.

Amanda gasped and both Jason and Joey looked on, round-eyed. Mark played with his roll, unconcerned.

"You're ten giant steps ahead again," Callie said, her face flushed.

"I'll wait for however long it takes for you to catch up," he replied, undaunted.

"I don't think it will be too long. Christmas might be nice."

"Remind me to kiss you later."

She smiled at him, her eyes shining with love. "Good. Now carve that turkey. I'm starved."

He laughed and began to carve. He stopped. The table groaned—and not because it was laden with food. Everyone was hungry.

"I forgot to say what *I'm* thankful for." He looked around the table. "I'm very thankful for each one of you, that you have come to me and we have made a family together. I'm thankful for you, Callie, because you came into my life and in a few short weeks made it complete. And I'm thankful that you love me. That's the greatest gift of all.''

Everyone smiled. Callie wiped at tears. Richard felt a few well up in his eyes.

''Turkey *now,* Unca 'shard!'' Mark shouted, then added, ''Peas.''

''Okay, okay,'' he said, putting actions to words.

The two little Pilgrim figurines on the table nearly touched hands. They had been listening and were pleased. Although the special request of the Holidays had been fulfilled with the four cousins, there was always room for one more, whenever he needed help.

into it," he said in... "Now that you've done it, what're you going to do? He learned that you've escaped. There's no place else to go?"

Jasmine wanted Chile when it came. Nathan let a deep sigh escape as...

"Nathan, what about...?" she asked. "Pete..."

"Nathan..." he said, putting arms around her...